A TY STONE THRILLER

HARD TRAUMA

FRANKLIN HORTON

ALSO BY FRANKLIN HORTON

ABOUT THE AUTHOR

Franklin Horton lives and writes in the mountains of Southwestern Virginia. He is the author of several bestselling post-apocalyptic and thriller series. You can follow him on his website at franklinhorton.com.

While you're there please sign up for his mailing list for updates, event schedule, book recommendations, and discounts.

ACKNOWLEDGMENTS

This book would not have been possible without the folks who help produce the final product, including my long-time editor Felicia Sullivan and my cover team at Deranged Doctor Design.

I would also like to thank my proofing team: Dawn Figueiras, Carrie Bartkowiak, Randy Cornell, and Laura Keysor.

I had some dear friends who reviewed the accuracy of the military scenes: Angie Heath, Steven Heath, and Wynn Parkinson. Any mistakes in that department came from my own imagination and not from their efforts to keep me straight.

Finally, I'd like to thank the veterans who inspired this book. No one better understands the idea of public service than those willing to make the ultimate sacrifice for the people back home.

HARD TRAUMA

1

Two Years Earlier

TYLER STONE WAS RUNNING a five-man team in the northern part of the Helmand Province, Afghanistan. Their mission was to conduct reconnaissance on a village where the Taliban was rumored to be stockpiling weapons. They'd been in position for three days and pinpointed a cave with a lot of suspicious traffic. Ty was fairly certain the crates being hauled into the cave didn't contain cases of beer and bags of pork rinds.

Sometimes their job was to find the weapons and call in an airstrike. They'd paint the target with an infrared laser and air support would blow it back to the Stone Age. This mission was different. They were there to collect photographs and coordinates, then transmit the data back to command. Supposedly, folks higher up the chain would use that data to extrapolate a more complete picture of the supply chain in the region.

The mission was going smooth as glass, which made everyone

jittery. Once they transmitted their data, they were ordered to return home. That was when they paid the price for the previous lack of complications. They were rucking out on a goat trail when their mission was blown in the same way so many other covert ops in the Afghan hill country were compromised.

Shepherds.

Up until that point, they'd done everything right. They'd gathered their intel, avoided detection, and sustained no casualties. The two teenage shepherds wore drab pajama-like clothing and carried herding staffs, looking like two kids who'd just wandered out of some biblical tale.

"Keep moving," Ty ordered his team. "Kamran, handle this."

Kamran, their "terp"—interpreter—approached the boys and gestured wildly, warning the young men to remain silent or they'd be killed. Perhaps it wasn't the approved, politically-correct method of requesting cooperation from locals but it was often the most effective. Ty kept his team moving while Kamran assured the shepherds that men would come back and wring their necks like scrawny desert chickens if they sounded the alarm.

The terp made a good show of it but you never knew how those threats would work. Sometimes the locals resented the Taliban for some atrocity they'd committed on their village and they'd keep silent. Other times, more scared of the Taliban, they'd raise hell, sounding the alarm as soon as you were out of sight. Ty thought they'd actually pulled this one off until they hit open terrain and he chanced a look back at the village thorough his M151 spotting scope.

"Son of a bitch," he growled.

"What is it?"

Taco, a weapons sergeant, shaded his eyes and tried to make out what he was looking at. He was a tall dude, wrapped in tattoos and muscles, the man just as battle-worn as his gear. His nickname had nothing to do with ethnicity but instead came from his last name, which was Bell. "Please tell me that's just a dust devil."

"That's a negative, Taco. I've got at least two dozen armed riders headed in our direction. Those fucking shepherds sold us out."

Taco shook his head in disgust. "Why am I not surprised?" He threw up his rifle and studied them through the scope.

Ty packed up his spotting scope. "We need to haul ass."

"Should we engage?" Taco asked. "If I can't drop them, I can at least scatter them. Slow them down."

"Negative on that. While we're engaging, the rest will close around us and we'll get penned in. Then we won't be going anywhere."

The two men ran to catch up with the rest of their team. Ty flagged down his commo sergeant, Hoot. "See if you can find us a ride out of here!"

A chopper could light those Taliban cowgirls up and haul the team back to base. Command was expecting their request for exfil, anyway. Surely someone was monitoring their op and waiting for the call.

Ty watched Hoot's face while he talked, and after two minutes of agitated jabbering, he knew there was a problem. He started to get a sinking feeling in his gut. "What's the hell's going on?"

Hoot whipped off his headset, looking pissed. "Everything is grounded. Major fucking storm on our ass. Could be tomorrow before shit settles down."

"Great," Ty mumbled. "You tell them we had our own storm to worry about?"

"Affirmative. They suggested we request the QRF if we needed them," Hoot relayed, referring to the Quick Reaction Force.

"Bernie's unit is on QRF now," said Taco. "You know he won't put anyone at risk. They'll drag their ass and get here tomorrow so he doesn't take casualties."

"Do it," Ty said.

Hoot got on the radio and passed on Ty's request. Ty could soon tell Hoot wasn't having any more luck with this than the exfil request.

"QRF says they'll contact command and advise us when they have their orders," Hoot repeated.

Ty shook his head in disgust. He scanned the horizon and in the distance found the storm Hoot was referring to, a dark mass emerging on the horizon ahead of them like some enormous beast. "There's your dust devil, Taco."

"I still say we dig in and engage them. We got this. We can take them." Taco's speech was rushed. They were all huffing and puffing from humping heavy gear at a rapid pace, their adrenaline pumping. After sitting in those hills for three days everyone was jacked up and ready for a fight. Running didn't taste good on anyone's tongue.

"Negative," Ty said. "They pin us down and there'll be a hundred of them surrounding us by tomorrow. They'll pound us with rockets and there won't be enough left to bury. We're going to outrun them, or at least try to."

"You got to be kidding me," Hartsock said. He was MARSOC, or Marine Special Operations Command, and had embedded with Ty's team before. They got a laugh out of it because his name was Hartsock, making him Hartsock from MARSOC. Sometimes that shit was funny when you had nothing else to laugh at, but at the moment, nothing was funny.

"I'm open to ideas if you got anything," Ty said.

"I don't think we can outrun them. Those horsemen will ride us to ground," Hartsock said. "We need a defensible position."

Ty raised his shemagh and mopped at his face. "They pin us down, we die," he countered. "We're going into that storm. They probably won't follow us in there, but if they do, they'll lose us. Once we get on the other side, we'll hunker down and call for a pickup. Maybe someone will be flying by then."

"*If* we come out on the other side," Taco griped. "We'll be blind in there. We could go around in circles and run into the enemy head-on."

"We're better than that," Ty told him. "We tighten up and make sure that shit doesn't happen."

Despite any reservations they had, Ty was in charge. They followed orders and ran toward the storm. Ty could see his men glancing nervously at the approaching weather conditions while monitoring the other ominous cloud rising behind them. Ahead was a menacing blizzard of dust and wind. Behind, a band of murderous

Taliban intent on torturing them to death and posting videos of it on the internet. This was a solid team, tough men used to suffering, but Ty could tell the ticking clock was wearing on them. No one liked being sandwiched between those two threats. They were truly caught between a rock and a hard place.

They closed on the great storm as it closed on them. The wind picked up immediately and Ty began to have second thoughts about his decision. This was not thunderstorm wind. This was stepping out into a hurricane wind. Dirt pelted them like a sandblaster, making any exposed flesh burn as it was abraded away.

Although they had goggles over their eyes and filthy sweat-soaked shemaghs wrapped around their faces to filter out the dust, it was a futile effort. Their ears filled with grit and dirt. Before long, their clothes were covered with so much dust that each man looked like a boulder risen from the barren landscape and marching around of its own accord. It would be perfect camo if they survived, but that was a big ask.

Ty shouted at his men to stay together but the buffeting wind drowned out his voice. As they finally lost sight of the pursuing riders, the swirling storm consumed them totally. There was the faint sound of rifle fire behind them. Their pursuers were giving it one last college try before they lost sight of the enemy, sweeping the storm with blind barrages of AK fire.

"Anyone hit?" Ty barked.

No one answered. He doubted they even heard him. Ty caught their attention and directed them through hand signals to change course. He didn't know whether the Taliban riders would charge into the storm or balk at its approach. While he doubted they would risk it, they were dogged fighters and it remained a possibility. The team slogged onward, the men shoulder to shoulder so that no one got lost.

Just as he thought it couldn't get any worse, Mother Nature said, "Hold my beer" and they were startled by a bolt of lightning. Thunder shook the ground like mortar fire. If there was anything worse than a dust storm, it was when it intersected with a thunderstorm. The product was what you might expect. It rained mud.

A torrent of muddy rain slammed into them. It was like being hit with a firehose and they were quickly drenched, their sodden gear doubling in weight. Ty frantically yanked his shemagh down off his face, the damp cloth making him feel like he was being waterboarded. Mud streamed into his mouth, bitter and gritty. He used the back of a glove to swipe at his goggles but it was futile. He couldn't see shit and they were running blind.

He was seriously beginning to question the wisdom of charging into the storm. Hell, could people drown while walking upright? It was starting to feel like a possibility.

Inside the storm, the conditions had not only impaired their visibility but had greatly reduced the amount of light reaching the ground. In those twilight conditions, with mud-encrusted goggles, Ty was placing tremendous focus on the terrain under his feet and keeping his men close. Touch was the only sense still working at full capacity. He noticed the terrain change under his feet and it stopped him dead in his tracks.

He grabbed Hartsock, the man nearest him, by the shoulder and pulled him to a stop. One by one, the men slowed their companions and circled up.

"I think we're on the road!" Ty screamed, trying to overpower the wind.

"How the hell can you tell in this mess?" Taco demanded.

"I can't be certain but the surface feels different. It felt like there was a shoulder at the edge. Let's head south."

Ty could barely see any of his men but he got the distinct feeling that they were looking at him like he was an idiot. That was a fair assessment of how he felt at the moment. "That way," he said, pointing in the direction his smeared GPS assured him was south. "Move!"

They resumed their cautious advance and marched through the blinding slurry of desert mud. Ty took a sip from his hydration bladder, trying to rinse out his mouth, and it was vile, the bite valve nearly as muddy as his boots. Then, as quickly as the storm hit them, they walked out of it.

Except they weren't completely out of it. Instead, they'd wandered into what appeared to be the eye of the storm. All around, completely encircling them, was the turbulent spinning blackness of the mud storm. They'd somehow landed in an insulated bubble of calm in the middle of it.

"Dude, this is fucking weird," Taco said, spinning slowly, watching for the Taliban horsemen to come pounding into their little oasis at any moment. "I don't like it."

"Spooky," Hartsock mumbled.

Ty took the opportunity to try to clean his goggles, smearing the mud from a thick coating to a thin veneer that he could almost see through.

"It won't last," Kamran assured them. "A minute or two. The storm is moving too fast."

Aware that he was correct, Ty signaled the men to start moving again. They were halfway across the eye, on the surface of the road, when he saw a reflection in the darkness ahead of them. "What the hell?"

"What is it?" Hartsock asked.

"I thought I saw something," Ty said. "A light or some kind of reflection."

Then it was on them and there was no time to bolt for cover. They threw up their weapons and leveled them on the black Mercedes Sprinter van. It skidded to a stop in front of them, mud dripping from every surface. Inside, the wide-eyed man and little girl stared out through the smeared windshield at what probably looked like aboriginal mud men surrounding them with guns.

The terrified driver raised his hands in panic. He was screaming, jabbering, but Ty couldn't hear a word of it. He moved around the driver's side, his weapon never leaving the man's face. Hartsock did the same on the other side. Ty heard the sliding door roll open on the far side as Hartsock checked the rear of the van. Ty pulled the driver's door open and turned off the ignition. He scanned the driver's lap and checked around the seat for any weapons but didn't find any. The driver was frantically trying to explain something but Ty didn't understand a word of it.

"Kamran!" he barked. "Get over here!"

The terp rushed to his side and looked from Ty to the driver.

"Tell him we need a ride. Now!"

Kamran spent a moment nailing down a dialect the two shared, then relayed Ty's request.

"No," the driver replied in English

"Uh, he said no," Kamran replied.

"I think I understood that part," Ty growled.

"He says he's Pakistani and here on business. He's already late for an appointment."

The rain began to pelt them again as Ty stewed on their predicament. The eye was passing and the storm was nearly back upon them. He was not letting this vehicle pass unless he and his men were aboard it. Command would frown on stealing a vehicle, regardless of their situation. They never wanted you to do anything that might end up on the evening news. Ty was struggling to figure out a different approach, a bribe or threat that might make the driver acquiesce when a gunshot split the air.

Ty flinched and flattened himself against the vehicle, head swiveling for the source of the shot. Then he saw the column of Taliban riders had burst into the eye of the storm as well. They may have looked like a sodden mass of swamp creatures but they were deadly and only seconds away. Ty swung his rifle and tore off several shots in their direction. The rest of the team did the same.

Negotiations were over. Ty made a command decision, shoving the driver out of the seat and onto the floor. "Get in!" he bellowed, and his team scrambled for the side door, exchanging gunfire with the approaching riders as they piled in.

The terrified young girl screamed at the top of her lungs.

Taco pounded the back of the driver's seat. "Go! Go! Go!" he barked.

There was the rattle of more gunfire and one of the back windows shattered, spraying the interior with pellets of safety glass. Ty turned the key but it wouldn't start and his heart sank. They were dead.

"Go!" Taco demanded.

"I'm trying!"

"Wrong gear!" Kamran shouted, leaning forward to place the shifter into the Park position.

Ty could have punched himself in the head. God, he was an idiot. Apparently he'd turned the key off when the van was in Drive so it wouldn't start. He tried the key again and it fired right up. Ty stomped the gas pedal and the van slewed, the tires spinning on the mud road. He eased off until they gripped and the van lurched forward. The girl, still in the seat beside him, emitted another bloodcurdling scream. The sound was grating on Ty's nerves. There was enough chaos without her adding to it.

"Take her!" Ty instructed her father, the man apparently too petrified with fear to act. He hadn't moved since Ty shoved him onto the floor between the seats.

When the Pakistani man didn't react, Ty shoved him, jarring him from his paralysis. He gestured at the girl. The father's arms shot forward and collected his daughter. He pulled her to the floor with him and shielded her with his body. Her scream became a keening whine of terror, melding with the general state of chaos.

More gunfire sprayed the back of the van, punching holes in the sheet metal and remaining glass. Ty had hoped to gain distance from the riders but they lost visibility as they re-entered the storm and he couldn't go much faster than they could. If he got the van stuck or went off-road and hit a rock, they were dead. Hartsock and Taco were wallowing on the floor, trying to peel off their soaked packs, slippery with mud. Hartsock came out of his gear first and rolled to his knees.

He aimed through a jagged hole in the rear window and started pounding out controlled bursts of 5.56 fire at the pursuing Taliban. The sound of the automatic fire in the enclosed space of the van was deafening. They all had hearing protection stashed somewhere in their gear but who the hell had time to look for it?

"Get'em, cowboy!" Taco hollered, finally making it to his feet and joining the fight.

He ripped the muddy goggles from his head and tossed them to the side, raised his boot, and stomped the shattered pane of glass from the opening on his side of the rear door. The addition of a second shooter only intensified the noise and bedlam in the van.

"Kamran! Ask him where this fucking road goes!" Ty bellowed, unable to judge the volume of his own voice since he couldn't hear shit.

The terp shoved the Pakistani man to get his attention and launched a barrage of questions at him.

One of the pursuing riders got lucky and swept the rear of the van with another burst of gunfire. Ty had the sensation of being touched on the shoulder. He thought Kamran might be trying to get his attention but he was afraid to take his eyes of the road.

Taco cried out and collapsed to the deck. The girl screamed and Ty caught a flurry of movement in his peripheral vision. He spun to see what the girl was screaming about and realized the touch on his arm was the sensation of her father's brain spraying onto the right side of his body. Ty was covered in gore, the dampness going unnoticed due to his already saturated clothing.

Ty roared from rage and frustration, pounding the steering wheel with his palm. He was splitting his focus between the road, where he couldn't see shit, and the back of the van, where he had no fucking idea what was going on. "Taco? Talk to me!"

"Thigh wound!" Hartsock barked. "Missed the artery. He's plugging it now. He'll live."

"Not if we don't get out of this mess," Ty countered.

The girl slipped from beneath the bloody crush of her father's body and crawled into the passenger side footwell, pressing her tiny body as tightly as she could into the cramped space. She was no longer crying, her eyes squeezed desperately shut, tears streaking her stained face.

There was a jolt as a wheel rode over the nearly invisible shoulder. He jerked his eyes back to the road and struggled to correct the van without losing control. It slid dangerously, the back end slewing left and presenting just enough of its side to the enemy that they pounded it with 7.62 rounds.

Ty glanced back and saw holes punched in the van's sidewall. He also noticed his terp gasping for air, frightened eyes opened wide. "Hoot!" Ty called to the commo guy. "Kamran's hit!"

Ty wasn't sure if Hoot could hear him or not. He had to be as deaf as the rest of them at the moment. He was in the back of the van trying to shoot out of the same holes Taco and Hartsock were but was having a hard time staying out of their way. There was too much flying lead in too small a space. Hot brass bounced in every direction and rolled around on the floor. It was like trying to stand on marbles.

"Hoot!" Ty repeated.

The commo guy heard him that time and sprang into action, checking the now-collapsed terp. "Got between his armor!" Hoot yelled. "I think he took one in the lung."

Ty whipped his head around in time to see Kamran emit a cough that sprayed a mist of blood onto his already dirty face and gear. "Can you get a chest seal on him?"

"Look out!" Hoot screamed, gesturing frantically toward the windshield.

Ty swung his eyes back to the road in time to see they had driven out of the storm and he was about to crash into a HUMVEE stopped directly in front of them. Ty locked onto the steering wheel with both hands and stood on the brakes. The heavy van went into a slide and stopped mere feet shy of the armored vehicle. There were groans and cursing from the back as men fought to get on their feet, hot rifle barrels scorching them through their clothing.

The second HUMVEE in the column had a roof gunner and his weapon was trained directly on Ty's window. They had no idea who he was or who the van belonged to. Ty raised his hand as soldiers spread around the vehicle, trying to figure out what was going on.

"We're Americans!" Ty yelled.

When one of the soldiers barked commands Ty gestured at his ears. He couldn't hear a thing over the persistent ringing.

They figured it out soon enough. About the time the soldiers realized there was an American beneath the mud and gore, the Taliban arrived on the scene. A soldier threw open Ty's door and pushed him into the floor, just as Ty had done with the Pakistani driver earlier. The soldier pulled the van around the column and the new arrivals opened up on the approaching riders. Ty grinned as the welcoming committee chimed in with their vehicle-mounted machine guns. They killed several of the Taliban before driving the remainder back into the concealment of the storm.

Ty knelt between the seats, watching the action. He was finally feeling a glimmer of hope they were going to survive this mission, when he noticed he was crouched on the arm of the dead van owner. He glanced toward the man's daughter, ready to give her an apologetic look for the misery they'd brought upon her. They'd not asked for this.

He was met with staring, dead eyes. A brilliant stream of scarlet blood traced the dusty crease of the child's face, her hair matted around an entry wound on her temple.

Ty had no idea what happened to him at that point. All he would remember later was feeling as if his electrical system had overloaded. He fell over backwards, his head hitting the sliding door. His legs were draped across the dead Pakistani and the wounded, gasping terp. Someone slid open the bullet-riddled cargo door and sunlight hit Ty in the face, blinding him.

Hands hooked under his arms and dragged him clear of the van. A medic was in his face asking him questions he couldn't hear to answer. He was covered in blood, mud, and it sounded like a freight train was pounding through his head. The medic put both hands on Ty's face and screamed a question at him.

Ty couldn't hear it but finally understood that he was being asked where he was wounded. He pointed to his ears.

The medic and another soldier began peeling Ty's gear off, searching for wounds despite his protestations. They poured water on him, looking for wounds beneath the dirt and gore. Ty turned his head toward the van and saw Hartsock stumble off, a bloody Taco leaning on him for support. Hartsock was being questioned by a soldier as he walked. Hoot came out under his own power but he'd taken a shoulder wound at some point and his arm hung at an odd angle.

The dead were left inside to be photographed. Those photographs would become part of the investigation that ultimately ended Tyler Stone's military career. Ty would never need to see those photographs to remember the scene that day. It was something he would never forget. It was something that would visit him in nightmares for the rest of his life.

2

Ty sat in his truck outside his sister's house and scanned the streets. Kids were home from school and adults were getting off work. There were too many cars coming and going. It took him a moment to acclimate to the level of activity. Every location, every area of operation, had a vibe and a particular flow. Ty needed to familiarize himself with that flow before he ventured out into it.

Women parked minivans and struggled with bulging grocery bags, children lined behind them like ducklings. Men straggled in from whatever job consumed their day, looking haggard and defeated. A retiree mowed his lawn from a pristine lawn tractor, a smile plastered on his face like it was the highlight of his day. Ty checked his rearview mirror again, decided this was as good as it was going to get, and jogged up Deena's driveway.

He climbed the brick steps and knocked on the glass storm door. The reply from inside was indecipherable, a chorus of both his niece and sister's voices yelling different things at the same time. He took it as an invitation to go inside. He found his niece Aiden seated at the kitchen island while his sister Deena stood before her in a bathrobe. She was trying to get ready but was being peppered with questions.

Eleven year old Aiden stopped her interrogation to regard Ty with that same look of disdain that eleven-year-olds give adults. It was eerily similar to the way cats looked at people, reminding them that, if they were larger, they would eat us and take over our houses. In this particular case, it was a look that said Ty had to prove himself worthy of Aiden's attention before he would be granted any.

Though she greeted him this way each time they saw each other, she always relented. With him having been deployed for so much of her life, she looked at Ty with the same reserved fascination she might use if some B-list celebrity she'd never heard of showed up at the house. She was intrigued but too cool to show it.

Aiden understood that Ty had been to a lot of exotic places and he was gone for long stretches of her childhood. She was aware he knew a lot of neat things like how to start a fire, how to tie knots, how to do first aid, and how to say hello in several languages. He could call someone a butthead in those same languages and had taught her how to do it. Her mother had not been as proud as Ty had.

He was proficient in martial arts and could do push-ups with her on his back. He could do pull-ups while she clung to his back like a monkey. She also understood that Uncle Ty's place was not child-friendly which made her want to visit his apartment whenever she could. She'd been there a couple of times but Deena usually found an excuse to keep her away, preferring that Ty visit her house instead. He didn't take it personally. It was easier than tidying up his own place, which he preferred to keep functional rather than pristine.

"Where are you eating tonight?" Aiden asked her mother, her voice firm. She sounded like a parent questioning a teenager about a date.

"I don't know yet," Deena replied. "We haven't decided."

"Is it someplace good?"

"I just said I don't know where I'm going. That means I don't know if it's someplace good or not, but I would assume it is. I hope my friends wouldn't take me to some crappy restaurant for my birthday."

"Is it someplace I'd like to eat?" Aiden continued.

"If I don't know where I'm going, how do I know if it's someplace you'd like to eat or not?"

"I don't want you eating anywhere without me that I might like," Aiden stated. "That's not fair at all."

Deena sighed. "So what you're saying is that you want your mother to have a *bad* dinner because the only way she's allowed to have a *good* dinner is if you're there to enjoy it?"

Aiden grinned broadly and nodded. "That's exactly what I mean."

"You apparently take after your Uncle Ty," Deena said, winking at him. "He was exactly like that as a child. If Ty wasn't happy, no one was happy."

"Don't believe her," Ty stage-whispered to Aiden. "Your mother is just mad because our parents liked me better."

"Oh, that's exactly it," Deena replied with an eye roll.

"It's okay, Uncle Ty. I know Mommy isn't taking me because she's ashamed of me," Aiden said, wiping at a fake tear.

She was good. If you didn't know the kid, you'd think she was truly heartbroken. Ty knew she didn't mean it. Her mother also knew she didn't mean it, but it was the kind of comment that a parent couldn't leave standing.

"You know that's not true," Deena said. "My girlfriends are taking me out to dinner for my birthday. It's just adults and there won't be any children present."

"Wow, I never knew there were so many *other* parents who were ashamed of their children too. Maybe someone will start a special home for us. Someplace we'll be loved and treated nicely. Someplace with puppies and all the ice cream you can eat."

Ty gestured at Aiden. "Come on, devil child, we better get out of here before you get in trouble. Your mom needs to finish getting ready."

Aiden slipped off her stool. "Okay, let me get my stuff."

"We're going to the movies and to get something to eat. How much *stuff* do you need?"

Aiden looked at Ty as if he had no concept of the societal burdens of an eleven-year-old girl. She stalked off and came back with something that was half purse, half backpack.

"You're taking all that?" he asked. "You planning on camping somewhere along the way?"

"Come on," she said, ignoring his question. "Let's go before Mommy says more mean things to me."

"I didn't say anything mean!" Deena exclaimed.

"Hug your mother," Ty reminded her.

Aiden gave her mother an appraising serious look. "I'm not sure she's worthy at the moment."

"She's worthy. Do it before she makes you stay home with a mean old babysitter that smells funny and makes you play Scrabble."

Aiden conceded, hugging her mother and heading for the door. Ty hugged his sister then rushed off before Aiden got too far ahead of him. Even though this was her house, in her neighborhood, he cringed at the way she confidently burst from the door and started down the driveway without so much as a glance at her surroundings. It was like he was on an executive protection detail with a particularly uncooperative client. Despite the subtle hints he gave her about personal safety, Aiden had no situational awareness at all. He was going to have to work on that.

He struggled to dial it down a notch and not helicopter over her. People tended to dislike the hovering. Besides, they were in the United States, in the peaceful little town of Abingdon, Virginia. While it was a relatively safe community, Ty wasn't sure any place would ever feel safe to him again. If he lived on a thousand-acre ranch in the mountains of Montana he would continue to check for bad guys when he went out the front door. He would react the same way if he lived in a one-horse town with thirty-eight people and no stop signs.

That was how he was wired these days. His little bubble of ignorant bliss had been punctured a long time ago. There would never again be a time in his life where he was as casual and happy-go-lucky as Aiden had the privilege of being. He'd seen too much of the world, gotten his hands too dirty.

They drove twenty minutes to the shopping center with the movie theater she liked. It was the peak weekday hour. Kids were being dropped off by parents who either wanted them out of the house or were tired of listening to the begging. There were families there to see movies together and groups of teenagers slinking around, enjoying their lack of adult oversight.

"I'm hungry," Aiden said as they got out of his truck and the scent of popcorn hit her nose.

Her voice startled Ty. He was lost in the chaos and sensory overload of the parking lot. There was a movement, a lot of people, and too many places to hide. Every situation had a rhythm and he was quickly assessing this one. Was it simply a shitload of people doing people stuff or was there threat present? No matter where he was, he always had to ask himself that basic question.

"We'll get you some popcorn in a second," Ty said. "Enough to fill a bathtub if you can eat that much."

Aiden made a curious face as the image played through her head. The movie she wanted to see was a fairly new release, and the afternoon matinee showing already had a line waiting for tickets. Ty expected there would be more lines at the concession stand inside the busy theater. Great. Lines and crowds spelled stress and discomfort for him but he'd agreed to do this. Deena needed a night out. She hadn't had many since the divorce. He'd promised her he'd do it. He *needed* to do it. It was a normal thing that normal people did and he wanted to be a normal guy again.

Looking back at his military career, the things he'd done over fourteen years of service, this was minuscule by comparison. How could going to a matinee with his niece be such a big deal? It wasn't, and he had to quit making it into something bigger than it was.

Buckle down, he reminded himself. *You got this.*

The ticket line was irritating. He didn't like strangers standing directly behind him, their presence looming over his personal space. It was one of the sensations he had the most trouble with in the civilian world, the awareness that someone was directly behind him and he was unable to keep an eye on them. In regular life, the situation was unavoidable. You couldn't just turn around and stare at the people behind you in line. That got weird. It was never a problem in the military. Someone that close was a brother, a man you could trust. A man who'd lay down his life for you with the expectation you'd do the same for him.

The slower moving concession stand line was even worse. Sounds from the adjoining arcade filled the concession area with a barrage of sound effects – beeps, chirps, and firing lasers. Ty was getting antsy, shifting on his feet, anxious to get into the theater and be seated. Maybe then he could chill out a little bit. He'd close his eyes in the comforting darkness and take some deep breaths, use some of those relaxation strategies they kept pushing on him. He needed to find his happy place, although he hadn't had much luck with that. Perhaps he didn't have a happy place. Could be that all he had was a dark and angry place. That was how it felt sometimes.

It didn't help that there was an action movie playing in one of the theaters. The ultra-realistic sound system shook the walls with gunshots and explosions, the sounds pulling Ty in like a nightmare. It was remarkable how the explosions in that theater, rattling the walls and making the floor tremble, sounded like they were being shelled.

The sound made Ty increasingly uncomfortable. He felt exposed and vulnerable, like he should be doing something, *anything,* to get them out of there. He needed to get Aiden somewhere safe before a round hit the building. At any moment they could be trapped in a pile of rubble with all these people. A line of sweat trickled down his back.

The people ahead of them got their popcorn and drinks, then moved on. Stuck there in his head, Ty didn't notice the line moving. He didn't notice that Aiden had already stepped forward and was waiting on him to join her. What Ty did notice was the man behind him reach forward and peck him on the shoulder.

"Go on, buddy," the guy said. "Wake up."

That unexpected physical contact was exactly the wrong thing for the man to do. Ty didn't hesitate. He didn't think. He spun and trapped the man's outstretched arm beneath his left. His right shot to the man's throat and locked onto it. He swept his leg, and took him to the floor hard. It was pure reflex, the product of over a decade of training. He had every intention of shoving the man's voice box through his spine when he caught himself.

He saw the man's shocked expression. He swept his surroundings and took in the stunned faces of the man's family. He took in the sea of other dumbfounded faces in the concession lines. This was not the kind of thing you saw at the Movie Mall Twenty. Everyone stood there frozen in that awkward moment, uncertain of how to back up from it. Ty certainly had no clue and the man in his grasp was too scared to even breathe.

"Uncle Ty?" It was Aiden, her quiet voice breaking the spell.

Ty released his grip on the man and stood. The other man got awkwardly to his feet, brushing at his clothes. Ty didn't help him.

"Don't touch people you don't know," Ty warned, his voice barely above a whisper.

There were a lot of people were staring. It was uncomfortable attention.

"We want the bottomless popcorn with lots of butter," Aiden told the concessionaire. She'd already moved on. "What do you want to drink, Uncle Ty?"

He turned to the counter and hesitantly gave his drink order. Rattled, he took a napkin from a dispenser on the counter and mopped at his forehead. They got their jumbo tub of popcorn and two overpriced drinks, then turned around to find two security guards waiting on them. Behind them was the man Ty had dropped, standing with his wife and their two confused young boys. Ty knew he'd screwed up.

"Sir, we're going to have to ask you to leave the premises."

There was a day when Ty would have given these guys a run for their money. He would have called them names and warned them they were biting off more than they could chew. The fact there were two of them meant nothing to him. Odds never concerned him. The problem was that Ty was currently employed as a security guard too.

He worked for a different company but it was the same crappy job. Any of the slights he would have thrown in their direction would have applied to him equally and he didn't want to go there. He'd heard it all before and hated it when people treated him like a second-class citizen because he was a security guard. There was something about that uniform that made you a magnet for assholes and anyone with something to prove. People talked real tough when they knew you couldn't fight back.

The other side of the spectrum was that the uniform sometimes made you invisible. People were programmed to ignore you in the same way they did homeless people. They didn't make eye contact, didn't speak. Somedays Ty craved that invisibility.

The only thing that made him reconsider taking the high road was the smirk on the face of the man he'd taken to the floor. Ty had already calmed down, the moment had passed, but that look stood ready to inflame his anger all over again. He was pretty certain if he tossed his drink forward the two security guards would jump to the side. That would leave an open channel to the smirking man and Ty could finish what he'd started. On the other hand, there was Aiden and the trust his sister had placed in him. He didn't want Aiden to see him hauled off in handcuffs.

"Sir, I'm not asking again. If you don't leave right now we'll call the police and have you removed. Please don't make a scene in front of these children."

Ty released a long sigh, trying to blow off this new stream of tension, but it would only go down so far. He glanced at his niece and found her staring back at him with large, curious eyes. Not disappointed, not angry, simply watching and waiting to see what he'd do.

"Let's just go, Uncle Ty. Mommy will be mad if I have to go to the hoosegow."

Ty couldn't help but smile. "Where did you ever learn a word like that?"

"Uh, you taught me."

The nervous security guards insisted on following them out the door and all the way to his truck. Ty could sense their relief. They didn't want to fight him. He and Aiden didn't particularly hurry, enjoying their popcorn and drinks as they walked. Ty gave a little wave to the security guards as they pulled out of the lot. He noticed one of them snapping a picture of his tag number. He was uncomfortable with that. The best case scenario was they would ban him from the facility. The worst was that he might get a visit from the cops tonight.

They drove to a park less than a mile away. They found a rickety wooden picnic table, its peeling green paint carved with initials. They had a picnic of popcorn and gigantic sodas.

"Your mother is going to be so mad at me," Ty said, slurping from his cup. He'd been mulling it over while watching Aiden toss popcorn kernels to a chunky gray squirrel.

Aiden snapped her head round and looked at him like he was crazy. "How's she going to find out? *I'm* not to tell her. Are *you* going to tell her? 'Cause that would be *dumb*. I'm just saying."

"Well, I didn't exactly plan on it but I assumed you might since it was probably the most interesting part of the evening. Isn't that what kids do? They tell their moms about their day and stuff?"

Aiden narrowed her eyes and stared off into the distance. She almost looked like a wizened old trapper recalling a particularly hard winter. "I learned a long time ago you can't tell mothers everything."

Ty grinned. "You learned that a long time ago, huh?"

She nodded and shoved so much popcorn in her mouth that she couldn't close it. She nodded and chewed, struggling to speak, popcorn falling out of her mouth. "Yeah, I figured that out pretty quick after I started elementary school."

"You told on yourself?"

"A few times," she admitted. "Then I figured it out."

"You know, you're a pretty sharp cookie. You might be a force to contend with one day."

She frowned at him. "What does that mean?"

"It means you're smart enough to be dangerous. It means you're so smart that the things you say will make people mad at you sometimes. You'll understand things about people and smart-aleck comments will come out of your mouth before you can even stop them."

Aiden smiled at that, relishing the thought that she had a tool of torment in her arsenal of which she'd previously been unaware. "I think that already happens sometimes."

"I'm sure it does."

She took a drink from her vat of soda and gave Ty a serious look. "So why did you get mad at that man? Did he do something to you? I didn't see what happened."

"What man?" Ty's head had wandered somewhere else and it took him a moment to find his way back.

"Duh? The one in the popcorn line? How many other men have you laid the smackdown on today?"

Ty frowned at her choice of words. More disturbing to him was how he could have forgotten the situation that had just taken place? If violence was that inconsequential to him, was he even fit to be wandering around in normal society? He wondered sometimes. It was part of what he was trying to come to terms with.

"No, he was the only one today. Lines make me nervous. The guy touched me and it startled me. I reacted before I had a chance to stop myself." He started to add that it was a "war thing" but didn't know if that would mean anything to her. He certainly didn't want her to think there was something wrong with him. He didn't want her to be scared to be around him. While he wasn't the most sensitive guy in the world, that would hurt.

"Are you a ninja?" she asked.

Ty laughed. "No, definitely not a ninja."

"Have you ever in the past been a ninja?"

He admired the way she rephrased the question. She was sneaky. "Not exactly."

"Well, that was a ninja move. You dropped that guy like a bad habit."

"Where do you learn these expressions?"

Aiden shrugged. "I don't know."

"I overreacted because he startled me. There was nothing cool about it. I shouldn't have done it. It wasn't the right thing to do and you should never act like that. Just because I did it doesn't make it right."

"I know. Mom said you get like that sometimes," Aiden admitted. "She said I shouldn't jump out of the dark and scare you."

Oh great, Ty thought. *She already knows there something wrong with me.*

He smiled warmly at her. "Definitely not. I might wet my pants and I'd be embarrassed."

Aiden thought that was hilarious. She held her belly and laughed.

"So what do you want to do, kid? I don't imagine you want to sit here and talk to me all evening. Would you like to go to a movie at a different theater?"

She looked doubtful. "Can we do that?"

"Of course we can. You think they've got wanted posters for me at every theater now?"

She shrugged. "I don't know. They might." She was fighting back a smile, the edges of her mouth twitching.

"Let's go."

She looked at her drink and popcorn. "Will they let me take this in at a different movie?"

"I doubt it. Toss the popcorn out for the squirrel. It'll make him happy and I'll buy you some more at the next movie."

Aiden dumped the greasy bucket to an excited looking squirrel and they threw their trash in a rusty green can. Ty took a deep breath.

Let's try this again. Going to the movies with your niece, take two.

"That squirrel is going to get really fat. I bet he won't be able to get back up that tree when he's done," Aiden said.

3

"Try calling her again," Barger suggested.

They were in Richmond, Virginia. The RV had been parked in a Wal-Mart parking lot all night and she'd done nothing but call and send messages since they got there. She groaned. Barger was getting on her nerves. "I've been calling. She's not answering."

"Why the hell is she not answering? You've been talking to this girl for months, right? She said she would go. Why isn't she here?"

"Fuck if I know. Yes, I've been talking to her for months. Yes, she said she wanted to come. We've been planning this for weeks. She was supposed to be *right* here but she's not. What do you want me to do about it?"

Barger had no answer for that. "Maybe she doesn't see us?" He scanned the parking lot outside the window.

"Seriously? We're the only RV here. We're the biggest damn thing in the whole parking lot. If she were here, she'd have no trouble spotting us. She's just not here."

"Then where the hell is she?"

Tia pushed herself up from the leather recliner. She couldn't listen to Barger any longer. He was like a broken record. She ambled stiffly to the table and grabbed a pack of menthol 100s. "I need a smoke."

She left the frustrated Barger pacing around the narrow confines of the RV. He was getting on her nerves with his ranting and stomping around. How was she supposed to know what was going on? She'd done this dozens of times and it always went the same way. Everything went like clockwork.

Until this time.

She lit a smoke and walked around, though she didn't go far. She was fifty-five years old now, ate poorly, and drank too much. She was overweight and her hips hurt with every step. She wiped her forehead with the tail of her tank top. The parking lot was not only hot, but humid in a way they didn't experience in Arizona. It was like she was slowly being steamed to death, like a stalk of broccoli. She didn't know how people could live here. The whole place was flat, hot, and miserable.

While she walked, she scrolled through her phone, a sharply-pointed green nail clicking as it tapped the screen. The girl's name was Kellie and the two had been in regular communication up until yesterday. Kellie had accepted her invitation and was ready to come live with her. Tia had come all way from Arizona based on her word. They were supposed to meet last night but Kellie hadn't shown. They'd been there for nearly twelve hours and Barger was getting nervous. He said he needed to get back home. Tia wanted to get back too, but she didn't want to leave empty-handed.

Although she and Kellie usually communicated via Snapchat, they also used text messaging, Facebook, and Instagram. She leaned against the shady side of the RV and checked Snapchat again. Her message had still not been read. She went to send another and received a message that she'd been blocked.

What the hell?

She went to Instagram, both to check for any updates and to send a message through that app. The account she was looking for was gone. Tia went to Facebook and found the same thing. All of Kellie's social media accounts had been deleted. This was not good.

Tia went to her messaging app and confirmed that none of the text messages she'd sent since arriving in town had been read. She had one thing left and it was something the two had never done. It was something she'd never done with any of the girls. She clicked on Kellie's contact and chose to dial a voice call.

She raised the phone, her anticipation growing with each ring. It was not a person who answered. After several rings, an automated message informed Tia that the number she was attempting to contact was no longer in service. Either Kellie, or someone acting on her behalf, had made it impossible for them to contact each other.

Tossing the cigarette butt into the parking lot, she shoved the phone into her sweaty bra and clambered inside the RV.

Barger looked at her expectantly. "Anything?"

Tia waved him off. "We might as well get going."

Slouched in the dinette booth with a bottle of water and a bag of chips, Barger looked at her with surprise. "What? We're leaving without her? What about that stupid puppy you promised her? The damn thing pisses all over the place. I'll never get the smell out."

Tia shrugged. "She either cut ties with me for some reason or they were cut for her. We probably don't need to be sitting around here any longer. If her parents caught her packing, they might go to the cops. Who knows what she told them?" She ignored his comments about the puppy. It was just a prop, insignificant in the bigger picture.

Barger cursed and ranted as he made his way to the driver's seat. She let him blow off steam, then settled into the passenger seat when he finally shut up. He started the engine, put the large vehicle in gear, and pulled out.

"So, I guess we're headed home?" His tone was clipped, his anger apparent.

"Guess so," she said. "I have other prospects but none are anywhere near our route. None were so far along in the process as Kellie."

Barger didn't care about that part of it. Those were Tia's problems as far as he was concerned. "I still get paid, right? I mean, I did my part. I did what I was supposed to do."

She didn't answer him. The asshole always had his hand out. He had no appreciation. No respect.

"I mean, you being successful was never a condition of me driving," Barger continued. "I've got fuel expenses, plus lost time on the job. This cost me money."

"It cost me money too," Tia retorted. "You think I don't got shit to do? You think I lay around all day eating Doritos and watching telenovelas?"

Barger was silent. That was exactly what he thought.

Tia could tell he wanted to say more but was biting his tongue. She was aware he saw her as a washed-up old lady. He forgot who she'd been. Sometimes she had to remind him but right now she was just sick of him. They'd spent too much time in tight quarters over the last couple of days.

"You could at least pay for a tank of gas," Barger mumbled. "I've paid for everything."

Tia waved him off. "You put it on your card."

"I get a bill for that card!"

"I'm an old lady on a fixed income. I have to watch my expenses."

Barger snorted. "Yeah right."

"How about you just hush and let me keep working on this. I'll see if I can move one of the other prospects along."

"I'm not going out of my way unless it's a sure thing. I've got shit to do at home. Jobs that pays the bills."

"Grumble, grumble, grumble," Tia mocked, tapping at the screen of her phone.

Barger shut up and stewed in silence. Tia sent a few messages and scrolled through updates. When they were rolling down Broad Street, she got up from her seat and went to the back of the RV. She shut herself into the tiny bathroom with a purse the size of a shopping bag. She lowered the lid of the petite plastic toilet and dropped heavily onto it. She lit another cigarette and fished an embroidered silk pouch from the depths of her bag.

From the pouch, she removed a statue around four inches tall and reverently stood it on the edge of the sink. It was a skeleton dressed in a robe like the grim reaper, complete with scythe. The skeleton held a globe in its outstretched, bony hand. Tia removed a bottle of perfume from her purse and sprayed some at the base of the statue as she prayed. The Bony Lady liked nice things.

Tia took out a tiny bottle of tequila from her purse. She splashed an offering at the base of the statue, then tipped the bottle up and finished it off. She had a better altar at home but sometimes she needed to speak to Holy Death when she was away. She carried the statue with her everywhere she went, along with some of the things Santa Muerte liked. She was fond of apples, but Tia was out. She would buy another the next time they stopped.

The RV swayed as Barger negotiated the onramp, pulling onto the interstate. Tia pinched the statue between long green nails, making sure it didn't fall over. "You have always blessed me, Holy Death. You have protected me against all enemies. Have I earned your displeasure? Have I failed you somehow?"

Tia stared at the blank orbital sockets and the impassive expression on the little resin statue. It wasn't that she expected a verbal response, though it would have been nice. It would make things so much easier. Tia began to pray in earnest, two splayed fingers locking the statue to the edge of the sink. She bowed her head in deference and spoke low, a whispered supplication. When the cigarette burned down to her fingers, she tossed it into the shower where it scorched the plastic base. Barger would be angry but he was a *cabron*, a bastard. To hell with him.

She resumed her prayer and it was an hour before the words stopped coming. When she was done, she was drained, lightheaded. She kissed the top of the statue and replaced it in the pouch. She tried to stand but found it difficult to gain the necessary momentum in the narrow space. She locked a hand over the lip of the sink and finally managed to heave herself upward.

She checked herself in the mirror but wished she hadn't. It was an old habit and she was certain she was less to look at than she'd once been. She was fat and wrinkled. She wore too much makeup, but there was not enough in the world to hide what time was doing to her. She wore cheap stretchy clothes that were comfortable but not particularly flattering due to the egg-shaped body she'd developed in middle-age. It was the body of her mother and grandmother. There was no escaping it. On top of it all, she added lots of gold jewelry so people would know she was someone.

Santa Muerte had brought her so much but she knew that restoring her youth, her beauty, was even beyond what The Bony Lady could do.

4

Ty had his normal lousy night of sleep, plagued by nightmares. Nothing helped that. They were always something disturbing, dreams in which he saw the faces of the dead, either recalled from memory or imagined. Sometimes he dreamed he was in a fight for his life and didn't have the gear he needed. Other times it was confined spaces with the sensation that he was suffocating. This time he'd been trying his best to run away from a threat while his feet felt like they were mired in quicksand. No amount of running gained him any ground.

The nights could be so exhausting that sometimes he didn't know why he bothered to go to bed at all. Not sleeping brought its own problems, though. After a day or two he started hallucinating. If he didn't find the nightmares in his sleep, they would seek him out in his daily life.

He took a quick shower and threw on his security guard uniform. By 0730 hours he'd sucked down an energy drink and was starting his first patrol around the Petro Panda Travel Plaza. The facility was a fancy truck stop about twenty minutes north of Abingdon, Virginia, on the interstate. It was the only job he'd held since his discharge, a little over a year ago. It wasn't a great job, not even a good one, but the duties were manageable. It was something he could do without having to think a whole lot.

He hoped that one day he could get into law enforcement but figured he needed to deal with some of his issues first. He didn't want to go to the effort of becoming a cop and then screw it up because he lost his temper. If anything, the experience at the movies with Aiden stood as a further reminder that he had things he needed to deal with.

It was late spring, the day already hot and humid. Ty could tell by the sun pounding on his face that it was going to be a hot one. Truckers who spent the night there wandered inside for showers and breakfast. Every few minutes the drone of idling trucks was broken by the intercom announcing that the next shower was available.

The smell of exhaust was so heavy that Ty wondered if he could inhale enough of it to kill himself. How much would it take? He'd known people who ended it that way and it seemed like a peaceful way to go. Just go to sleep and never wake up. It was less traumatic than a gunshot or hanging. It also left the body more presentable for the funeral, assuming he hadn't already alienated anyone who might attend.

While Ty didn't consider himself to be suicidal, there were times he found himself dwelling on it. He wasn't adjusting well and there didn't appear to be any route between where he was now and where he wanted to be. He let that morbid thought-bubble wither on the vine and tried to concentrate on his surroundings.

Very little went on at the Petro Panda at this time of day. When he worked the night shift he had to watch for the lot lizards, prostitutes who made a living selling their services truck to truck. He also had to watch for local drug dealers intent on making a little money off bored truckers stuck there for the night. On the day shift he might have the odd fender bender or a shoplifter to deal with. Most days, though, it was just a matter of walking in circles and being visible.

Visible yet invisible.

Lately he'd come to wonder if this was the wrong type of job for him. There was nothing to do but walk around and think. It gave him too much time to dwell on his situation, too much time for the darkness to fill his head. Perhaps he'd be better off with some thoughtless factory job where he'd hopefully stay busy with some inane task that required just enough of his mental faculties to prevent him from getting carried away by his thoughts. There were a few factories around that might fit the bill but he hadn't gone as far as filling out any applications yet. He wasn't sure he could sit in one place all day. At least being a security guard allowed you to move around.

Over the next few hours, things perked up considerably. On a beautiful Saturday, this time of year there were lots of people on the road. At some point the Petro Panda was overrun by a girls' softball team rolling in on an activity bus covered in banners. They must have been on their way to a tournament. Multiple carloads of parents and grandparents accompanied them with more slogans scrawled on their windows in wide, white letters.

Ty recognized the name on the bus as being from a local middle school. A group that size would congest things for a while. They would cause long lines at the bathrooms as everyone took care of business, and long lines at the cash registers as everyone stocked up on drinks, chips, ring pops, and gummy bears for the road. Even without this group, the pumps were active with a steady stream of weekend travelers. In the truck section, semis and RVs were fueling up at the diesel pumps. He hoped all the activity would provide a distraction and make the day go faster.

Around 1000 hours he took his morning break, wandering to the far edge of the parking lot and taking a seat at one of the metal picnic tables. He'd been thinking about taking up smoking because it would be the perfect activity for filling his break time. He'd tried smoking before but it impaired him physically, and in the military his life had been about training. He wasn't certain that mattered anymore. He continued to hit the gym obsessively but it wasn't like he was training for missions. A little drop in his cardio functioning wasn't likely to get him killed these days.

From the corner of his eye he caught an irregularity at the gasoline pumps. It was something he learned watching crowds when he was patrolling in the war. Places and activities had a certain rhythm to them and when that rhythm changed it could mean something was going on, something he might need to be concerned with. In Iraq and Afghanistan it could mean insurgents were infiltrating a crowd and something bad was about to happen. It could mean he'd interrupted something shady and villagers were attempting to hide it from him.

At the Petro Panda, the rhythms were different. Fueling vehicles had a particular rhythm. People filled their tanks and leaned against their cars. They cleaned trash from their vehicle and shoved it into the truck stop's big red cans. Sometimes they went inside the store and sometimes they didn't. What they did *not* normally do was run around frantically from vehicle to vehicle in a state of panic.

Ty jogged toward the distressed woman. She was in her mid-thirties and well-dressed in casual clothing. Her hands were shaking and she was on the verge of utter hysterical panic.

"Excuse me, ma'am, is something wrong?"

She spun toward Ty, her eyes taking in his uniform and recognizing him as someone who might be able to help. "I can't find my daughter." Her speech faltered, like she was embarrassed at the turn of events, like it was somehow her mistake.

Ty smiled at her reassuringly. "Don't worry, ma'am. This is a big place and kids get lost here all the time. We'll find her. What's her name?"

"Gretchen," the woman said, wringing her hands together.

Ty pulled the radio from his belt and relayed that information to the manager on duty.

In a matter of seconds, there was an announcement over the intercom, the sound blaring over the entire property. "*Gretchen, could you come to the register at the front of the store, please? Your mother is looking for you.*"

"What's your name, ma'am?" Ty asked.

"Heather Wells."

"Heather, I'm Tyler. Gretchen will probably show up at the

register any minute. You give me a description and they'll be on the lookout for her."

"She's ten years old. She's wearing a blue shirt with a yellow frog on the front. She's got on white shorts and flip-flops. Green flip-flops with sparkles. I hate them because they don't match anything but she loves them."

Ty nodded, passing on that information to the manager. Heather hurried off, calling her daughter's name and asking other patrons if anyone had seen her. Heather's manner was polite but continued to verge on the fringe of panic. Ty empathized but was certain Gretchen would pop up at any moment. This happened at least once a week during the summer. The missing kids were always in a bathroom stall, playing a video game, or had slipped back to the car when their parents weren't looking. Ty had witnessed quite a few spankings from embarrassed and relieved parents intent on teaching their children a lesson about running off without permission.

Heather rushed back to Tyler's side. "I don't see her!" There were tears in her eyes this time. "There's so many kids around here that no one's sure if they've seen her or not. All these kids are wearing blue shirts."

Ty nodded thoughtfully. She was right. The softball team had on blue shirts. Their supporters and siblings were wearing matching blue t-shirts. It was a sea of blue everywhere you looked. A ten-year-old girl in a blue shirt was not going to stick out at all in this crowd.

He raised his radio. "Has Gretchen shown up at the register yet?"

"*Not yet,*" replied the manager. "*We're on the lookout. I just sent someone around to check the bathrooms.*"

Ty was beginning to get concerned. Usually it didn't take this long. Most of the time the announcement over the intercom was all it took for the kid to come running. Gretchen had probably been missing for about five minutes at this point.

"Heather, lock your car so nobody steals your stuff. Does your daughter have a phone?"

Heather indicated the child didn't. Regardless of Ty's opinion on whether a ten-year-old needed a cell phone or not, it certainly would have made things easier if she had one. They could call her and, if worse came to worst, use it to track her location.

"Okay, then I want you to get your phone and text me a picture of Gretchen."

They walked to Heather's car and Ty gave her his number. When he had the picture, he instructed Heather to go wait by the cash register while he made another pass of the parking lot. He wanted to show the picture around and see if it jarred anyone's memory since the description of her appearance was so vague.

"Fuck that," Heather spat. "I'm looking for my daughter." With that she tore off, peering inside every car she passed. She made a tearful appeal to people along the way, showing them the picture she'd just sent Ty. "Have you seen my daughter?"

So much for being on the verge of panic. She'd crossed over to full-blown terror. Ty radioed in to the manager again. "She show up?"

"*Not yet. Usually it doesn't take this long. We've checked the bathrooms, the shower facilities, and even the stock room.*"

"Why don't you go ahead and call the police. It shouldn't take this long. A little girl would have responded to the intercom and there's nowhere here you can't hear it." Ty was concerned something else might be going on but he didn't want to guess what. None of the options were anything he wanted to put into words.

"*Are you sure?*" the manager asked. "*Maybe we should give it a little longer.*"

"No, this feels wrong," Ty said. "Call them now."

"*Okay, but it's on you.*"

He stared at his radio like he wanted to reach through it and throttle the manager. "I don't care. Just do it! Also, announce that description I gave you and ask if anyone has seen her."

"*I don't know about that, Ty. It might scare the other customers,*" the manager replied. "*We don't want to make them think something bad is going on.*"

"Something bad *is* going on. Do it or I will."

"*Dude, I'm not sure if we're supposed to do something like that. I don't want to lose my job.*"

"What if this was your kid?" Ty asked. "What would you want?"

"*Fine*," she replied.

"Jesus," Ty mumbled, shoving the radio in its pouch. What was it with people?

Heather passed him again, shouting her daughter's name as she rushed by. She must have made a full circuit of the store. The line of vehicles continued to exit the parking lot as more were coming in.

Seeing Heather in such a state of panic made Ty realize that, despite his frequent anxiety, he felt nothing but focus at the moment. A calm had settled over him. It had to be his training kicking in. As it did, he understood he needed to control this scene. He needed to lock the Petro Panda down.

His mind raced. He ran toward the diesel pumps and stepped in front of a semi headed toward the exit. Ty waved his arms to flag the driver down. When he rolled his window down, Ty jumped onto the running board. "Hey, I've got an emergency. I've got a missing kid and I need to shut this place down until we find her. Can you block the main entrance with your rig? I don't want anyone going in or out."

The driver looked doubtful. "Buddy, I've got a schedule to keep."

"It's a fucking kid," Ty barked. "Can you help or not?"

Deciding Ty was not a man who took "no" very well, the driver waved his hand and nodded. "Okay. I'll do it. The main entrance?"

"Yes," Ty said, hopping down. "I'll get someone else to block the truck entrance once you've pulled out."

The driver headed off to get his truck into position. Customers would not be happy about this. Ty rushed off and found a second driver willing to block the heavy truck entrance. Although no one wanted to be delayed this was an emergency. People would have to show a little understanding. Just as Ty got every entrance secured, his radio crackled.

"*Ty, I need you to get out front,*" the manager said. "*There's a truck stuck across the entrance. People can't get in or out.*"

Ty whipped out his own radio. "He's not stuck. I put him there. He's blocking it until the police get here."

The manager grew irate. "*You can't do that! I'm pretty sure it's against policy and probably against the law. You can't just hold people pris-oner against their will. You're not a cop!"*

Ty ran back toward the store. He hadn't heard the manager broad-cast the description of Gretchen over the intercom like he'd asked. He was starting to get pissed at the lack of cooperation. He also needed to make an announcement about the reason for the blocked entrances to quell any panic. He pushed through the glass doors on the back side of the truck stop and found a crowd of angry people demanding answers. They were surrounding the cash registers and the manager, an overweight woman with curly 1980s hair, looked scared. She caught Ty's eye as he burst through the door and her fear turned to anger. Her look made it clear this was all his fault.

He pushed his way through the crowd and joined the staff behind the counter. He took the microphone connected to the public address system and turned it on.

The manager gave him a warning look. "Honey, you're on your own here. I tried to warn you."

"Did you at least call the cops like I asked?"

"Yeah."

Ty raised the microphone to his mouth. The manager held her hands up in a gesture that she wanted no part of this, rushing off toward the back office and leaving Ty to deal with the situation. He had no problem with that. It was exactly what he intended to do.

"Excuse me, folks, but I need you to bear with us for a moment. We have a missing child and I need your help in locating her. Her name is Gretchen."

While he was giving her physical description, Ty heard sirens approaching. Help was on the way.

5

_____

L ess than a minute after ending his speech over the intercom, Ty was speaking with two county deputies and a Virginia state trooper outside the store. They demanded the trucks blocking the exits be moved before they addressed the situation with the missing girl.

"You can't hold these people prisoner," an exasperated deputy said. "What the hell are you thinking?" He'd been bombarded by several dozen customers anxious to get on their way.

"I was securing the scene," Ty said. "We at least need to get their information before we let these people go. We need to know who was here when it happened."

"We don't know that anything even happened yet," the trooper said. "She could have just wandered off. That's usually the case."

Ty struggled to keep his cool. "Officer, we deal with lost kids on a regular basis but they're always found in a few minutes. It's been at least ten minutes now."

"Did you lock things down as soon as the woman alerted you her child was missing?" the trooper asked.

Ty shook his head. "No, like I said, things like this happen and the kids _always_ turn up. We searched for her first. We made an announcement over the intercom. I started to get concerned when we went past five minutes. There were cars coming and going that whole time."

"We can let these people go ahead and leave," the trooper instructed the deputies. "If you don't mind, can one of you get a list of names and tag numbers in case we need to follow up with them in the future?"

One deputy headed off toward the main entrance, speaking to agitated customers as he went. He got the truck driver's contact information first, then instructed him to move his rig out of the way. The truck driver was relieved to get going, tired of angry patrons threatening him.

"I'm going to speak to the mother," the trooper told Ty. "Can you give the deputy here a statement?"

Ty pointed in Heather's direction. "That's the mother there. Her name is Heather Wells. Her daughter is Gretchen."

Heather was sobbing into her phone, frantically gesturing as she explained to someone what had taken place. The second deputy moved closer to Ty, pulled up his sagging belt, then drew a notebook from his pocket.

"Are there more officers on the way?" Ty asked.

The deputy raised his eyes to Ty, then went back to jotting down the date in his notebook. "Why don't you let us do the police work, Mr. Stone? There's no call for us to bring in additional officers yet. Now tell me exactly where you were when you learned about the missing child."

"I've been here since 0730 hours. I had just gone on my morning break, which is at 1000 hours."

There was a change in the deputy's facial expression. It wasn't quite a smirk but a look that implied *of course you were on break*. He jotted the information down. "That's ten o'clock, right?"

The condescending implication that Ty hadn't been doing his job made his blood run hot. He checked the deputy's name badge. "You take breaks don't you, Deputy Puckett? You think crimes don't happen when you're on break? You think crime comes to a stop every time you pull into the fucking Krispy Kreme?"

The deputy raised his eyes from his notebook, surprised at Ty's vitriol. "Was that necessary? We're trying to find a missing girl here. What I don't need is any more of your attitude."

Ty struggled to rein in his impatience. "I know exactly what we're trying to do here. I was doing it before you showed up. Let's get back to doing it and quit bullshitting about it. You're wasting time."

Deputy Puckett gave Ty a warning look. "I don't appreciate your language. If you think we're wasting time, what would Mr. Security Guard suggest the real cops do differently?"

"I would suggest the *real* cops get more men out here."

"Are you done with the attitude?"

Ty didn't respond, giving the deputy a hardnosed stare.

The state trooper interrupted their standoff. Heather Wells was sobbing in the background. The trooper had seated her in his car, the door open. "Deputy, do you all have a female deputy or a victim's assistance officer who might be able to help out with her? She's in a bad place. She doesn't have family close and she's going to need someone."

Deputy Puckett clicked the mic at his collar, leaned toward it, and relayed the trooper's request to the dispatcher.

"Do you have access to the security camera footage or is that archived at the corporate level?" the trooper asked Ty.

"I can access it here but it's backed up at the corporate office over the network."

The trooper gestured at the deputy. "Can you keep an eye on the mother while we check out the video?"

Deputy Puckett agreed but pulled the trooper aside for a moment. Ty had no idea what was being said but assumed it was something about his attitude. If they didn't start looking for this girl, his attitude was only going to get worse. The deputy was the one with the attitude as far as Ty was concerned. In his experience, everybody got pissed on by somebody. The FBI pissed on state troopers, troopers pissed on deputies, deputies pissed on small town cops. All of them pissed on security guards.

"Come on," the trooper said when he was done, leading Ty toward the store.

The truck stop had its own tiny server room housing all the electronics required to operate the complex facility. Credit card processing, point of sale equipment, inventory management, and Wi-Fi all ran out of the room. A table held a workstation and monitor. Sitting down in two folding chairs, Ty and the trooper ran the video back to the point where the mother parked at the gas pumps with her child. The mother fueled the vehicle and then it appeared that both needed to use the restroom so they headed inside, where they encountered the long line that had built up due to the softball team and their families.

The two got separated waiting to get in. The mother allowed her daughter to go into the restroom first and, as a result, the child was out before her mother. Heather stated that she instructed her daughter to wait on her outside the restroom, but the child had not obeyed. The security footage showed her wandering the aisles looking at candy and toys. In one view the girl made it to the front of the store and stood there looking around, presumably waiting on her mother.

Out of nowhere, a broad smile crossed Gretchen's face. She stood up on her toes and flapped her hands with excitement. She could barely contain her glee and skipped toward the door with no sign of hesitation.

"Can we see where she went? Is there a view of that?" the trooper asked.

"Yeah, there's a lot of views. It may take a second to figure out which number camera corresponds to which view. I don't have to access this very often. Usually we're just dealing with shoplifting so I'm accessing inside footage."

Ty clicked the mouse around the interface, eventually changing camera views and rewinding to the appropriate timestamp. It turned out to be incredibly difficult to pick the small child out in the various outside views. The shots were all wide angle, attempting to capture the most area possible with a single camera. While that made sense for the company because it saved on the number of cameras required to cover a given area, it rendered the images nearly useless. They were grainy and distorted.

The footage was color, but not streaming real-time. It was more like a series of rapid snapshots taken every couple of seconds. The child was there and then she was a foot away, then a foot further away. This too was a cost-saving measure. A lower frame-rate required less storage capacity than recording full-motion videos. Data storage wasn't such a big deal for a small facility with a half-dozen cameras but this place had sixty cameras. The Petro Panda chain itself had hundreds of truck stops with thousands of cameras. At a corporate level that meant a lot of storage was required and storage cost money.

"My God," the trooper said, "there's kids everywhere. What color shirt was she supposed to be wearing?"

"Blue," Ty replied. "Same color as—"

"The softball team's shirts," the trooper finished.

It was true. The footage showed kids everywhere, most wearing blue shirts. With the low image quality, one blue-shirted child didn't look a whole lot different than the next. They changed views and found the bus from the softball team blocked the camera view to the front of the store. That one might have been helpful. Other views showed kids clustered everywhere taking selfies, group shots, and horse playing. Families and parents were mingling among the kids. The players were constantly running on and off the bus, scurrying around like ants.

"It's chaos," the trooper mumbled.

Ty could only nod in agreement.

Fifteen frustrated minutes later they agreed that those few seconds of Gretchen heading toward the door with a broad grin on her face were the last images of her the cameras had captured. That particular camera was intended to capture a clear image if anyone robbed the store. It produced a high resolution picture that could be distributed to the news or law enforcement. None of the other cameras had a clear view of the child after she separated from her mother, nor did they have the resolution to zoom in and closely study the image. Collectively, it wasn't much.

"Can you print those screenshots?" the trooper asked.

Ty clicked a few onscreen buttons and the color images sputtered from a nearby inkjet printer. When the first one dropped into the tray, the trooper snapped a picture of it with his phone and texted it out to someone.

"Are you issuing an Amber Alert?" Ty asked.

"Not at this time. We don't have enough information for that. We don't even know if she's in a vehicle. It'll just go out as a missing child report for now. I've got detectives showing up any moment, though."

"It's probably too late," Ty said. "If someone snatched her, she's gone. They wouldn't stick around."

"What makes you so sure of that?"

"I served in Special Forces when I was in the Army. That's how they trained us to do it. Snatch and grab. Use chaos to your advantage. Don't stick around."

6

Within two hours the Petro Panda had blossomed into the epicenter of a missing child investigation. The Virginia State Police brought in an RV fully outfitted to serve as a mobile command center, and pop-up awnings were erected along one side of the parking lot to shelter investigators from the heat.

The sheriff's department brought in a tracking dog and Gretchen's mother had provided them with an item of clothing for scent tracking. The dog handler appeared hopeful but Ty held little hope for this approach. With thousands of people going in and out, there was no way the scent of that one child was not corrupted. Despite that, the dog handler jogged behind his bloodhound as it wandered around the massive parking lot trying to do its job.

Local television news crew filmed this with great interest. They were constantly struggling to find dramatic stories and they'd hit the jackpot today. While he thought their approach a little sleazy, Ty understood the importance of their cooperation. Getting Gretchen's picture out on the news was critical. They needed millions of people to recognize her face if they saw it.

The local search and rescue unit had shown up and was combing the surrounding area. Tyler understood they wanted to help but he thought this too was a wasted effort. There simply hadn't been enough time for Gretchen to get very far before they started looking for her. If she'd been wandering around the fringes of the parking lot or walking away from the truck stop someone would have spotted her. Everyone would have heard the announcements about a missing kid.

Ty's replacement was called to come in early so Ty would be available to assist the investigators. He spent a lot of time beneath one of the pop-up tents giving the same statement over and over again. He was getting frustrated and ready to go home when a tall, whip thin lady in her late fifties approached him. She wore a badge on a lanyard around her neck and extended a hand toward Ty.

"Mr. Stone, I'm Lieutenant Whitt with the Virginia State Police. I'm an investigator assigned to this case."

Ty shook her hand.

"I understand you caught a little grief about locking down this scene?"

Ty nodded. "There were a lot of pissed off people but they calmed down once I had a chance to explain the situation to them. Well, most of them did."

"That's okay," said the lieutenant. "Managing a crime scene sometimes inconveniences people. The public just has to deal with it."

"I wish I'd thought to do it sooner."

"Don't beat yourself up over it. You had no reason to think it was anything other than a kid who'd wandered off from a parent. You kept a cool head in a tough situation. Where'd you learn to handle a crowd like that?"

"Iraq and Afghanistan."

"What branch?"

"Army."

"Thank you for your service, Mr. Stone. I retired from the Marine Corps myself. I was a drill sergeant at Parris Island. I find myself bossing folks around on a regular basis. It's hard to leave that life behind us sometimes."

Tyler smiled at that. He could imagine the hard-earned demeanor of a drill sergeant didn't go away magically upon retirement. "I'm glad to help in any way I can, but I'm ready to get out of here. It's been an incredibly stressful day and I'm beat. How much longer do I need to stick around?"

The lieutenant rocked back on her heels and shoved her hands in her pockets. "There's no reason you can't go, Mr. Stone. We have your statement and your contact information. If we need anything else from you we can find you."

Ty got to his feet. "Thank you. I hope you find her as soon as possible."

Lieutenant Whitt removed a business card from her pocket and extended it to Ty. "If you think of anything else, please contact me."

Ty slipped the card into the pocket of his uniform shirt. "I'll do that."

"One more thing, Mr. Stone. Despite pissing a few people off, you handled yourself pretty well. Have you ever considered a career in law enforcement?"

"I've considered it." It was on the tip of his tongue to mention he had some personal issues he wanted to work out first but he let it go. She didn't need to know that. She might ask the nature of his personal issues and he didn't want to go into it. Then again, being military, she might understand.

"Well, you might think about it. Sometimes that military experience is a good match for a law enforcement career."

Ty thanked the lieutenant, shook her hand, and went on his way. He was tempted to speak to Heather before he left, to wish her luck in the search for her daughter, but she was being interviewed by another news crew, offering a tearful plea that anyone who knew the whereabouts of her daughter should come forward. Ty went on to his truck. She probably didn't want to see him anyway. As far as he was concerned, he'd failed her and her daughter.

7

Ty got in his truck and experienced a wave of relief. Even though he hadn't pulled out yet, simply being in familiar space, in the safety of his truck, produced an immediate, comforting effect. He started the engine, then plugged his cell phone into the charger, noticing he had several missed calls from his sister. He was too emotionally drained to call her back at the moment. He assumed she must have heard about the missing girl and was checking in to see if he had any information.

Despite being exhausted, he desperately needed to wind down so he headed for the gym. Besides the shooting range, it was the only place he ever went on a regular basis. It was a reflection of his military career. Work, gym, and train. It had become so ingrained in him that, even now, as a *nobody*, he couldn't put it behind him. His routine was all that kept him grounded.

He drove straight to the gym and whipped his truck into a parking place. He unlocked the door, grabbed his gym bag, and was starting to get out when it hit him. Where was his paranoia? Where was the hyper-awareness of his surroundings?

This was the first drive in a long time where he had not constantly monitored his mirrors. Usually his anxiety rose slowly over the course of his drive. When he'd reached the gym this time, he simply parked like anyone else.

Like a normal person.

He didn't circle the parking lot to check out the other vehicles, hadn't watched to see if he'd been followed. He'd even opened his door with no regard for who might be out there in the parking lot. That *never* happened.

Rather than being upset at his own lack of situational awareness, Ty was intrigued by his lack of symptoms. He was aware paranoia was a byproduct of the anxiety, which was a byproduct of the PTSD. He wondered if it was the exhaustion after the long day. Perhaps he was distracted by his concern for the missing girl. It showed how much his symptoms were a part of him that their absence was so noticeable.

His phone, sitting in the cup holder, rang. The noise startled him. He reached inside, tipped the phone in his direction, and saw it was his sister. Unlike most people these days, he never took his phone into the gym. He had no interest in taking pictures of himself posing in front of the mirror.

Not knowing how long he'd be inside, he thought he'd better go ahead and take the call. Otherwise, he wouldn't be able to enjoy his workout, knowing she was burning up his phone. He slid back in the truck, shut his door, and took the call. "Hello?"

"How was work?" she asked, an odd, clipped tone to her voice.

Ty sensed an underlying tension. She'd likely heard the story on the news and, having a child roughly the same age, it hit home to her. "Shitty day. I guess you saw the story on the news?"

"No, I haven't seen any news today, Ty. What was on the news?"

"There was a girl who went missing from the truck stop. I thought she'd just wandered off from her mother but we never did find her. There were cops and search teams all over the place. They're still looking for her. They think she might have been abducted."

"Don't they have security cameras? Didn't they pick up anything?"

"We have them but the quality isn't great and the place was overrun with kids at the time. There was a bus with a softball team and all their parents. The last footage we got showed her going outside despite her mother's instructions. We don't know why. There was no shot of what she did when she got outside and we didn't find any more footage of her."

"How old was she?"

"Ten," he replied.

Deena was silent at that. Ty was certain she was processing the exact same thing he had, with Gretchen being so close to her own daughter's age. So close that it was hard not to put herself in that mother's shoes. Where was the mother now? What was she going through? Was she alone in some hotel room, having to call people and tell them what happened? Were they judging her, thinking she was a bad mother for letting this happen? Would there eventually be a happy ending to this story or was this woman's life over?

Those were the things racing through Ty's mind, the places he assumed Deena was going too, but he was wrong. She had her own concerns and she couldn't hold off any longer. *"Well, the reason I haven't watched any news today is that I spent a good deal of the day on the phone. I had a few fires of my own to put out."*

"I'm sorry," Ty replied, unable to imagine that her day had been any worse than his. He tried to be a good brother and listen, though his emotions were so screwed up anymore that he didn't know how to respond half the time.

"So how was the movie last night?"

He immediately got a sinking feeling in his gut. "Um, same as we told you last night. It was a goofy kid's movie. Aiden loved it and I was glad she loved it. I didn't get half of the jokes but that didn't matter because she had a good time." Yeah, he was leaving out a few details. He knew that but he wasn't yet certain that *she* knew that.

"That all you have to say about it?" The way she said it confirmed his worst suspicions. She knew.

"Yeah. That's pretty much it." Wrong answer.

"That's far from it, *Ty!"* she said, her voice rising. *"This morning I found myself tagged in a video on Facebook. Apparently another parent shot a little video on her phone at the Movie Mall Twenty yesterday. She*

tagged me because she thought I should know that my daughter was nearly in the middle of a brawl."

Ty chuckled, an automatic reaction. Suppressing it would probably have been the smart thing to do but he didn't catch it in time. "It was hardly a brawl, Deena."

"I don't know why you're laughing because there's nothing funny about it! Is that all you have to say for yourself?"

"Have you talked to Aiden about this?"

"I have," Deena replied. *"She's grounded for lying to me. I certainly hope you didn't put her up to that."*

"I didn't put her up to anything. I would never put her in that position. She suggested that we probably shouldn't tell you about it and I didn't object. We decided it was the prudent course of action."

"You what? *You seriously thought an eleven year old child's judgment overrode the need to tell her mother about something like this?"* There was utter disbelief in her voice. *"What does it say about your judgment that you agreed with her?"*

"She's not your average eleven-year-old, Deena. She's a sharp kid."

"That's no excuse. So what even happened this time, Ty? She said she was ordering popcorn and everything went quiet. She turned around to look for you and you'd dropped some guy like a ninja. You had him on the ground choking him out in front of his family."

Ty sighed, trying to push the anxiety out, but it wouldn't go. "From a child's perspective that's a reasonable description of what took place, but I didn't actually choke him. I used a hand on his neck to guide him to the ground. It's different."

"But why? How the hell does someone go to a children's movie and end up choking another parent in the popcorn line?"

"I was feeling a little freaked out and he put his hands on me. You shouldn't touch people you don't know. That's a basic rule of civilized society."

"I'm not sure you're much of an expert on the rules of civilized society, Ty." Deena lowered her voice and hissed at him. *"Is this is a PTSD thing?"*

Her tone made it sound like some kinky habit she was loath to ask him about. Although it was a legitimate medical condition, her tone was far from that of his sister asking him how he was dealing with an illness. It was accusatory and angry. He'd been luckier than most in that his PTSD had not isolated him from his family. He'd remained close to his sister but he understood that was not the case for everyone. Many others with the condition hurt and alienated the people around them until they had no support system left. That was where the real trouble began. Then there were fewer voices to compete with the ones telling you to hurt yourself.

"Ty, are you even listening to me?"

He snapped back. "I'm here."

"Being here is not the same as listening."

"I'm...listening," he replied with a firm voice. "But I am not in the mood to be lectured. You were not there."

"No, I was not there, but I've been to the Movie Mall many times and you know how many choking incidents I've seen? NONE! No beatdowns in the popcorn line. None! Ever!"

"Okay, I understand you're angry. What's the damage and how do we fix it?" It was a very practical, military way to respond to the situation. It was done. It had happened and there was no fixing that, no taking it back. It was time to move on and do what needed to be done in the way of damage control. Perhaps he could help with that.

"Ty, I was tagged in the video because they recognized Aiden. All the parents at her school have probably seen it. I tried to get the woman to take it down but it's too late. Other people have posted and shared it. It's probably spread through the whole community by now. People have a sick fascination with those kinds of things."

Ty was behind the curve on social media. Much of the public obsession with it had taken place while he was deployed and had larger concerns, like staying alive. Even though he'd gotten into it over the last couple of years, he felt like a novice sometimes. Yet he did understand the basics of his sister's concern. If she had been tagged in the video, people connected to her could see it, and it could be shared indefinitely. People she worked with could see it, Aiden's friends might see it, their parents would see it, people Aiden played sports with could see it.

"I have to go," he said. It wasn't like he had somewhere to be but he was done talking. He was at the point where ugly things were going to come out of his mouth. Rationality was about to go out the window. It was time to cut this off.

"Ty, we're not done here."

Ty's frustration boiled over. "Look, there's nothing I can say that's going to make you happy right now. I don't know what to tell you. The guy put his hands on me and I lost my shit. I was stressed out because there were so many people around and so much noise. I apologize. If that's not good enough for you..."

Deena sighed, understanding that she'd pushed as far as she could. *"Okay. Do you think you should consider going back on the meds, though? You weren't nearly as angry then."*

Yeah, he wasn't angry *then* because he could barely function on those meds. In fact, he could barely hold a thought in his head. They turned him into a drooling idiot. "I'll consider it, Deena. I have to go."

"Good night, Ty."

They ended the call and he sat there simmering in the parking lot. He accepted she was right to an extent. What he couldn't tell her was that the anger was part of what kept him alive anymore. Those drugs that calmed him also left him less able to resist the demons. Some of them even listed increased risk of suicidal ideation as a side effect. He'd quit taking the meds because he sensed he was losing the fight. It could be that there were better drugs that the doctors hadn't tried yet.

Something told him that, in his case, meds weren't the answer. They might be a bandage but they couldn't fix him. Whatever that solution was, he'd have to find it himself.

8

Ty had some second thoughts about working out after his call with Deena but decided it was probably the only thing that was going to make him feel better. He spent two hours burning through a heavier than usual routine, and the simmering rage inside him fueled his muscles. When he left the gym, the sun had set and it was nearly dark. His body was completely spent. His legs were wobbly and he couldn't imagine there was a muscle group he hadn't exerted.

Despite the endorphins generated by his workout, his symptoms began creeping up on him as he walked across the dark parking lot. Whatever respite he'd been granted by the day's events was short-lived. He'd parked in an isolated section of the lot and there were no other cars around him. That was comforting in that it offered no place for people to hide. If anyone was waiting on him, he'd see them coming.

He used the remote to unlock his door and slipped inside the truck, immediately locking it. He opened the center console and confirmed his Glock was where it was supposed to be, started his truck, and drove home with a constant eye on his surroundings. If someone followed for too long, he slowed until they were forced to pass.

When he reached his townhouse apartment, he parked in his usual spot and studied the lot. It was late and most folks were settled in for the evening. The lot was well-lit and, as far as he could tell, it only held the same vehicles he was used to seeing every day. Ty was wearing his clothes from the gym and there was nowhere to conceal a Glock. He removed it from the center console and laid it in his open gym bag, leaving it unzipped in case he needed quick access to the weapon.

He climbed the steps to his townhouse, unlocked the door, and stepped inside. When he relocked the front door he did not turn any lights on. He retrieved his Glock from the gym bag and activated the weapon light. His unit was two stories and he efficiently cleared each room. Although it wasn't something he had to do every day, he found it easier to relax when he was certain there was no one else in the house. He lived alone and the house had never been broken into. Nor had there ever been anyone in the house uninvited. He had no reason to feel the way he did, yet that didn't change anything.

Everyone had little rituals that helped them feel comfortable and got them through the day. This was one of his.

More comfortable now, he left his handgun on the coffee table and unpacked his gym bag, throwing his dirty clothes in his laundry basket. He took a quick shower, put on clean clothes, then went to the kitchen to find some food. Because he was too tired to make any significant effort, he dumped half a box of cereal into a large mixing bowl.

He added the necessary amount of milk, grabbed a spoon, and headed for his computer. Ty didn't have a lot of local friends. Actually, he didn't have any. He'd only moved there to be close to his sister after his discharge. As a result, his online community constituted the bulk of his social life. Most of his friends were not people he'd recognize if he passed them on the street. Many of them he only knew by the avatars or thumbnail images that represented their account on Facebook.

Ty crunched cereal while his laptop booted. He was aware cereal wasn't the healthiest option, though it was a staple of his diet. He should be making a protein smoothie. That was what his muscles were asking for, but it took more energy than he had on tap at the moment. Besides, this was supposed to be the healthy kind of cereal. There were no bright colors, no prizes inside, and it looked like livestock feed.

When his computer booted, he logged into his email and then Facebook. He had dozens of new emails, all of them either bills or junk. He had ten new private messages on social media and over fifty notifications. Ty used social media to keep up with some of the folks he served with. He was part of several groups set up for veterans. Some were specifically for members of his unit, while others were targeted toward the special operations community. Some groups were public, others private.

By far, most of Ty's online interactions were in a group called Wasteland for Warriors, or as it was affectionately known by its members, "the Wasteland." The group had an enormous membership, over 30,000 members, though most were simply lurkers. The group was focused on people who'd served in Iraq and Afghanistan.

The group had a particular vibe that would probably not be understood by folks who hadn't shared their particular set of experiences. One thing pointedly different about the group was the abundance of dark and morbid jokes. It was battlefield humor and beyond. There were jokes about dealing with the VA system and military life. There were friendly jabs exchanged between different branches of the service. There were memes about spouses cheating while a loved one was deployed, and members compared medical conditions and symptoms.

There were also jokes about the most disturbing aspect of having served in that conflict. That was the high suicide rate among the returning veterans. It was truly at epidemic levels. Not everyone responded to counseling. There was a general dislike of mood-altering medications, though they worked for some. There was a nearly universal disdain for having to deal with VA medical centers, which could often be as depressing as the condition itself. For many the *only* thing that kept them sane was the ongoing support of their community, the brothers and sisters who'd gone through the same thing.

The Wasteland, and other groups like it, despite their irreverent approach, actually saved lives. Not a day went by that a veteran didn't post a message he was having a particularly trying day and needed folks to talk him off the ledge. The use of the word "Wasteland" in the title of the group did not refer to the field of battle. Instead, the Wasteland was the mutual terrain of damaged relationships, struggles with family, difficulty maintaining employment, and the fight to survive when those whispering voices told you it might be better to go ahead and end it all.

Sometimes an especially desperate plea would be posted in the group. A member would share that the demons were winning, they were done fighting, or that it wasn't worth it anymore. Everyone knew what that meant. It meant the desire to end one's life had become irresistible.

In such a case, despite the haphazard and callous nature of the group, they pulled together like a team, just as they'd been trained to do. They mobilized with the single-minded intention of dragging their lost brother or sister back from the precipice. They started by using Facebook to track down people who knew the at-risk person in real life. They would scour their friends list for people who could make a call or go by and visit them.

If they couldn't locate anyone with a personal relationship, they had computer-savvy members who would take it to the next level, working to find a home phone number or physical address. If they were successful, members of the group would start calling in an effort to get the person on the line. If someone got through, that person might spend hours talking to the member in distress. They would post constant updates to the Wasteland that the individual was safe. Meanwhile, while that one person had them on the line, other group members would continue to work toward finding local people, whether friends or family, who could further assist.

It was strangers helping strangers. Ty had done it too. More than once, he'd climbed into his truck in the middle of the night and driven hours to a member's house because of a Wasteland post. These were not people he knew. Acting off addresses obtained by other Wasteland members, he'd shown up and knocked on doors, fully knowing that there was a man behind that door with a gun in his hand, ready to end it all.

When all else failed, as a last resort, they would involve local law enforcement and ask them to do a welfare check. It seemed like an extreme step but the measure had saved lives. They knew this to be a fact because several members later posted to the group that the life-line thrown to them by their fellow Wastelanders had been the only thing that kept them alive. It was a strange thing, that such a group with its crude humor and dark posts was a ray of hope for so many.

As he scanned the posts, Ty found no especially distressing situations taking place that night, which was good. He wasn't certain he had the emotional energy left to assist with something too challenging. That was okay too. Had there been someone in trouble, there were plenty of people ready to step in and help.

Crunching cereal, he read posts and commented on them. He answered the private messages. Most were from people with whom he'd formed a bond. They were friends and kept tabs on each other every day. While Ty knew some people didn't consider online friends to be *real* friends, he saw it differently. It was the closest thing he had to a community since leaving the military and these people were the closest thing he had to friends.

Ty yawned and realized the day's adrenaline surge was finally winding down. It was like someone had yanked his plug from the wall. He needed to go to bed. He closed his internet browser. The wallpaper on his computer desktop was a picture of him and Aiden making goofy faces. It reminded him of the call with Deena.

He wondered if he should go take a look at the video she was tagged in. He didn't want to, but perhaps it would help him understand her reaction. If nothing else, he should probably see how bad it looked.

He reopened the internet browser and returned to Facebook. He and Deena didn't interact on social media very often, their circles being entirely different, but they were connected, allowing him to keep up with pictures of Aiden's latest adventures. After clicking his way to Deena's page, it didn't take very long to track down the video. She'd attempted to block it from her page but new people kept tagging her in it. Before Ty could even decide if he was ready to watch it, the video started playing automatically.

The shaky cell phone footage did not show what precipitated the event. It didn't show the man touching Ty, nor did it show how he dropped the man. That probably happened too fast for someone to start recording it. Where the video began was with the man flat on his back and Ty's hand at his throat. He had to admit it didn't look good. The video followed as the security guards escorted him and Aiden from the theater.

The video didn't bother him that much but he wasn't happy they'd caught Aiden in it. It wasn't her fault her uncle was wound a little too tight. Neither she nor Deena should be punished for the things he did. He realized that was part of the collateral damage of him being close to them. Sometimes he went off and people in the blast radius got burned. It was all the more reason he probably shouldn't be close to them, perhaps even to people in general.

He started reading the comments posted below the video and it got even worse.

"OMG, Deena, is that your brother?"

"Someone like that should not be around children."

"I wouldn't let him take my child to the movies."

"That man clearly has anger issues."

Rage surged in Ty's chest, making him want to shove his fist through his laptop screen. Failing that, he considered responding to each of the comments with profanity but that would only make matters worse. It would embarrass Deena even further and it would probably lead to more people sharing the video. Everyone loved that kind of drama. Certainly the video appeared to be getting enough attention already. The number of people who'd viewed it was appalling. Even worse, nearly a hundred people had shared it to their own social media pages. Ty had gone viral in the worst possible way.

He placed his laptop on the coffee table and stretched out on the couch, grabbed a blanket draped across the back, and pulled it over his body. He laid there staring at the ceiling. This clearly wasn't working out, this whole "life" thing, this whole "being close to his family" thing. How could be have been so effective in the military and so inept now?

A black hole opened in his chest and he felt himself slipping inside. The sensation was hard to describe. It was emotional and physical at the same time. He wondered if the people who chose to check out and end it were the smart ones. How much more of this could he take? Not once in his military career had he ever considered giving up. It wasn't in his vocabulary. No matter how difficult the training, how hopeless the mission, or how painful his injuries.

Now he was ready to.

He looked around for his Glock. It was just out of reach but he could lean forward and get it. He hated to put Aiden through it but perhaps it was the merciful thing to do. Why keep embarrassing her? Surely as she got older she'd become more acutely aware of his short-comings. She'd start avoiding him, just like he heard from so many other folks in the Wasteland.

The comments posted below the video played through his head: #PSYCHO, #angerissues, #PTSD, #madman_at_the_moviemall.

He couldn't help but think that the energy of all these commenters would have been better spent sharing information about Gretchen Wells. The world had become such a narcissistic place. He thought of all the people he'd seen taking selfies at the gym and while he was at work. Were all those selfie-obsessed people from the Petro Panda sharing information about the missing girl tonight or were they posting their own stupid pictures?

Ty sat upright on the couch. Had any of those pictures taken at the truck stop been posted to the internet? Had they been shared like the video of him at the movies? If so, were there any clues hidden in them? He threw off the blanket and reached for his laptop.

Five hours later, Ty was still sitting there. He'd long since exhausted the ink cartridge in his printer, producing the stack of pictures sitting on the corner of his desk. Beyond that point, everything he found had been saved to a folder on his hard drive. He'd discovered and followed dozens of hashtags related to the softball team's trip. He'd used the breadcrumbs of social media to check the pages of parents and grandparents to see if they'd taken any photos at the truck stop. As a result of those efforts, he'd amassed a very thorough gallery of high-resolution images much sharper than anything produced by the security cameras.

He'd not found the missing girl in any of them, but the backgrounds of these photos definitely deserved more attention. They caught people filling their vehicles, people wandering in and out of the store, and dozens of license tags belonging to patrons who were at the store during that time period. It was a wealth of information he had to assume was previously unknown to the investigators.

His search wasn't limited to a single social media site either. Some people's profiles were set so that posting a photo to one site led to it being simultaneously being posted to their other profiles at the time. Ty followed rabbit hole after rabbit hole. He wondered if the police had explored this angle. He probably needed to contact the lieutenant he'd spoken to at the Petro Panda. He had her business card somewhere. He could copy the pictures onto a USB drive and leave a set with her.

When he finally turned the computer off, he realized the sun would be up soon. He needed to get in bed before that happened. He had a hard time sleeping once daylight arrived. He crawled into bed and found he didn't have any trouble turning his thoughts off this time. The black maw of depression did not threaten to swallow him and he was soon fast asleep.

9

After a couple of hours of hard sleep, Ty woke up feeling like shit. He had that same thick-headed stupor that often accompanied a bad hangover, except he'd had nothing to drink last night. This was simply the after-effect of a late night after a very long day. He tried lying in bed a little longer but the train had left the station. He couldn't get back to sleep. It took him a few minutes of staggering around the house in a groggy state to orient himself to time and place. It was only after a strong cup of coffee that the gears in his brain meshed together and the events of the previous day came back to him.

After finishing the entire pot of coffee, he decided to go for a run. He switched to running clothes since running in your underwear was frowned upon. He strapped an elastic cell phone holder to each bicep. The one on the right side contained his phone and driver's license, while the one on the left contained a compact .380 pistol. Ty didn't go anywhere without the means to protect himself or escape capture. It was one of his *things*.

He preferred running on trails to running on pavement, so he hopped in his car and drove the ten minutes across town to the head of a popular trail. He parked in the gravel lot and stashed the keys inside the fender well when he was certain no one was looking. The first mile of the trail was always the most congested. It irritated him but he understood it would thin out as he got further from town.

There were ladies in yoga pants speed walking with strollers or token Labrador retrievers. Silver-haired retired couples walked together in matching track suits, fastidious in monitoring their pace, distance, and heart rate. A determined but limping man who must have been in his seventies was walking off his knee replacement. After a mile, Ty left them all behind. It was just him and the occasional cyclist.

He inserted a single earbud, unable to relax if he wore two because it made him feel vulnerable. He loved the serenity of the deep woods. The trail, a former railroad bed, took him into a hardwood forest and along several creeks. The perfect accompaniment for this tranquility was the grungy metal of The Melvins. He selected a playlist on his phone and hit Play.

The plan was for six miles, three out and three back. Ty was barely two miles into his run when his phone started ringing. He probably could have ignored it if not for the incessant beep in his earbud. Recalling the events of the last day, he decided it could be something important. He slowed to a walk and checked the screen. He didn't recognize the number but he went ahead and answered it. "Hello?"

"Hey, is this Ty Stone?" There was a forced exuberance in the voice, like the man was selling cars or insurance.

Ty immediately regretted answering the phone. He hated breaking pace nearly as much he hated talking on the phone. "It...is," he huffed.

"I haven't caught you at a bad time, have I? You sound a little winded."

"I'm out for a run." *As if it's any of your fucking business, whoever you are.*

"Well, you might need to slow it down a little bit. You sound like it's kicking your butt."

The last thing Ty was interested in was fitness advice from some stranger on the telephone. It made him want to crawl through the phone and demonstrate what getting your butt kicked was actually like. He experienced a flush of anger. "Who is this and what do you want? I'm a little busy at the moment."

"Okay, we'll get right to it. This is Butch Flynn. I'm head of Human Resources for the Petro Panda. I work out of the corporate office in Nashville."

Human Resources? What the hell did they need?

He wondered if they wanted to thank him for his performance after the abduction yesterday. They'd done things like that before, recognizing employees who'd risen to the occasion when some unusual circumstance had taken place at their facility. Just last year they'd given an award to an employee who went the extra mile in the recovery effort after a tornado. Before that, they'd recognized an employee who saved someone in the parking lot with CPR.

"What can I do for you, Mr. Flynn?" Ty asked, continuing to walk, not wanting to let his heart rate drop completely back to its resting pace.

"Mr. Stone, I'm afraid the company has some concerns with the manner in which you performed your duties yesterday. That thing you did with the trucks, closing off the parking lots, constituted a serious safety violation in our eyes. You put our customers at risk and that's just something we can't allow. For that reason, we're going to have to let you go."

Ty stopped in his tracks. "Excuse me?"

"Yes, it's unfortunate. I understand you thought you were doing the right thing but you were acting beyond your authority. Everyone at Petro Panda has a role and you ventured beyond the scope of yours. Had you called corporate and briefed a manager, we could have offered guidance. We could have provided technical assistance and steered you in the right direction. Instead, you decided to play cowboy and go rogue. We can't have that."

"You've got to be fucking kidding me," Ty said, unable to push back the anger now. "There was no time for that. The state police investigator *complimented* me on my actions. They agreed that locking down the scene was the right thing to do."

Butch sighed. *"I understand that, Mr. Stone. They have the authority to take action like that, but you don't. What they agree with or don't agree with is totally irrelevant as far as the company is concerned. They don't run the Petro Panda."*

Ty wanted to climb through the phone, grab this Flynn character by the necktie, and bash his head against his desk until it popped. He took a deep breath and tried to control the anger in his voice. He didn't want to give the asshole the satisfaction of knowing he'd rattled him.

"You know, it might get interesting when the media gets ahold of this," Ty said. "I met several reporters yesterday. There are probably some at the Petro Panda right now. I'm sure they'd love to hear about you guys terminating me for helping secure the scene. That kind of thing doesn't play well in the media."

The asshole sighed again and Ty knew it was for dramatic effect. *"It's unfortunate you feel that way but think carefully before you act, Ty. The manager at your location said you made her feel unsafe yesterday. You ignored her recommendations and behaved in an aggressive, perhaps even reckless, manner. I'll go as far as to say that she felt threatened. If you issue a statement, we'll be forced to do the same."*

"You're a fucking asshole," Ty growled. "I hope we get the opportunity to meet in person one day."

"Careful," Butch warned. *"I'd hate for you to say anything that might be mistaken for a threat. You wouldn't want to give people the impression you're unstable, would you? That certainly wouldn't help your case."*

Ty hung up. He started to unleash a yell of primal rage but it would probably terrify some other runner out enjoying the day. They'd call the cops and complain he'd made them feel uncomfortable. That was just what he needed. How had he gotten to the point in his life where everyone was scared of him? It was a world of assholes and he was tired of them all.

He resisted the urge to throw his phone deep into the forest. He started The Melvins again and crammed the irritating thing back into the phone sleeve on his bicep. He had a lot more stress to burn off now.

Fucking perfect.

The only good thing to be said about it was that the anger pushed the depression down. As long as he was hating someone else, he hated himself a little less.

He started out at a jogging pace. Fueled by caffeine and hate he was soon burning down the trail at a full sprint, his respiration functioning with a mechanical efficiency. Sweat streamed from his body and slung from his pumping arms. His eyes burned down the trail, narrowed with a furious intensity. He imagined Butch Flynn was ahead of him on the trail, like a carrot dangling from a stick. If he ran just a little harder, he'd catch him. When he did, he'd beat him like a piñata full of Skittles.

10

Back at the trailhead, Ty sucked down two bottles of water while he walked off the run. He circled the perimeter of the parking lot, turning his situation over in his head. His stomach was in knots but he wasn't sure if it was his pace or the state of his world. While he hadn't particularly enjoyed being a security guard the work was comfortable. The routine was familiar and it came easy to him. It paid the bills. Then there was the infuriating manner in which he'd been terminated.

The other question was whether this might impede him finding another job. Most large companies like the Petro Panda, terrified of a lawsuit, were hesitant to pass on too much information when contacted by a potential future employer. Most had a pat answer they provided, such as stating whether the former employee was re-hirable or not, or whether they performed their job duties as required. He didn't know what Petro Panda might say about him.

Bastards.

His bank account was in good shape. He hadn't had many expenses when he was in the military so most of his money went into savings. He wasn't married and didn't have a house. He'd never fallen into that trap of needing an expensive car, the latest gaming console, or the biggest flat screen television. His only spending habit was that he enjoyed going to the range and shooting firearms. He owned several but demonstrated restraint there too, not purchasing so many that they became a burden to him. He bought good weapons, good accessories, and good ammo.

Ty tossed his empty water bottles into a garbage can and slouched on a park bench. He needed to find some way to redirect this anger or it was going to get him in trouble. He couldn't simmer on a low boil all day. He pulled out his phone and opened the photos. The last was one he snapped of Lieutenant Whitt's business card before he left his house. He committed the number to memory, then switched to the keypad and dialed her number, leaning back to watch the parking lot while the phone rang.

"Lieutenant Whitt," the voice answered.

Ty recognized the efficient, authoritative tone of the former drill instructor. "Hey Lieutenant, this is Tyler Stone. I'm the security guard from the Petro Panda. We met yesterday."

"Hello, Mr. Stone. How's it going?" Her tone was friendly but business-like.

"Not so hot, to be honest, but that's not why I called. I had some information I thought might be of use to you."

"Did you remember something that might be relevant to the case?" Whitt asked, hope in her voice.

"Not directly," Ty replied. "My sister and I were discussing social media yesterday, and it made me think of something. I remembered that while the softball team was there, both the girls and their parents were taking tons of pictures. This was around the same time Gretchen disappeared. I thought there could be something relevant in the background of those pictures."

Ty didn't get into the reason he and his sister were discussing social media. He was mad enough already without adding yesterday's anger into the mix.

"Well, I appreciate that. We have the contact information for everyone who was here when we arrived yesterday. I'll have someone reach out to them and see if they have anything that might be helpful."

"I might be able save you a couple steps there. After I thought of this last night, I couldn't get it off my mind. I don't sleep all that well. Anyway, I was up late last night copying pictures from various social media sites and there were quite a few taken at the Petro Panda during that window of time. I didn't spot the missing girl in any of them but that doesn't mean there might not be some clue I missed. I saved them all to a USB drive, if you want a copy."

There was a long pause on the other end of the line. Ty began to wonder if this was a bad move. Did it make him come off as creepy or suspicious? He was aware that criminals sometimes inserted themselves into investigations, trying to be helpful. At least that was what he saw on television. Was that how he was coming across? Was he trying too hard?

Ty cleared his throat. "Okay, if you're not interested, I'm sorry I wasted your time. I just couldn't get this out of my mind last night and had to look into it."

"No, I'd definitely be interested in seeing what you put together, I was just surprised by the initiative you took. That's quite a bit of effort. Anything that saves us legwork moves this investigation further down the road. In fact, I'm at the Petro Panda right now. We have a command center set up here. Could you swing by today and drop that USB drive off?"

"I will if I'm allowed on the property."

"Why wouldn't you be allowed back on the property?" Whitt asked.

"Petro Panda terminated me about an hour ago. They basically accused me of putting our customers at risk by locking down the travel plaza yesterday. They said I was overstepping my authority."

"Was this a local thing or did it come down from the corporate office?"

"It was corporate. I got a call from some asshole...excuse me... *guy* named Butch Flynn who said he was the head of Human Resources."

"I'm very sorry about that, Tyler. Are you going to appeal it? Is there anything you can do?"

Ty watched a young woman struggling to extricate a jogging stroller from the trunk of a tiny car. "Mr. Flynn gave me the impression that I should go quietly. He said if I made a big deal out of this they would portray me as being unstable, saying I made my manager uncomfortable with my aggressive behavior and that's why they had to let me go."

It was Whitt's turn to be disgusted now. *"That's bullshit."*

"No kidding."

"So when do you think you can run that by?"

Ty held his phone so that he could see the clock on the face. "1300 hours?"

"1300 hours it is. See you then."

Ty got up off the bench and headed toward his truck. The woman with the jogging stroller had finally got the complicated contraption unfolded and settled a baby into it. The kid was wearing a fancy tracksuit with tiny, nearly round running shoes. Ty was smiling at the goofy outfit until he caught the woman frowning at him. He averted his eyes.

Jesus Christ, he thought, *why do you dress the little guy so goofy if you don't want people laughing at him?*

11

T y headed home for a quick shower. He fixed lunch, resisting the temptation to pour himself another trough of cereal. Instead, he fixed toast with peanut butter and honey, something he thought was damn near akin to a delicacy. He chased it with another bottle of water and a tall energy drink.

With a clean body, a full belly, and a caffeine buzz, he headed to the Petro Panda to meet with Whitt. The scene was no less crowded than it had been the day before. It was a Sunday so the parking lot was crowded with travelers. The Virginia State Police command center RV was parked in the side lot, surrounded by folding tables and pop-up awnings. There was an assortment of law enforcement officers, both in uniform and in variations of off-duty cop-wear. Two TV news vans indicated that the missing girl story was fresh enough to get airtime.

Ty gave the command center a wide berth and parked at the far corner of the parking lot, the same place he usually parked when he was working. He locked his truck, confirmed the USB drive was in his pocket, and started across the hot parking lot. He'd nearly reached the command center when he was intercepted by Brock, a former coworker who was apparently the security guard on duty today.

"Hey, Ty!" Brock yelled, loping across the parking lot in Ty's direction.

Ty gave a reserved nod. "How's it going, Brock?"

The tall, lanky man shrugged. "Oh, you know. Just working. Living the dream. What are you doing here?"

Ty pointed toward the command center. "I'm meeting up with one of the investigators."

Brock looked away, suddenly uncomfortable. "Yeah, about that... I was notified I'm not supposed to allow you on the property."

Ty rolled his eyes. "You're fucking kidding me, dude. Seriously?"

Brock nodded sheepishly. "Just doing my job, man. I'm sorry. For what it's worth, I think you did the right thing."

It was only then, as Brock started to piss him off, that Ty noticed how relaxed he'd been between his home and the Petro Panda. There was none of the normal anxiety he experienced on a drive. He hadn't been paranoid or hyperaware of his surroundings. Now that relaxed state left him with the abruptness of being shoved under freezing water. He was suddenly anxious, angry, and felt under attack again.

He took note of Brock's posture. The man was totally off guard. Ty was certain he could take him. He was ready to fight back against these people attacking him. Brock was open and Ty could probably drop him with a single punch. Two at the most.

"Mr. Stone, there you are," Lieutenant Whitt said, breaking Ty's train of thought.

Ty was not so far gone that he didn't realize Whitt's arrival was a good thing. With all those cops there, he'd end up in jail for sure if he attacked Brock. The Petro Panda would probably press charges if he created a disturbance on their property. He needed to chill.

Tighten up, Ty.

"Hey, Lieutenant, Brock here was just telling me I'm banned from the property. I have a feeling he was getting ready to escort me back to my vehicle. I'm afraid I'm not going to be able to stick around and meet with you."

Brock looked at Whitt uncomfortably. "Yeah, it's not me. I got a call from corporate. From the head of security. The order came straight from him."

"I just got off the phone with your corporate office," Whitt said tearing into Brock. "I think there's a Mr. Butch Flynn who's in his office right now trying to duct tape his ass back together after I got through with him. I don't appreciate the way Mr. Stone here is being treated. He served this nation in the military and was the first person on the scene yesterday to understand the importance of locking it down. You get your head of security on the phone and you tell him Mr. Stone is critical to our investigation right now. If you try to remove him, I'll arrest you for interfering and I'll close this station as a crime scene. Do you get me?"

Brock flushed red. Lieutenant Whitt's drill instructor background had just reared its head. Ty could tell this was a woman who had elevated the act of dressing someone down to a fine art form and that she enjoyed every single second of it.

"Yes, ma'am," Brock said.

"*Ma'am*? Do I look like your mother or grandmother, son? It's Lieutenant or Lieutenant Whitt to you. Are we clear?"

"Yes, Lieutenant Whitt."

"Good. Now you hustle your ass back inside that store and relay my message to your boss. You do it now and then you stay out of my way."

Brock did as he was told, spinning on a heel and sprinting back toward the store.

Ty couldn't help but grin. "I can tell you've done that a time or two."

"I held back. If I dialed it up a notch, I could have cussed him for ten minutes and not repeated myself. The state police have less tolerance for that kind of behavior than the military did, though. I could also tell you were looking for an opening. I was afraid I wouldn't get over here before you laid his ass out in the parking lot."

"I was considering it," Ty admitted. He reached into his pocket, found the USB drive, and held it out to Lieutenant Whitt. "These are the pictures I was telling you about. I'll get out of your hair. I know you're busy." Ty started to back away to return to his truck, but the lieutenant beckoned him with a wave.

"Wait a minute. Not so fast. Why don't we take a quick look at these in the command center? I need to document your process for finding these images. It also might be helpful if you could put them in perspective for me. You might recognize the location where they were taken quicker than I can."

"Sure," Ty said. "It's not like I have to go to work or anything."

The two fell into step heading across the hot pavement to the command center.

"I guess you heard me say that I just got off the phone with your HR guy?" the lieutenant asked.

"Yeah, I was going ask you about that."

"I can't make them hire you back, Tyler, but I made it clear that firing you was a pretty shitty thing to do. I told him that you didn't know about my call and that he certainly couldn't stop *me* from leaking news of your firing to the media. I told him they should reconsider their decision because I could make them look pretty damn bad if I wanted to. I'm old, grouchy, and don't give a shit anymore."

Ty shrugged. "Working here was a lousy job anyway. I'm not sure I want it back, to be honest."

"So what are you going to do with yourself? You don't seem like the type to just lay around and do nothing."

"I'm not sure yet."

"There's always the State Police Academy. If you don't want to be a trooper, there's always the conservation police or local law enforcement. It's good work."

They reached the command center before Ty felt pressured to respond to her suggestions. The muffled sound of a generator emerged from behind the RV. Lieutenant Whitt led Ty through the other officers, beneath the shade of an awning, and into the air-conditioned comfort of the command center. There were flat screen monitors tuned to the news and displaying information from several computers. An array of radio equipment allowed the command center to communicate with anyone they might need to reach. A metal locker bolted to the wall held several rifles and shotguns.

Whitt led Ty to a countertop mounted along a wall and gestured for him to take a seat on a stool. She grabbed a metal folding chair and sat beside him, opened a laptop in front of her, and plugged in Ty's USB stick. The antivirus utility scanned the drive, then opened the folder containing the images. Deciding the laptop screen was too small, the lieutenant plugged a cord into one of the laptop ports so the image was displayed on a larger monitor mounted to the wall.

She had Ty walk her through how he'd come to the conclusion that social media might help him find pictures of the scene. She took thorough notes, writing down hashtags he explored on the various social media sites. Ty knew that law enforcement undoubtedly had the know-how to use this means of investigation but their efforts were probably focused in more traditional directions at the moment.

"Have there been any clues at all?" Ty asked. "Any progress?"

"Off the record, the parents just went through a nasty divorce. Of course, that's pretty common now and doesn't particularly mean anything significant, but we haven't been able to locate the dad."

Ty's eyebrows went up at that.

Whitt waved it off with her hand. "That doesn't necessarily mean anything," she said. "The dad's friends said he's supposed to be on some off-roading trip in the backcountry of Utah. There's no cell reception and it's pretty remote. We've got local law enforcement looking for him but there's been no leads yet. He's currently the main focus of our investigation."

"It's usually somebody that knows the victim, isn't it?" Ty asked. "That's what they say in the crime shows."

"Unfortunately yes."

12

Ty spent nearly two hours in the command center going over the pictures with Lieutenant Whitt. Later, at her request, he repeated much of the same information to an investigator from the local sheriff's department. When he finally stepped from the air-conditioned RV into the sweltering heat of the afternoon, Whitt tried again to encourage him to consider law enforcement as a possible career.

"I'll admit that part of it is I'd like to help a fellow veteran," Whitt said. "That's not all though. You have an enthusiasm for investigation. You can't teach that. You either have it or you don't."

"I'll think about it," Ty said. "Thank you." He appreciated her effort but didn't feel capable of making any life-changing decisions at the moment. He didn't know where he wanted to go from there. Part of him wasn't certain if he even wanted to keep going at all.

As he headed back across the parking lot, he saw Brock taking a break on a picnic table, smoking a cigarette. He gave Ty a tentative wave. While Ty suspected it was meant to indicate there were no hard feelings, Ty had hard feelings. He gave Brock the finger. It was a childish gesture, but he hadn't had a lot of satisfying moments over the last few days. He'd take his gratification were he could find it, even if it was immature.

He left the Petro Panda, got on the interstate, and headed back into town. He punched a button to dial Deena and the sound of the ringing phone emerged from the speakers in the truck. It took her four rings to answer, long enough that Ty had to wonder if she was dodging his call. When she finally did answer, the tone of her voice indicated he may have been correct.

"Hey, Ty."

She sounded tired, though he couldn't tell if it was physical or mental exhaustion. He was afraid to ask because he was pretty sure, whichever it was, he was responsible for it.

"Hey, Sis. How's it going today?"

"Are you sure you want to know?" Her response sounded sincere, with none of the edge he'd braced himself for.

Apparently he wasn't the only one having a rough day. "I was wondering if I could take you and Aiden out to dinner," he offered. He didn't really feel like it but he wanted to reconnect with them. It was something he needed to do.

"I don't know, Ty," she replied. *"I'm not so sure it's a good time. I wouldn't be very good company."*

"Neither of us is good company. Aiden makes up for that, though. She's got enough personality for the three of us."

"That's true."

"Listen, I'm sorry, Deena. I watched the video last night. I know it looks bad and I read some of the comments. I saw that people were giving you a hard time. I wish I knew what to do."

"You don't know the half of it."

Ty figured she was referring to the phone calls she said she'd been getting from "well meaning" friends. "Deena, I probably wouldn't have gotten so angry yesterday if not for what happened at work. I kept thinking about what I would do if it were Aiden missing. I couldn't push it out of my head. I still can't."

"I know. It probably wasn't the best time to spring that whole mess on

you, but I was a little overwhelmed. Your actions impact me, Ty, and they impact Aiden."

Although Ty understood that was true, this was new territory for him. He wasn't used to having to tiptoe around people's feelings. In the military, he had a responsibility to his team but they weren't sensitive. If you stepped on someone's feelings, they got over it. He liked that life better.

The only reason he'd ended up living in the same small town as his sister was out of a sense of duty. With their parents dead, neither of them had anyone else to depend on. He thought they might be able to help each other out. Deena was recently divorced and they didn't have any other family around. Since she was always needing help getting Aiden somewhere or picking her up, being able to assist with those little things helped give him purpose, giving him a mission, and helped pull him out of the murky waters of his own head. Despite this rough patch, he wasn't ready to give up on that mission.

"How about I pick up a couple of pizzas and bring them over? Would that be okay?"

"Sure," she relented.

"Beer?"

"Make it Dos Equis."

"It's a deal."

They hung up and he placed a call to their favorite pizza place.

13

The parking lot at Bella's Pizza was a little over half full. Ty backed into a space at the farthest corner of the lot and sat there for a moment to get a feel for the place. He slid out the door of his truck and headed across the parking lot, instinctively scanning the parked cars. He saw no one sitting inside and watching him, no one crouched between cars waiting to jump him.

Inside, there was no line. He was able to quickly pay for his order and get out the door. He made a quick stop at a drugstore with a good beer selection and picked up Deena's beer. Fortunately, on a Sunday afternoon, the drugstore was dead as disco. He was the only car in the parking lot and the only customer in the store. Still, he was glad he was armed. Drugstores were sketchy these days. Too many lowlifes who would beat down a cancer patient to steal their medication.

On Deena's street, he parked in front of her house and did a quick assessment of the scene around him. It was small-town Sunday stuff. People were washing cars, kids were playing in yards, and men were mowing lawns. When he got out, he could smell grilling steaks and hear music playing from down the block. He started to unholster his Glock and leave it in the truck but couldn't bring himself to do so. He grabbed the pizzas and the six-pack of beer, then headed for the house.

With his hands full he used his toe to tap on the storm door. Aiden came running to let him inside. She pushed the door open and stood outside holding it while he eased in with the wide boxes.

"I didn't tell her, Uncle Ty," she whispered. "I swear I didn't."

Ty looked at his niece and caught the serious look on her face. She was worried he'd be mad at her. "It's okay, sweetie. I know you didn't. We're good. You didn't do anything wrong."

Her face brightened and she grinned at him. He regretted causing her to worry about it. None of this was her fault. It was just one more reminder of the pain he caused the people around him.

Ty made his way to the kitchen. He handed the beer off to Deena and set the pizza boxes on the island. "One supreme, one pepperoni, and a six-pack of beer."

Deena busied herself with napkins, paper plates, and silverware. "Aiden, get yourself a bottle of water from the fridge."

"What if I wanted a beer?" she asked, a challenging inflection in her voice.

Deena gave her a sharp look. "Would you prefer a spanking?"

"I'll take the water," Aiden replied, though she knew as well as Ty did that the odds of her getting a spanking were pretty low.

Deena slid two slices of pepperoni off onto a paper plate. She handed it to Aiden, then tore loose a paper towel and extended it to her daughter.

"My hands are full," Aiden complained. "Carry it for me."

"Open up."

Aiden frowned and opened her mouth. Deena stuck the corner of the paper towel in Aiden's mouth. She clamped down on it and started mumbling through her closed lips like an unskilled ventriloquist.

"Maybe this will keep you quiet for a while," Deena said. "You go in there and watch TV while you eat. Uncle Ty and I need to talk."

Normally, Aiden would have protested. She wanted to be where Uncle Ty was. She also wanted to hear any adult conversation that might be taking place under her roof. The fact that she didn't complain indicated she understood exactly what this conversation was about. It was about Uncle Ty knocking that man down at the movie theater and she wanted no part of that uncomfortable chat. That didn't mean she wouldn't eavesdrop from the next room, though. She was more than willing to absorb it from a safe distance.

While Aiden wandered from the room, mumbling through the napkin in her mouth, Deena opened two beers. She slid one across the granite island to Ty and took a long drink off hers. She didn't have the opportunity to drink very often and the almost desperate way she took that first hit off the bottle gave Ty an indication of how she was feeling. She was stressed.

"First off, I'm sorry that whole thing happened," Ty said, diving right in. "I know it's no excuse, but there was this action movie playing when we were in line. You know how those sound systems are now. Everything is so realistic. There were explosions and gunshots. I got lost in my head, and the next thing I knew, his hand was on my back. I didn't even think. I just reacted. By the time I figured out what was going on, the guy was on the floor."

"In front of my daughter," Deena said, setting her beer down on the granite with a loud clink.

"If it's any consolation, Aiden was probably the least shocked person there. She had no reaction whatsoever. She just continued placing her order like nothing happened. When they asked us to leave, she took it in stride. She's a pretty together kid. Probably more together than me at this point."

"You've got to get help, Ty." Deena looked down at her pizza but didn't pick up a slice.

Her imploring tone tore at him. "We've been down this road. I know I've got...symptoms, but I'm not even sure if this is actually PTSD. The condition is different for everyone. When I went to the VA medical center they put me on so many drugs I couldn't function. I'd never considered suicide until then, but every day I knew I was one step closer. I can't explain it, but it was like those medications didn't only shut down the bad voices in my head, they shut down *all* the voices, even the ones telling me to fight back."

Deena gave him a wry smile. "You do have PTSD, Ty. You need to admit it. You need to *accept* it. Those doctors are professionals. They have more experience than anyone in dealing with this. Those meds have to be safe. They're not going to give you anything that will hurt you."

Ty burst out laughing. "Maybe they wouldn't *intentionally* give me something that would hurt me but veteran suicide is an epidemic. You think none of those guys are on medication? If medication was the answer, veterans wouldn't be dropping like flies. There's got to be another answer and we just don't know what it is yet."

"Well, what are you gonna do? You can't go on like this. You're going to hurt someone."

Ty gave his sister a wary look. "You can't start looking at me like that. You can't start treating me like I'm this time bomb that's going to blow up when you least expect it. I can't handle that."

"It's not just about what I think, Ty. When people in this community see a video like that, they don't want you around their children. That's what they're telling me. They worry about you dropping Aiden off at school. They worry about you being here if she has friends over. That's what I've been dealing with since this video was posted. I've been trying to defend you and I don't know how much longer I can do that if you're not going to get help."

That stung. He couldn't stand the thought of people thinking he was a danger to their children. If he was that unstable, he'd go out to his truck and end things right then. Truthfully, he thought he'd been doing better the last twenty-four hours. His mind had been so preoccupied with the child abduction that he'd been distracted from his symptoms. He was less paranoid and less obsessive about the little rituals that kept him safe. He had fewer thoughts of hurting himself.

While he didn't understand why the preoccupation with this missing girl helped him, it definitely did. He sensed it was more complicated than simply keeping him busy. If that were the case, he could take up a hobby like leatherworking or basket weaving and make his symptoms go away. Yet he knew that wouldn't work. He'd tried structuring his days before, obsessively filling every minute of the day with some all-consuming activity, and it hadn't worked. He'd heard of other people trying the same thing and it wasn't working for them either.

Ty took a sip of his beer and set it on the counter. "Let's eat." He wasn't particularly hungry, having lost whatever appetite he had due to the nature of their discussion. Eating would provide a distraction, perhaps allow their emotions to settle some.

Deena slid him a paper plate and he pulled a single slice onto it. A firm knock on the back door startled him and he whipped in that direction. There was a woman he didn't recognize standing there with a fuzzy gray puppy cradled in her arms. The lady was in her sixties with short white hair. She gave a quick smile and waved in Deena's direction. Deena smiled back, then walked to the door to let her in.

"Hello, Nancy, who is this?" Deena asked, cooing at the puppy and stroking it on the head.

"This is my new little baby. Her name is Percy and I wanted to bring her over so Aiden could see her. I know how she loves puppies."

"Aiden!" Deena called. "Come here."

"What is it?" Aiden yelled.

Ty smiled at Aiden's weary tone.

"Come here!" Deena repeated.

In a second, Aiden came skating into the kitchen on her sock feet. When she saw the puppy, her eyes widened and an expression of pure joy overtook her face. She threw her hands in the air and literally danced toward the puppy.

The gesture, Aiden's exuberance, floored Ty. He stood there for a second with his mouth hanging open. "I've got to go," he said.

Deena looked at him curiously, petting the puppy. "You just got here. You haven't even eaten a single bite and *you* brought dinner."

"I just remembered something I had to do."

Deena left Aiden cradling the puppy and came to her brother's side. She put a hand on his shoulder and lowered her voice. "Are you sure you're okay?"

"I am. Seriously. There's just something I have to do right now and it can't wait."

Deena let out a long, disappointed sigh, not yet done with the conversation they'd been having. "Sure. Whatever. Call me later."

"I will. I just have to run right now." He waved at Aiden but she barely glanced in his direction. He'd been totally upstaged by the puppy.

14

Ty raced back to his townhouse, driving a little too fast. He whipped into the parking lot, nearly clipping a light pole, and roared into the first parking space that caught his eye. He didn't go through his normal ritual of backing into a space and perfectly centering his vehicle, nor did he sit there for a moment taking in his surroundings before he rushed to his front door. There was no time for that. Aiden had reminded him of something he'd seen in those hundreds of pictures he spent the night downloading. If he could just find the right one.

He unlocked the door and rushed inside, not even locking it behind him. He also didn't take the time to clear the house, going directly to his desk. He removed the holstered Glock from inside his waistband, plunked it down, and powered up his laptop. While he waited, he grabbed the stack of printed pictures and started shuffling through them.

The very top image was not one he'd printed himself. It was the one the state police had handed out at the travel plaza, the one taken as Gretchen left the store. It was the "have you seen this child" picture, the high resolution image of Gretchen with a wide grin on her face, her jubilant hands in the air. That very picture was half of the reason Ty rushed home. He was struck by the similarity between that image and the expression on Aiden's face when she'd seen that puppy at the back door. They were exactly alike. He set the picture to the side. It was only half the equation.

His laptop finished booting and he logged in. He went back to the printed pictures, urgently shuffling through them and tossing the discarded images into the floor beside him. He didn't know exactly what he was looking for, but he hadn't seen it there. He turned back to his computer and opened the folder on his desktop. Inside, he'd saved a digital copy of all the photos he'd printed, as well as the additional pictures he'd been unable to print when he'd run out of ink.

He double clicked on the first picture and it opened up to fill the screen. He dropped a finger to the arrow key and tapped it, advancing through the images. "No, no, no," he repeated as he scrolled through them.

Ten images.

Fifty images.

One hundred images.

Then he found it. The two hundred and sixty-second image of three hundred and sixty-nine. He stared at the picture. The reason he'd had such trouble recalling it was that the element prickling his memory was not the focus of the image. It was not the three smiling girls with their lips puckered up. It was merely a blip in the background. In all of those three hundred and sixty-nine images, there were thousands of such vignettes randomly captured in the backgrounds. There were tired men filling gas tanks, mothers rushing children to restrooms, old men with orange fingers, bags of Cheetos, and bottles of Mountain Dew. Yet this one background detail paired perfectly with the expression on Gretchen's face.

Ty took up the printed picture of a smiling Gretchen in one hand and held it alongside his laptop screen. He could imagine that these two images were the far extremes of a single, larger scene. Gretchen, inside the store, represented one end. The other image, displayed on his screen, could logically represent the other half of what had taken place. It was the half no one had seen or understood, but Ty was certain he understood it now. If he was right, and these two images were captured at the same moment, the expression on Gretchen's face was the result of the puppy in the background of the image on his screen.

Behind the three young girls posing for the picture, a woman was standing at the rear of a smaller RV. She leaned against the spare tire holder, cradling the puppy in her arms. She was wearing cheap white sweatpants and a white sweatshirt. Her gray hair was pulled back in a ponytail. She appeared to be in her fifties but it was hard to tell. Her skin was deeply lined and it looked like some of her years had been hard ones. Ty could make out a stocky man fueling the RV but could not see his face due to the angle of the camera.

The woman was looking toward something off-screen, but Ty couldn't see her eyes because of dark wraparound glasses. He did recognize the location where this picture was taken because of the number on the fuel pump. That told him exactly where the woman was looking. She was eyeing something toward the main entrance of the store, possibly Gretchen.

There was something slightly disturbing about the picture, though. The smile on the woman's face did not look like someone kindly returning the joyous smile of a child. To him, it was an expression of satisfaction. It was the look of a predator watching prey wander into its trap.

Ty picked up his phone and dialed Lieutenant Whitt's number. She picked up on the third ring.

"*Lieutenant Whitt.*"

"Hey, Lieutenant, this is Tyler Stone again. I found something I think you'll be very interested in." Ty was in high gear, his mind racing with the urgency of the situation, and he needed the lieutenant to get on board. Time was wasting. When she didn't answer, he prodded, "Hello? Lieutenant Whitt?"

"*Mr. Stone, I appreciate your effort to be helpful in this case but the nature of the investigation has changed. New information has come to light and the FBI is now the lead element in this investigation.*"

Ty could hear a lot of bustle in the background. The level of activity at the command center had increased since he left there. It sounded like there were more people and they were engaged in an animated conversation. "What happened?"

"I'm not at liberty to discuss the details of this case, Mr. Stone. The FBI will be making a statement in the morning at a press conference. I suggest you tune in if you want to follow the case."

Ty didn't like the sound of that. Lieutenant Whitt was behaving differently, and she didn't sound interested in anything he might have to offer. While he certainly had no official role in this investigation, he was certain he had insight that might prove helpful. He needed to get it out because a little girl's life may depend on it.

"I think I figured something out, Lieutenant Whitt. Something you guys may have missed in those pictures."

"Hold on a damn minute," Lieutenant Whitt said, frustration growing in her voice.

In the background, Ty could hear her excusing herself and a chair banging. He heard the sound of a door shutting and diesel engines rumbling in the background. The lieutenant had left the command RV and stepped out into the parking lot. He could hear her breathing into the phone and the rhythm of her steps. She was putting distance between her and the rest of the investigative team. Perhaps she was interested in hearing what he had to say after all.

He couldn't have been more wrong.

"Did you not understand what I said?" she growled. *"We're not interested in hearing anymore about pictures, social media, or your theories. We don't have time for it."*

Ty was stunned at the change in her demeanor. He'd sensed the two of them had a connection, that the fact they were both veterans had given them an understanding of each other. "Um, I'm sorry. I just thought you'd be interested." He didn't know what else to say.

"I understand you were trying to be helpful. I appreciate it and I know the girl's family would appreciate it. This is an FBI matter now, though, and they don't *appreciate it. They have their own people and their own theories."*

"Is there someone else I could speak to?"

She gave a frustrated sigh. *"Are you not getting me, Tyler? There's no one you can speak to. There's no one interested in your theories,"* she said through gritted teeth. *"This is the point where you back yourself out of this and go on with your life. I empathized with your situation and tried to give you some guidance but I can't make you follow that advice. It's up to you whether you do something with it or not."*

Ty heard what she was saying, and under normal circumstances he might have been a little pissed. She made it sound like she'd only humored him out of pity. While that stung, he needed to keep rolling, to keep moving forward. It wasn't about him, it was about Gretchen. He needed to get his information out whether she wanted to hear it or not.

"I know why she was smiling when she left," he said.

"I do too," Whitt replied. *"Because she saw a familiar face. Gretchen Wells saw her father in the parking lot."*

Ty was stunned. "I thought her dad was in Utah."

"We all did."

"How do you know he was there? How can you be sure? Did you find him in those pictures I sent you? In the security camera footage?"

"Goodbye, Mr. Stone. I'll ask that you don't call me again. If I have any questions for you, I have your number." The line went dead.

Ty lowered the phone to his desk. He picked up the printed picture and held it alongside his laptop screen one more time. They could think what they wanted, investigate whoever they wanted. He simply had to confirm one piece of information to know that he was on the right track. He needed to speak to Gretchen's mother and find out if she was obsessed with puppies like Aiden. If she was, he needed to find the woman in the picture. She may have seen what happened in the parking lot. If Gretchen indeed went with her father, this lady may have seen it happen.

He didn't care what Lieutenant Whitt said. He couldn't let this go.

15

Tia knew she had the girl the moment she reacted to the puppy. She hadn't targeted her specifically, nor singled her out. Any of the girls would have been sufficient and there were so many of them right there at the gas station. Since things had gone so badly in Richmond, she had prayed non-stop. She was certain Holy Death would provide and she had.

She couldn't take a child by force in this crowd. It had to be the right child at the right time. They had to find a girl who melted at the sight of puppies. A child like that would enter the RV eagerly if she thought there were more puppies inside. Tia understood that a clean, well-dressed child like this one had probably been instructed to stay in the store. She probably had a mother in there shopping or using the restroom. For the ones with puppy fever, as she called it, that would make no difference. The cuteness overwhelmed them. Some inner drive took over and all their good sense, all their obedience, evaporated.

The child danced toward her, eyes glued to the puppy. "Can I pet it?"

"Certainly," Tia said.

"It's so cute. What's its name?"

"Nemo," Tia said.

Gretchen beamed as if she hadn't heard a word Tia said, utterly engrossed in the warm ball of fur.

"You want to see its brothers and sisters?" Tia asked.

Gretchen nodded in that dazed way some children did around small animals. She would have agreed to anything. Tia could see it in those trusting eyes that bespoke nothing but good fortune. Nothing bad had ever happened to this child. No one had been mean to her or betrayed her. No one yelled at her or slapped her. She was clean and fed.

How nice for her.

Tia pointed toward the RV door, giving her surroundings a casual glance to see if anyone was paying particular attention. She'd chosen her position because she was blocked from the cameras. Despite the crowd, they were insulated. The school bus that was pulled alongside of them blocked their RV door from the storefront and most of other customers. No one would see their interaction.

Tia opened the RV door and smiled broadly as Gretchen climbed into the large vehicle. She could look friendly if she put some effort into it. "The puppies are in the back. There's a dog crate on the floor."

When Gretchen didn't see it, Tia pointed toward the door at the rear of the vehicle. She headed in that direction and Tia shut the RV door behind her, flipping the lock. She hurried to catch up with the girl.

Gretchen stood in the back bedroom, looking confused. "Where are the puppies?"

Tia shoved her down onto the bed and raised a hand as if to strike her. Gretchen cowered in fear and that pleased Tia. Even the threat of violence worked with this sheltered, innocent child.

"You do not make a sound," she hissed. "If you make noise or try to get away, I'll kill this puppy and then I'll kill you." Tia slid her hand around the dog's neck to show the girl she was serious.

Gretchen began crying. She tried to control it but could not. Tears had no effect on Tia. She'd seen enough in her lifetime to create a lake. As she hovered over the girl a door slammed toward the front. Soon after that, Barger started the engine.

Gretchen's eyes widened. "Where are we going?"

Tia did not answer her. Gretchen tried to get up and Tia kicked out, her sneaker connecting with the child's shin.

Gretchen fell back onto the bed and cradled her throbbing leg. "My mother will be looking for me. I can't leave."

The RV turned to the left and the movement forced Tia to steady herself against the wall. She was more at ease now that they were moving, putting distance between them and the scene of the crime. She stepped out of the room and put the puppy down in the kitchen area. She removed several items from a drawer by the kitchen sink and went back to the bedroom. The terrified child had not moved.

"Stick out your hands."

Gretchen hesitated, frozen with panic.

"Do you want me to kick you again?"

The girl obeyed this time and Tia snapped the handcuffs around her wrists. She enjoyed the way the girl looked at the cold metal bracelets. So terrified. So cowed.

"Am I being arrested?"

Ignoring her, Tia went back to the kitchen for a chain. Although it was thin, the kind that might be used to tie a dog out in a backyard, it was plenty strong enough that a child couldn't break it. Tia secured one end to the handcuffs with a tiny padlock, then secured the other end to a grab bar in the cramped master bath.

"They hurt," Gretchen whined. "They're pinching me."

"Get used to it. You have enough chain to get to the bathroom. Do you have a phone?"

Gretchen shook her head. You never knew these days. Sometimes they had them as soon as they could walk. Tia continued to search for her and found nothing. She could see the girl's revulsion at her touch. That was okay. She wasn't offended.

Tia returned to the kitchen and removed something from another drawer. She went back into the bedroom and tossed a bottle of water onto the bed. She held out a hand with two pink pills. "Take these."

Gretchen looked down at the pills, then back up to her. "I can't take pills. They make me throw up."

"Do I have to get the puppy?" Tia snapped. "Do you want to see me to hurt it?"

The child's hand shot out and Tia tipped the pills into her small hand.

"What are they?"

"They will make you sleep. It's the same thing you take for a bee sting."

Gretchen held the pill in front of her mouth, hesitating. Her eyes teared up. "I don't want to take it."

Tia whipped her hand back, ready to slap the child. "I don't care what you want, you little shit. You can take them or I'll shove them down your throat. You will *not* like that."

Gretchen put the two pills in her mouth, uncapped the water bottle, and started gagging as she tried to swallow them. She grimaced, then choked, but managed to wash them down with the water. Her face turned bright red and her stomach heaved.

"You throw up and you'll clean it up," Tia warned. She returned to the kitchen one more time, returning with a bag of chips and a candy bar. She tossed them on the bed.

"Where are we going?" Gretchen whimpered.

"To your new home."

"What about my old home? What about my mommy?"

"You'll never see your mommy again, kid. You might as well get used to that now."

Gretchen leaned over on the bed and began crying again. The medicine would kick in soon and she'd cry herself to sleep. Tia was fine with that as long as she kept the volume down. She hated sniveling, whiny children. The world was a cruel and miserable place. The sooner they learned that, the better off they'd be.

She left the room, closed the door, and slipped a padlock into the hasp they'd added to the bedroom door. She went all the way forward to the cab and sank into the passenger seat. Barger did not look happy.

"A little warning would be nice next time," he said.

"It was a target of opportunity. Santa Muerte led us here. She gave us a child."

Barger shook his head in disgust. While he had no place for that creepy religion and its weird practices, he knew better than to insult Tia. "There were a million people back there in that parking lot. Those places have cameras all over. That was too risky for me."

"That's why you're not in charge, Barger. You don't have the big balls. Someone had to salvage this trip. We don't drive four thousand miles and go home empty-handed."

"I think that other kid, the one from Richmond, must have got busted or something," he mused. "Her parents must have found the messages and took her phone."

"Eh, she may have got cold feet."

"It sounded like you had her hooked."

Tia did have her hooked and she wasn't sure why the whole thing went south. She had an eye for finding those troubled kids on social media because she'd been a troubled kid long before the internet came along. It wasn't hard to recognize them. Those postings they made and pictures they shared, their complaints, the kind of music they listened to. All those things helped her single out her targets.

She'd reach out to them and portray herself as the cool grandmotherly type. She'd offer advice, hint at smoking weed and partying. At some point, because she chose them so well, they'd all make that same comment.

"You're so cool. I wish you were my grandmother."

She'd tell them she could make that happen if they'd promise not to tell anyone. She'd groom them until she was certain they were committed, then she'd go pick them up and bring them to live with her. Despite their dreams of freedom, Tia's home wasn't the end of the road for those kids. It was only the beginning.

"This one's a little young, isn't she?" Barger asked.

"No. Not at all."

Barger let it go and kept his eyes on the road. It wasn't his job to ask questions. He was just the driver. This was her show. In twenty miles, he'd be in Tennessee, but it would take a lot more miles before he would be able to relax.

16

———

Ty wasn't sure what to do with himself. He'd lost his job and brought a lot of stress down on his sister. He'd come to this town solely for the purpose of helping her, but he was a doing a poor job of it. Trying to help find this missing girl was the most alive he'd been since being deployed. It carried the same life or death urgency, the same sense of purpose he'd experienced when fighting for his country. While it was a different kind of mission, it was still a mission. The question was whether he was willing to give it up or not.

Another part of his brain told him that the police had this under control. They didn't want his help, and there was no place for him in what they were doing. He wasn't so sure they were on the right track, though. They had their theories and he had his own. They were cops, trained for this, but he had an instinct that had served him well in his previous career. That instinct told him that the girl had gone outside because she'd seen that puppy.

That was only a suspicion. Also, it was based on Aiden and not Gretchen, the missing girl. He needed to call Gretchen's mother and confirm his theory. He could be wrong. Hell, it could be that she was obsessed with cats.

He dreaded calling the mother. She was probably being bombarded by people wanting to interview her or insert themselves into her life because of this tragedy. There would be crackpots calling and offering their theories on what happened. People like him. Even if he might be one of those crackpots that was not how he wanted to come across.

There were times in his military career when he'd been back in the U.S. on leave and had gone to visit the families of fallen brothers. It was not something he did out of his own need but because of promises made in the nervous build-up to a mission. They all assured each other that they would check in on a man's family if he didn't make it. Ty took that vow seriously. It was never easy, though. Opening the door into a family's grief was like opening the door of a blast furnace, nearly scorching your flesh from your bones.

He could always see that question in their eyes. Why had they lost their loved one when he was still alive? Although it was a natural question, it was never an easy one to be on the other side of. Ty wished he had the words to comfort those families, but he never did. While he hoped he might continue to be part of their lives, he was never certain how to do that. The loss of a loved one was not simply a position that a buddy could step in and fill on a part-time basis.

In the end, he felt like he probably did more damage than good. Those families didn't deserve to have him stirring around in their emotions. He needed to leave them alone and let them heal. He didn't know how to save them any more than he knew how to save himself.

Yet knowing all this, he picked up his phone and scrolled back through the text messages. He found the one from the unfamiliar number he'd received in the Petro Panda parking lot that day. It was the text he'd gotten from Heather when she sent him her daughter's picture to show around the parking lot. Before he could talk himself out of it, he tapped on the phone number and dialed it.

It rang twice before a groggy, slightly confused voice answered. *"Hello?"*

Ty immediately knew it was her, recognizing the strained voice from that day at the Petro Panda. "Hello, Heather, I'm sorry to bother you. My name is Tyler Stone and I'm the security guard who was on duty when your daughter went missing. I just wanted to follow up and see how you were doing."

Tyler knew it was a stupid line and he twisted uncomfortably as it came out of his mouth. How else would she be doing? Miserable. Suicidal. Terrified. Hopeless. All of those things.

He was such an idiot sometimes.

"*Hello, Mr. Stone,*" she replied. Her tone was apprehensive and cautious, as if it were totally unexpected and inappropriate for him to be calling her.

That was pretty much how he felt too, but he couldn't stop himself. "I know things have to be pretty bad right now. How are you holding up?"

"*Not very well. They tried to give me medication to help me sleep but I don't want to be messed up if they find Gretchen.*" Heather lowered her voice. "*They can't find my ex-husband right now and they're starting to think he might have had something to do with this. There's no sign that he was in this part of the country though. No credit card charges for gas, hotels, or food.*"

A voice somewhere in the background spoke to Heather, perhaps chastising her for giving away so much information to someone outside of the investigation. Ty should have realized there would be cops or the FBI there with her. It could be that they were expecting a ransom call, or some other attempt at contact, and here he was tying the line up.

"*I'm sorry, they're telling me I need to get off the phone in case she tries to call. Thank you for calling.*"

"Wait, can I ask you one question? I know it may sound totally irrelevant, but did your daughter like puppies?"

The sound of Heather's voice changed, an almost cheerful tone emerging as memories flooded forth. "*Why yes. She was completely obsessed and I promised her a puppy when we got settled into a house with a yard. They're all she can think about...*" Her voice trailed off, deflating as the warm memory was replaced with cold absence.

"Okay, I was just wondering. I'll be thinking of you. If there's anything I can do, just let me know."

"No!" Heather snapped. *"Why would you wonder that? Why would you ask me that? You weren't just wondering."*

Ty considered what to do. He'd inserted himself into the investigation and into this poor woman's misery. He couldn't simply ask her a question like that and not follow up. He decided to be completely honest with her.

"It's because of the look on her face as she was going out the door —the picture the security cameras caught. It's the same look my niece has when she sees a puppy. It just made me start thinking, that's all."

The line fell silent on the other end, that thought sending Heather down an unpleasant spiral. *"The police say the expression in that picture is an indication that she saw someone familiar. Someone she recognized. They think it might have been my husband."*

There was uncertainty in her voice now. Ty had introduced that uncertainty. He was responsible for that.

"Did she ever look at your husband that way before?"

"Not really," Heather replied. *"I tried to tell the police that she blames him for the separation. She probably wouldn't have gone with him."*

"Stay strong," Ty said. "Keep thinking positively. They'll find her." It was on the tip of his tongue to say *we'll* find her but he caught himself.

She hung up without replying and Ty put his phone on the desk. He opened his web browser and went to the Wasteland page, needing that sense of community.

He was making his way through the list of his notifications when he was startled by his ringing phone. He studied the display and recognized it was Lieutenant Whitt calling him. No doubt she'd somehow found out about him calling Heather. The last thing he was in the mood for was a drill instructor's ass chewing. He chose not to answer it. He was done with people for the day, perhaps even longer than that. He hadn't decided yet.

Ty tried to concentrate on his social media notifications. He'd been busy the last day and had missed a lot. Being part of the Wasteland group was the only thing in his life that made him feel like he was actually helping people these days. As screwed up as his own life was, he'd done some good in the group. He'd talked people off the ledge when the demons were winning. He'd chatted with folks online who just wanted someone to listen. He'd tracked down vets who'd gone dark when they thought they had nothing left.

Yet as important as that community was to him, his mind kept returning to those pictures. From the corner of his eye he could see Gretchen's smiling face in that printed photo. He couldn't ignore it. He picked it up, holding it to the side of his laptop screen, and again opening the familiar picture of the woman with the puppy.

The tag number on the RV was clearly visible. Even though the way the woman leaned against it made him think it was hers he couldn't just call up the police and ask them to run the tag on his suspicions. Even if he provided them with his information, their investigation was headed in an entirely different direction. They were looking at the dad, not a stranger with a puppy. His suspicions would be recorded and would languish on someone's desk until it was too late. Ty turned his laptop off and pushed away from his desk.

He went to the couch and collapsed onto it, staring at the blank television. The dark screen opened like a mouth to swallow him and he suddenly experienced the sensation of sinking into a pool of cold black oil. He was being swallowed into a joyless and unfeeling world that always felt permanent, inescapable. His return to civilian life was an utter failure. He'd been unable to succeed at even the most elementary task.

He'd brought suffering onto the only two people in the world who cared about him, Deena and Aiden. He'd put his sister in the position of having to defend him in a situation that was not defensible in their isolated little world. It was only going to get worse for him. He imagined there'd be a point where Deena no longer allowed him around his niece. Aiden would be hurt by that and the responsibility for that pain would come back to him. He should never have inserted himself into their lives.

There was probably only one answer.

He thought of going into the Wasteland and reaching out to his friends. It might be his turn to be talked off the ledge. It took a tremendous effort to pull himself up from the couch. It held him like a pit, the walls high and slippery. His limbs had doubled in weight. He went to his desk and retrieved the Glock, confirmed there was a round in the chamber, and carried it to his bedroom.

He sat on his bed for a long time, staring at that pistol. When he got up, he placed it on the bed and retrieved two duffel bags from the spare bedroom. One was the OD green one he'd been discharged with and the other was a long yellow one that could probably hold a body, though that was not a theory he'd tested. He crammed the green one with clothing, boots, and a jacket. The yellow one he packed with a sleeping bag, camping gear, and several different holster configurations.

He selected a soft gun case from the pile leaning against the wall in his living room. The case was padded nylon with long magazine pockets on the outside. He opened it to confirm that it contained his Tavor X95 in .300 Blackout. In his bedroom, he found the suppressor for the weapon, spare magazines, and subsonic rounds in the correct caliber. He slid a pair of binoculars into the yellow bag and packed away several boxes of 9mm ammunition for his Glock. He preferred custom loads from Maker Bullets that opened like spinning, razor-sharp stars but would not over-penetrate.

Ty grabbed an empty cooler from his spare room and took it to the kitchen. He packed what canned food he could find, a can opener, and anything edible that didn't require special care. He threw in some paper plates and roll of paper towels. There was a partial case of water on the pantry floor and he stacked that on the cooler, along with a Nalgene water bottle.

He packed his laptop and the printed pictures into a messenger bag, holstered the Glock, and went to his dresser for something with an edge. He selected a Benchmade side-opening automatic which he carried in a kydex sheath on his belt, positioned behind the Glock. He also tucked a custom karambit into the front left side of his belt. While for some folks this may have been overkill, Ty had been places and seen things. He never left the house without redundant methods of defending himself.

Ty moved his truck as close to his own door as he could get it and loaded everything, placing it all in the back of the crew cab. Though the windows were tinted, he spread a blanket across the load to hide it from any prying eyes. When he was done he locked the townhouse and checked his watch. It was late afternoon. If he was lucky, he might make it across the state of Tennessee before he gave out for the night.

17

Several times in the night Tia crept into the girl's room and forced her to take more Benadryl. She didn't know if a child that size could overdose on it. Usually she collected slightly older girls. If this one tolerated the Benadryl well, she'd transition her to something stronger soon. That made the girls so much more cooperative. No one on heroin or fentanyl ever fought back, at least not for long.

Tia heard no movement out of the back bedroom in the morning so she let the girl sleep. It was not out of compassion but for the sake of convenience. Sleeping children were less trouble. Later, when she heard the chain rattling, she was certain the girl was awake and moving around.

Tia went to the smaller half-bath beside the kitchen and retrieved something from a drawer. She went to the bedroom, removed the padlock, and shoved the door open. She held the scissors out in front of her and allowed Gretchen to study them, enjoying the fear in the girl's eyes as she no doubt imagined all the horrors scissors could inflict.

The stabbing.

The cutting.

The slicing.

"In the bathroom, now," Tia ordered.

Gretchen didn't react but Tia didn't think it was defiance. She was paralyzed by fear.

Tia leaned against the doorframe. "You can walk in there on your own or I can drag you by the hair. You choose."

When Gretchen finally stirred, Tia held open the door to the bathroom and she went inside, standing in the tiny space before the sink.

"In the shower," Tia said.

When Gretchen hesitated again Tia hurried her along with a smack to the back of the head. It was best the child learn that Tia was not scared to hit. Once they understood that, things always went smoother.

She stepped over the raised lip of the shower and Tia touched her hair, examining the length and the cut. Gretchen flinched away from her touch, the long, pointy nails, but Tia yanked her hair and she didn't move again. Tears rolled from her eyes, ignored by Tia.

The child's hair was soft and well cared for. A loving mother had combed it and washed it, she could tell. Tia raised a piece, pinching it between two fingers, and snipped. A foot-long piece of hair dropped to the shower floor.

"No," Gretchen whimpered.

Tia placed the scissors on the edge of the sink and the deliberate-ness of her actions should have been an indication of what was to come. Without warning, she struck Gretchen in the head with an open-handed blow. The girl fell against the side of the shower, covering her head. She sank to the floor, thinking the gesture of submission might protect her, but it did not. In fact, it could have been a fatal mistake.

Tia raised a sneakered foot and lashed out, kicking anywhere she could hit flesh. The child's weakness enraged her and she lost her temper, only regaining it when she almost kicked the girl in the face. Gretchen huddled beneath her, sobbing.

Tia lowered her foot to the floor. She never marked the face. It led to uncomfortable attention from strangers. It could lead the police to your door. On a more practical level, it impacted the price one got for a girl.

"Get up!" she hissed. "GET UP NOW! You don't tell me no!"

Tia didn't have to repeat herself. The child understood now that she was willing to inflict pain. She had no choice but to comply. Gretchen got to her feet, tears pouring down her face. She didn't move again while Tia efficiently cropped her beautiful long hair into a crude bob.

Tia left the sobbing girl in the shower and returned with a garbage bag. "Clean it up. All the hair. Put it in there."

When Gretchen had done an acceptable job, Tia turned on the shower and used the handheld sprayer to rinse her off, clothes and all. When she was finished, Tia went back to the main compartment of the RV, returning a moment later with several bottles. She snapped on a pair of rubber gloves and proceeded to dye Gretchen's hair an inky black. It was much the same color as Tia's own hair had been when she was younger. She could tell this whole process traumatized the girl. Apparently her hair was important to her. That was the old life and this was the new.

When Tia was done, she backed out of the shower and tossed Gretchen a grubby, stained towel.

"Get out of those clothes and put them in the garbage bag. There are new ones for you on the bed. Your name is Zarita now. It's the only name you will use."

Tia could not hold back a smile at the look on the child's face. Apparently the taking of her name was the last straw. She looked so hopeless at that moment. When Tia backed out of the room, she was staring at herself in the mirror. She seemed broken.

Exactly where Tia wanted her.

18

B arreling down Interstate 40 in Tennessee, Ty had plenty of time on his hands to consider what the hell he was doing. He kept telling himself that it was because Gretchen had gone missing on his watch, snatched while he was on duty. There was also the fact that she was so close in age to his niece and he couldn't imagine how he would react if Aiden disappeared. Added to that was the underlying selfish motive that he might have taken his own life if he hadn't gotten out of his house. As they said in the Wasteland, he was listening to the demons.

Ty had spent fourteen years in the military. He never imagined a life outside of the uniform. He enjoyed the brotherhood, the action, and being on the front lines of the battle between good and evil. Ty understood his decisions back in the mud storm in Afghanistan had cost civilian lives. Even worse, the life of an innocent child.

While there may have been a day in the past when the military saw the occasional civilian death as part of the cost of doing business, those days were over. There was no allowance for collateral damage in an operation. Someone had to pay for what happened that day. That man had been Ty.

Thinking about his service made him wonder how his brothers

and sisters in the Wasteland were doing. He wondered who was melting down today besides him. Surely there was someone else. Sometimes it was prompted by having to wait in line for a ridiculous amount of time, the stress triggering PTSD symptoms. It could be the result of a frustrating letter from the VA. It could be because of a bad relationship a member couldn't navigate their way out of.

Through all those things, the people of the Wasteland supported each other when it was appropriate and collectively set the member straight when it appeared they were at fault. It wasn't a perfect system but it was what they had.

He wondered if anyone was in real crisis. If so, he imagined there were other Wastelanders responding. The group always came together and rallied for their own. There was a senior member, a moderator named Jessica, who was usually on top of things. Like Ty, she was a frequent flyer who appeared to have no life beyond her job and the Wasteland. Sadly, that was probably true for a lot of them. Dealing with symptoms eventually restricted what activities they chose to participate in because everything stressed them out. Many of them had few relationships in their life as symptoms strained their bond with friends and family.

Thinking of Jessica reminded Ty of something that had once crossed his mind when they were trying to set up a welfare check on a vet in distress. Ty opened the Facebook Messenger app on his phone and dictated a private message to Jessica.

Hey, I'm on a road trip. Driving most of the day. Do you mind giving me a voice call on my cell? I promise it's nothing creepy.

As weird as it sounded, he was almost obligated to include that last line. For people with whom the entirety of your interactions were conducted online, asking someone to call you on the phone or to meet you in person was like a violation of protocol. It just wasn't done. Real world relationships stayed in the real world, online relationships stayed in the virtual world, and the two were never intended to cross. It was like matter meeting anti-matter in a science fiction movie.

Somewhere between Nashville and Memphis Ty pulled into a rest area. He'd consumed several energy drinks, which kept him awake, but had the side effect of making him need to use the restroom. He was also getting pretty wound-up from the caffeine overdose. It was past midnight, the rest area was well-lit but with few cars in the parking lot. There was a security guard in a booth with a little golf cart beside it. Most of the vehicles there were tractor-trailers parked for the night.

Ty went inside and took care of his business. When he came back out, the security guard was getting into the golf cart to make a pass around the property. "Excuse me, sir?" he said.

The security guard appeared to be around seventy years old and was startled by Ty addressing him. Apparently his shift was pretty quiet and he wasn't used to having to interact with people. "Yes?"

"I need to stretch my legs," Ty said. "Any problem with me running a few laps around this place?"

The old man grinned. "As long as I don't have to go with you."

"Not if you don't want to. Just wanted to let you know. Didn't want to startle you if I came running out of the dark like a crazy man."

The man started the golf cart and winked at Ty. "Yeah, white people get shot every day for running around in the dark, don't they?"

Ty gave the guard a nod of thanks and tore off down the concrete sidewalk that circled the facility. The night was comfortable with temperatures in the fifties. It was perfect for running. Ty planned only two or three laps but ended up doing ten. He only quit when he realized that he might keep at this all night if he didn't make himself stop.

He returned to his truck, unlocked it, and climbed inside. He sucked down a bottle of water, wondering whether he should try to grab a nap, but there was no way with all the caffeine banging around in his system. Besides, he was making good time and the roads were less crowded this time of night. Before he got back on the road, he decided to make a quick pass through his social media accounts. As usual, most of his notifications were related to activity within the Wasteland group.

There was some good-natured banter, friendly at this point,

between the different services. There were two men comparing notes, each trying to outdo the other on how badly they were being treated by their wives. Not to be left out, a woman jumped into the fray to complain about her husband. Reading their comments only reaffirmed to Ty why he preferred to remain single at this point in his life. He was scrolling through posts when his phone dinged with a message notification. It was from Jessica.

"Dude, does it have to be a phone call? I'd rather poke my eyes out than have to spend time on the phone. Whhhhhhyyyyyyy???????"

Ty messaged her back. *I'm driving. It has to be FaceTime or a voice call.*

An animated icon appeared indicating there was typing on her end. In a moment a message appeared. *"Then let's do FaceTime. Maybe it won't be so bad. At least I'm not having to listen to a disembodied voice."*

In a few seconds his phone started ringing and prompted him to accept or decline a FaceTime call from an Oklahoma number. He knew from Jessica's posts that's where she was located. He accepted the call, holding the phone up in front of his face so she could see him.

Her image slowly came into focus as the camera adjusted to the lighting conditions. He found himself facing a woman, probably in her early thirties, with blue hair and several facial piercings. Her elbow was propped up on a table or desk, her cheek resting in the palm of her hand. The pose made her look like a teenager.

"Can you do this and drive?" she asked. *"Don't want to be responsible for you piling up somewhere."*

"I pulled into a rest area. Too many energy drinks. Had to take a break."

She smiled at that. *"I work the night shift. I know all about it. Now tell me, what's so damn important that we have to break the electronic wall and talk on the phone like regular people?"*

"Can I be blunt? Maybe even a little nosy?" The question was purely rhetorical. He was already determined to be both of those things.

Jessica shrugged, a smile still on her face, but looking a little wary. *"You promised not to be creepy."*

He laughed. "I stand by that promise. I need to ask you about something personal. Something you've never posted online."

"Need to or want to?"

"Need to. What do you do for a living?"

If the question surprised her, she didn't break stride, didn't lose her smile. *"Why do you need to know what I do for a living?"*

"Because I've noticed that whenever we're trying to find somebody's info for a welfare check, you're always the person who comes up with the street address or which local law enforcement agency needs to be contacted. Is that a coincidence or does a girl have resources?"

She grinned. *"It's no coincidence. A girl* does *have resources."*

"I knew it."

"But look, I don't want my personal shit blasted out on the Internet. I'm not sure my work would approve of some of my online activities. Hell, they barely approve of me in person. That's why my ass works the vampire shift."

"Does this mean your name isn't really Jessica?"

She laughed. *"Exactly! And don't even ask my real name because I won't tell you."* She paused and her eyes rolled up in thought. *"Well, I might since I've seen your face and have your phone number. That makes you more real, I guess."*

"No worries. This conversation is completely confidential," Ty said. "I won't mention anything you tell me."

"Well, that's a start. So tell me why you want to know? What's so fucking important?"

Fueled by caffeine and mania, Ty launched into the story. "I've been working as a security guard at the truck stop. It's a shitty job but, you know, I have to work."

"I can relate."

"The other day a little girl around ten years old disappeared on my shift. I feel like I have a lead but the police aren't interested. Their investigation is going down an entirely different road. They're interested in the dad, but I don't think that's the case."

"Divorced or separated parents?"

Ty nodded. "Yep."

"It usually is a parent in those cases."

"I know. Bear with me. To make matters worse, the company that owns the truck stop decided that I overreacted because I locked the place down after it happened. They said I was being too aggressive and scared the customers, which is bullshit. They canned my ass, so now I got nothing but time on my hands. Since the police aren't interested, I decided to follow up on this lead before the trail went cold."

Either his story was convincing her or she was tired of hearing him talk. *"I work as a dispatcher,"* she admitted. *"I like the night shift because there's fewer people to deal with and it's where the crazy shit happens. There's a lot of the same rush you get from being deployed. I don't know if that's why I do it or not, but it helps me cope and it keeps me fed."*

"I think you're coping pretty well," Ty said. "You always have your head together. You give good advice and you've helped a lot of people."

"Eh, I'm a basket case like everyone else. I have my good days and bad days. You guys just see the good ones."

"You're not the only one, Jessica. Getting caught up in this missing kid thing and losing my job has me in a weird place. Not to mention I kind of went off the rails at a movie theater last week and it's caused some grief with the family."

"Just remember to ask for help if you need it. Don't wait until you're so far down in the hole no one can reach you."

"Roger that. So, are you able to run tag numbers?" Ty asked, cutting to the chase.

She raised an eyebrow at him. *"I like the way you just slipped that in there all casual-like. One minute you're talking about how great I am at dealing with folks in the Wasteland and then you ask for a favor."*

"I've never been accused of being smooth," Ty admitted. "You seem to have access to information, though, so I wondered if you were able to run a tag number. I have a vehicle that I think might be involved in this abduction, but like I said, the police aren't interested in my information at this point. They're sold on the dad and asked me to butt out."

"Why do you think they're wrong? I mean, they're detectives, right? They do this shit for a living."

"If I tell you, you're going to think I'm crazy."

Jessica shrugged. *"We're at home in the Wasteland. That pretty much makes both of us a little crazy, right? Besides, if you want my help, you're going to have to convince me that you have a compelling case."*

"I guess so," he conceded. "It was the look on the child's face. We have a clear surveillance shot of her leaving the store on her own to go outside. She had this *look*. I've seen the same look on my niece's face and I think I know what it means. I *don't* think it means she left with her dad, I think it means she saw someone with a cute puppy."

"Do you have any evidence that there was someone out there with a puppy?"

Ty nodded adamantly. "Oh hell yeah. I got a picture of a woman with an RV and a puppy. The picture shows her tag number. Can you run it?"

She sighed. *"Okay, I'll do it. I can run it as soon as I'm back at work but you have to swear you won't tell anyone. This is serious. They will fire me in a heartbeat if they find out. It's a good gig. If I lose it over a look and a puppy I'm going to be pissed. I'll be showing up on your doorstep."*

"That's why I wanted to ask you in person. I didn't want to put it in a message."

"Shit, you think that makes a difference? The NSA is all up in our phone calls."

"If you can look the number up, that would be fantastic. I'll owe you big time. I'm on my way to Arizona now to look into this."

"Wait...what? From where?"

"Virginia. I'm somewhere in Tennessee now. Probably hit Arkansas in the morning."

Jessica was shaking her head at him like he was indeed crazy, a knight charging out on a fool's errand. *"Dude, I'm not even going to argue with you. You got the number handy?"*

Ty gave her the tag number and watched her scribble it on a piece of paper.

"You're going to fucking owe me."

"I know. I'm headed in your direction. Maybe I'll stop in Oklahoma and buy you a big old steak."

"Yeah," she said with a grin, *"I'll believe that when I see it."*

"Well, I better get back to it. I have a lot of road to blow through."

"Just like a man. Get what you want and take off."

He winked. "You know it."

"Hey Ty, one more thing," she added before he could disconnect. *"Something I just thought of. There used to be a guy active in the Wasteland a few years back. His name was Cliff Mathis. He's involved in child abductions and human trafficking stuff. Like, he works for some international organization and does this shit for a living. He's one of the only Wastelanders I've ever met in real life because he did a training for our law enforcement on investigating human trafficking."*

"Human trafficking? There's no sign this is anything like that."

"If it's not the dad then it's a possibility."

"You really think so?"

"I don't know but I hear it from the cops I work with all the time. You'd be shocked how often human trafficking is a component of crimes like prostitution, drug dealing, and even shoplifting."

"Shoplifting?"

"Definitely. They smuggle these folks in, keep them prisoner, and then send them into stores to steal goods that can be sold. The traffickers don't care if the shoplifters get caught because there's plenty more people to replace them."

"Sounds like I need to do a little more homework. I had no idea."

"Call this guy, Ty. He'll probably talk to you if you play the Wasteland card. He knows a lot about finding kids."

"That might help," Ty agreed. "You have contact info on him?"

"It's at work. I have his business card. I'll shoot a picture of it and text it to you tomorrow."

"I appreciate it, Jessica. You have a good night."

"You too. Drive safe, Rambo."

Ty was smiling when he ended the call. He started his truck and got back on the road.

19

The next morning Ty awoke stiff and uncomfortable in the reclined seat of his pickup truck. Out of sheer will, he'd pushed until he crossed the Mississippi River overnight, but immediately turned into the first rest area he found on the Arkansas side. It was midmorning and he'd had a decent night's sleep for a change. His bladder was screaming for relief so he headed in to use the facilities, stretching as he walked.

When he was back at his truck, he grabbed a bottle of water and a package of Pop Tarts from the food box. He unplugged his phone from the charger and found a picnic table where he could sit for a few minutes. He needed to get his head together before he got back on the road. He tore open the Pop Tart and found it was strawberry, which would do. There were better flavors but it was what he had. He opened the water bottle, drained half of it in a single drink, and wished he'd brought a second one with him.

While he slept, he'd missed a call from his sister, another call from Lieutenant Whitt, and a text from Jessica. Before he dug into any of that, he opened his Facebook app and checked into the Wasteland. He replied to messages and reviewed the most active posts to see if there were any he was compelled to weigh in on. It looked like anyone needing help overnight had found it. The people in crisis had received solid advice and deescalated. As usual, the community was taking care of its own in a way that people outside the fence could never understand. It wasn't clinical or pretty to look at. It was quick and dirty problem-solving by people who understood. Field medicine for the heart and mind.

When he finished his Pop Tart and his bottle of water, he went back to his truck to get another of each. He retook his seat at the same picnic table and opened the text from Jessica. It was not the expected picture of the business card she'd mentioned.

I'm not back at work yet but I remembered the guy's website. I go in tonight and I'll get that other thing you wanted.

There was a link in the text and Ty clicked on it with his thumb. It took him to the website of a man named Cliff Mathis. The name sounded vaguely familiar. Perhaps he'd heard it in the Wasteland, but it was no one he could recall interacting with. He scrolled down the homepage to find that it contained a montage of images: women and children from all over the world, people in shackles, jacked up guys in tactical gear standing in dirty foreign compounds, and flex-cuffed men on their knees as they were lined up for arrest.

Ty scrolled a little further and found blocks of text explaining the story of Cliff Mathis and his organization. He called his company Door Kickers International and they were one of several veteran-operated entities who devoted themselves to ending human trafficking and sexual exploitation. Cliff's bio explained he came from a special operations background and entered law enforcement after receiving a career-ending injury in combat. He was so appalled at the pervasiveness of human trafficking that he encountered through regular police work that he wanted to devote his career to ending it. Finding no way he could do that within a law enforcement framework, he left that job to start Door Kickers International.

Ty was impressed to learn this was not just an organization dedicated to increasing awareness. The centerpiece was an operational division whose activities had earned the company its name. Backed by a team of American and international lawyers, the company worked with foreign governments and American law enforcement to take action against known traffickers.

This wasn't just writing stories and holding press conferences to shame ineffective governments. This was action. It was fast-roping out of choppers and, as the name implied, kicking down doors. The company had deep pockets and conducted investigations around the world. When they nailed down a target, his people took the risks and launched the operations. In foreign countries, local law enforcement or the military stepped in behind them to make the official arrests. Victims were freed, government officials got some good press, and Cliff's team moved on to the next job. There were always more jobs because there were always more victims.

Ty was fascinated by the website. There were dozens of articles and just as many videos. There were links to podcasts and television interviews, along with testimonials from individuals rescued by the team's actions, and statements issued by celebrity spokespeople. He could have sat there all morning and read through it, but he needed to get back on the road.

After one more round of stretching, Ty climbed into his truck and hit the road. He needed to fuel up, suck down some go juice, and put miles behind him. He hadn't dealt with the missed phone calls yet but he didn't want to start his day off that way. He was a little concerned about Deena. If he didn't contact her, she might panic and send the police to do a welfare check on him. The last thing he needed was the police busting down his door when he wasn't home to secure the place. He damn sure didn't want them pawing through his gun collection.

Deena, for as much as she cared about him, just didn't get it. She was like a lot of family members whose hearts were in the right place but didn't understand how to relate to their returning vets. She always expected him to stick a gun in his mouth or take some other drastic measure. That was only true part of the time.

He was aware from his experience in the Wasteland and from his buddies that a lot of returning vets struggled with the same demons. Of course, he knew they weren't *actual* demons. He didn't really think there was some supernatural entity speaking to him in his head and trying to sabotage his life. It was simply the term they commonly used to describe the experience of feeling like you were sinking and losing your ability to fight back. At least every couple of days someone in the Wasteland would post that the demons were winning. Everyone knew what that meant. It was a cry for help and the team pulled together to do what they could.

Ty navigated through his phone and clicked Deena's number. She answered with her professional voice and it was only then he remembered she would be at work this time of day.

"Hey, I'm sorry. I forgot about you being at work."

"It's okay, Ty. I was just kind of worried after the way you took off so suddenly yesterday. You had like one bite of pizza and bolted out the door. Is everything okay?"

It was one of those questions he didn't know how to answer. Things weren't exactly okay but he was in a good place at the moment. He decided to start with something concrete. "I got fired from the Petro Panda."

"Ty..." She groaned with a mixture of disappointment and sympathy.

"It's okay. It was because I shut the place down when the girl turned up missing. They decided it was an overreaction that put the public at risk, so they fired me. Turns out that locking the place down didn't make any difference. The missing girl must've already been off the premises by then. I think I did the right thing, though. If I had it to do all over again, I'd still lock it down. I'd just have done it sooner."

"Have you tried talking to them and making them understand why you did it? You could ask for your job back."

"That was my first reaction but it's actually a shitty job. It's not worth begging for. Especially when I know I was right. If that's the kind of people they are, fuck'em."

"So what are you going to do?"

"Right now, I'm going on a road trip."

He heard an involuntary inhalation on her end, like mild panic. *"You left town?"*

He had to laugh. "Did I need permission, sis?"

"Well, of course you don't need permission. I mean, you're a grown man and all. It's just..."

"Just what?"

She lowered her voice. *"You're not running off to do something crazy, are you? You're not going to...hurt yourself?"*

"Jesus, no!"

"I'm sorry, Ty. I had to ask. I know you get in these funks sometimes."

"No funking funk here, Deena. Just taking a road trip to clear my head. Might visit some buddies."

"Where are you headed?" That mother voice was coming out again.

"I'd rather not say. That way, if anyone asks, you don't have to lie." He was specifically thinking of Lieutenant Whitt contacting his sister if he failed to answer her calls, though that was probably a long shot. He was likely nothing but a footnote in their investigation at this point.

"Why would anyone ask about you, Ty? You didn't knock off a liquor store, did you?"

"Not lately."

"So you're not going to tell me where you're going?"

"No, not right now. But I'll stay in touch. I'll be coming home soon so don't worry."

"If you say so," she said, not sounding as if she believed him.

They said their goodbyes. After ending the call, Ty reviewed his recent calls again, staring at Lieutenant Whitt's number. He wavered back and forth as to whether he should make the call or not. He decided to pass, closing the display on his phone and placing it in the cup holder.

20

T he day after cutting Gretchen's hair, Tia went into her room and tweaked the style. She snipped any stray hairs she'd missed and tried to comb it into something resembling a professional cut. It wasn't perfect and that was fine. It just had to be good enough. When she was satisfied, she backed away from Gretchen and held up her phone.

"Face me, Zarita."

She took several pictures, trying to find a flattering angle in the poor light. "Turn to your left." She snapped more pictures, turned the child, and then took more of the other side. When she was done, she retrieved a bottle of water and another candy bar from the kitchen.

"What's your name?" Tia asked.

Gretchen hesitated, then muttered, "Zarita."

Tia tossed the food and water on the bed. There was no praise. Tia didn't give praise. She withdrew from the room and locked the door behind her, then went forward to the cab and settled into the passenger seat.

After studying the pictures she'd just taken, she opened an encrypted email application she used for communicating with her contact, attached three images to an empty email, and sent them. She stuck the phone in her bra and stared out the window. "I just sent the pictures."

"Good," Barger said. "The sooner this is over with, the better."

"If you're losing your nerve I can always hire someone else," Tia said, tired of his complaining.

His lack of response gave her his answer. Barger liked the money. He couldn't give it up any more than she could. She also sensed he was a little scared of her, which was good. He should be. She gave the email a few minutes to work its way to its destination, then dialed a number on her phone.

"Hello?"

She recognized the voice. She didn't know his real name but they called him El Clavo, *the nail.* He'd earned that name by his practice of leaving the bodies of his enemies nailed to prominent buildings. That sent a certain kind of message, which was exactly what he was after. El Clavo was a member of the Jalisco Cartel New Generation. Tia's son Luis had made the introduction. She didn't know where El Clavo stood within the hierarchy of the cartel but assumed he must be a low-level player since she was able to call him directly. She showed him respect, though, because even a low-level player could be plenty dangerous.

"It's Tia. Check your mail."

"Hold on," he said. *"Putting you on speaker."*

She waited, knowing he was clicking around his phone and opening the email she'd just sent.

"This is a different girl," he noted.

Tia sighed. She'd gotten ahead of herself and sent him a picture of the girl she was supposed to pick up in Richmond, which hadn't panned out. "That a problem?"

"No," El Clavo replied. *"It may affect the price, though."*

"Hell, she should bring more."

"Eh, the young ones are more complicated, Tia. That's a specialty market with more risk. If I assume more risk, I pay you less money."

Tia hated these cartel bastards but what could she do? If you wanted to be a player, they controlled the court. "Well, the other deal fell through and this is what I got. I don't know what happened. You know how shit goes."

Trafficking wasn't a business for the rigid and inflexible. Every day was something new. You had to be able to think on your feet and improvise. El Clavo understood that. Tia understood that. Barger, not so much.

"How old is she?"

"Ten or eleven, I'd guess. I haven't asked."

El Clavo let out a low whistle. *"How soon can you be here?"*

Tia tipped the phone away from her mouth. "Barger, how soon can we get there?"

He shrugged. "Probably middle of the night tomorrow. Could be the day after. Depends on how tired I am."

Tia relayed the information into the phone.

"You see, that's a problem," El Clavo said.

Tia rolled her eyes. Everything was a problem with this one. "What's the problem?"

"You were supposed to be here tonight. I have cargo headed to San Diego tomorrow for the West Coast circuit," El Clavo said. *"If she ain't here then, she'll miss that ride. I'm not sending more girls until next week and I damn sure ain't babysitting her until then."*

"You could make a special trip," she offered. "It might be worth it."

"I don't make special trips."

Tia was ready to give up but he was her only market for this kind of thing. She had no idea where she'd look for another buyer. "You *are* interested though, right?"

El Clavo paused. *"Yes. Next week I'm interested. This week, not so much."*

Tia sighed but knew there was nothing she could do. This was her problem, not his. This was not a man you disrespected, either. It was best she not push her luck. Santa Muerte had delivered the girl to her. She would help solve this little problem too. "That's fine. I'll call you next week." She ended the call.

Tia tipped her head back and closed her eyes. The world had

been a better place before the rise of the cartels. She resented the way they'd moved into her city and took over her neighborhood. Before they came along, she'd been a boss, one of the few women running a gang in the city. At the time, when they drove her out, she'd been lucky to escape with her life. Now, she didn't feel so lucky. What had they left her with?

To make matters worse, her own son went to work for them. Luis made more money than she'd ever made. He had his fancy house and his fancy ranch outside the city. Anytime she asked him for something, like the introduction to El Clavo several years back, he acted as if it was an inconvenience. He tossed favors like they were scraps of meat and she should be appreciative.

"What the hell are we supposed to do with her for a week?" Barger asked. "People are going to be looking for her. She'll probably be on the news."

"I'll take care of it, Barger. You just do what you're paid to do. I'll deal with the rest. Besides, this is your fault. You drive like an old lady."

"I'm sorry if I have to take breaks," Barger snapped. "I can't do more than ten or twelve hours a day. My back starts hurting."

"You complain like an old lady too."

"You want to help drive? We could drive straight through if you'd help out."

"Yeah, whatever," Tia replied, her mind elsewhere. She was already thinking of someone she could get to replace Barger. Someone younger and more able to handle long hours behind the wheel. Someone better looking would be nice too. Barger was old and fat. She got tired of looking at him.

21

Ty made decent time on the highway. At some point, Deena sent him a long text expressing her concerns and letting him know he should contact her any time day or night if he was considering "something drastic." He appreciated her concern but not her sense of drama. Lieutenant Whitt tried to call him twice and he ignored it both times. On her second call she left him a voicemail, but he'd yet to listen to it.

He texted Jessica.

What time do you go into work?

Not until midnight, was her speedy reply.

That was a long way away but he supposed it didn't matter. He was at least a day away from Arizona. That made him begin to consider what he was going to do when he got there. Was he going to set up surveillance on the house? Was he going to barge in and demand to know where Gretchen was? Worse yet, what was he going to do if she wasn't there and this had all been a wild goose chase?

Ty stopped in Oklahoma for a power nap at a rest area. When he awoke, he charged through the windmill-spotted grasslands into northern Texas, eventually hitting the yellow-brown dirt of New Mexico. If his day went as planned, he would get a hotel room outside of Albuquerque just as Jessica was going into work. Before he settled in for the night, he hoped to have the name and address belonging to that RV.

When the sun disappeared over the horizon ahead of him and full dark settled on the highway, Ty began to tire. He was road-weary and needed a caffeine boost. He took an exit offering several options, including a Petro Panda. Part of him was determined he would never give up any more of his hard-earned money to that business ever again. Another part of him might get a wicked charge out of stopping there. He even considered taking a selfie in front of the store and sending it to that dick from human resources.

"What store am I at now, Butch? Take a guess. Where's Waldo?"

In the end, the familiarity of the Petro Panda won him over. He knew the layout of the pumps, knew the restrooms were clean, and he also knew they stocked his favorite energy drinks and they were on special right now, two for four dollars. He pulled into the well-lit facility and fueled up. While the gasoline pumped, he emptied the trash from his truck and shoved it into the Petro Panda cans. After what they'd done to him, they could damn sure haul off his trash.

When he was done at the pump, he pulled his truck into a space at the side of the parking lot, went inside, and purchased his energy drinks and some junk food to keep him awake, struggling with whether to go with Mike And Ikes or Hot Tamales. He decided to buy both.

On the walk back to his truck, a bag of caffeine, chemicals, and sugar dangling from his arm, his phone rang. He checked the display and saw it was Lieutenant Whitt again. This time he decided he'd answer it, but for purely selfish reasons. If the call pissed him off, it might help keep him awake while he pushed through this last stretch of road.

"Hello?" he said, his voice neutral and intentionally pleasant, ready to absorb whatever she threw at him. He was the kid surrendering to the fact he was going to get a spanking and ready now just to get it over with.

"Good evening, Ty. It's Lieutenant Whitt."

"Why, I *thought* I recognized that number."

She ignored his sarcasm and didn't sound as angry as he'd expected. *"I assumed you must recognize it since you've been ignoring my calls."*

"Well to be honest, Lieutenant, after the weekend I've had, I wasn't interested in another ass-chewing. If I wanted to feel bad about my life I didn't need your help doing it."

"I actually wanted to call and apologize for going off on you the other day. Things have been a little stressful. No one likes a missing child case. No one likes the FBI coming in, telling them they're incompetent, and shoving them out of the way."

"Then it was a shitty weekend for all of us."

"Most days I don't give a shit how I treat people, but you and I both served our country. I feel like I owe you a little more respect and considera-tion than I might give the average civilian. I'm sorry."

Ty tossed his shopping bag into the driver's seat of his truck, went to the back of the truck, dropped the tailgate, and took a seat in the cool night air while he talked. "I appreciate the apology."

"With that in mind, I want to let you know why I wasn't interested in hearing your theory about what happened to Gretchen. This is strictly between us, and if you ever tell anyone, I'll deny we had this conversation. Anyway, the divorce between Gretchen's parents isn't final yet. He told her he was going camping and off-roading somewhere in the area of Moab, Utah, and that he would be out of cell range for a week. When one of the husband's friends saw the story on the news that Gretchen was missing, he called her mother and spilled the truth."

"Did he admit that her dad took her?" Ty asked. He couldn't accept that was the case. Could his intuition have been that wrong?

"Not quite. The friend said that Gretchen's dad wasn't really going to Moab. He was driving down to Mexico, looking at a place on the Gulf of California with his girlfriend. He's wanting to move out of the country when the divorce is final."

"Have you been able to track him down?"

"Not yet. Apparently he was keeping things low-key because he didn't want Gretchen's mother to know about the girlfriend or *his plans to leave*

the country. We did confirm that his passport was used to cross the border into Mexico. He's not using any of his credit cards, though, and we don't have a name on the girlfriend to monitor if they're using hers. We're looking into that."

"So you're still leaning toward the dad taking her?"

"I think it's fairly obvious," Lieutenant Whitt said. *"They've probably smuggled her across the border somewhere and have no intention of returning. The dad is going to start a new life in Mexico and wanted his daughter there with him."*

Ty didn't believe it. His instinct told him he was right. She'd been abducted by strangers, most likely in the RV he was chasing. While it may not be logical, his gut told him those people knew something, and he was not going to stop until he found them.

"You don't believe it, do you?" the Lieutenant asked, sensing Ty's reluctance to buy into the theory.

"You have your gut feeling and I have mine," Ty replied.

"Well, this is the consensus of the FBI and the Virginia State Police. The mother was pretty much in agreement with us until you planted that seed of doubt about the puppy. If this doesn't pan out, I'll give you a call and we can discuss your theory."

That response told Ty all he needed to know about her attitude toward his theories. She had no interest in hearing them and put no credence in them. Although she may have felt bad about the way she treated him, she continued to dismiss his theory about Gretchen's disappearance. He understood that with every passing day the odds of recovering Gretchen became slimmer. By the time they realized they were on a wild goose chase, the trail would be cold. He couldn't let that happen.

"Well, thanks for the call, Lieutenant Whitt. I'm heading out of town for a while. Good luck with your investigation. I'm sure you all have it under control." He figured his sarcasm might be showing a little bit but that was okay.

"I might advise against that, Mr. Stone. That was the other reason I was calling you."

"Why? Am I a suspect now?"

"*Not in this matter. A deputy did inform me today that you're being charged with assault for an incident at a movie theater. Does that ring a bell?*"

Ty's heart sank at that news. It was the last thing he needed. "There was an incident with another patron in line last week. He put his hands on me and I reacted as trained."

"*Then as a law enforcement officer I would advise you not to leave town, Mr. Stone. Your interests would best be served by turning yourself in and making a statement. I'm not sure that the argument you were 'reacting as trained' will get you very far.*"

"I'll take that under advisement," Ty replied, knowing he had absolutely no intention of doing either of those things. He was not turning himself in and not making a statement. He was going to Arizona. He could deal with the rest of this mess later.

"*You take care, Mr. Stone. Good luck.*"

Ty hung up without a goodbye. He hadn't expected that incident at the theater to materialize into anything. He was used to being around men who would dust something like that off and take it as a lesson learned. He forgot sometimes that not everyone was that way. For some folks, everything was a legal matter. Fucking lawyers. They'd ruined the world.

He got in his truck and cracked open an energy drink. He selected a Five Finger Death Punch playlist on his phone and turned it up loud. He needed to elevate his mood and keep it up. He had one more reason to be depressed now. If the demons returned, they would be excited by this latest development. They loved to peck at you while you were down. Hopefully the music would keep them away.

22

Ty was running on fumes by the time he reached Santa Rosa, New Mexico. He'd been talking out loud to himself for over an hour, driving with the windows down to keep himself alert. He finally reached a point where nothing was working and decided he needed to find a hotel immediately. He was ready for a real bed and a shower.

He chose a well-lit two-star motel where he could park directly in front of his room, not wanting to leave his rifle in the truck nor carry it through the lobby of a hotel. That sometimes drew unwanted attention. Lots of it.

After he'd paid for his room, he parked in front of his door and observed the parking lot. There was no one moving around. He grabbed the gear he needed for the night, locked his truck, and went inside. The room was small but clean, with two beds, and plenty of southwest colors in the decor. Though the bed was tempting, he didn't even sit down on it yet. If he did, it was all over. He'd fall asleep sprawled out and fully-clothed. He was determined to take a shower first.

He took a hot one and collapsed across the bed feeling human again. Before sleep could take him, he grabbed his phone off the nightstand and shot Jessica a short text.

You working?

In seconds she texted him a photograph of what he assumed to be her computer screen. It was the results of his license tag search. There was a name and address in Tucson.

He texted her back. *Thank you very much. I owe you.*

It's in Tucson. That's where Cliff's office is, she texted.

In his delirious state, the name didn't ring a bell. *Who's Cliff?*

Former Wasteland dude. Human trafficking guru.

How had he forgotten that?

Sorry. Exhausted.

No problem. Get some rest. Just let me know how it goes. And be careful.

Will do, he replied, then plugged his phone in to charge. He resisted the urge to log into the Wasteland. He was too tired to get sucked into it right now. He also resisted the compulsion to immediately begin planning his op in Tucson now that he had an address. He double-checked that all the locks on the door were secured, then jammed a wedge beneath it. He carried a plastic wedge in his gear exactly for this purpose. It would prevent the door from being opened even if all the locks were defeated.

He clipped a gun light onto the rail of his Glock and placed it on the nightstand, turned the lamp off, and settled into the stiff sheets. The bleach-smelling pillow was too small and it made his nose burn, but he was too tired to care. Despite his exhaustion, thoughts bounced around in his head. They were not the organized, structured thoughts he normally had but chaotic, fleeting streams of ideas that resembled ants pouring from a disturbed anthill.

This was not Ty's first rodeo. He'd participated in hundreds of operations over his career, mostly in Iraq and Afghanistan, but on other continents as well. Mission planning was a big deal in that life and there were lots of support personnel backing it. You were rarely on your own. Unless, of course, you were stuck in a mud storm and no one wanted to risk getting dirty or losing men.

This time he had no support personnel. There was no team

backing him. That information on his phone and the pictures from social media were all the intel he had. It wasn't much to go on, and he was going to have to wing it. The last time he did so was in that mud storm and the burden of what happened then weighed heavily upon him. In fact, he had nightmares about it nearly every night.

This needed to turn out better. If anyone died, it needed to be that lowlife scum who stole children. Ty was even fine with losing his own life. Some days, it was barely worth holding onto anyway.

23

While Ty had somehow managed to keep his shit together through the long days of driving, it eventually caught up with him. It could have been the lack of sleep or the depressing motel, but something snatched the rug out from under him. He awoke with a growing pit of blackness at his core. He could feel it expanding, parts of him crumbling into it like a widening sinkhole in a Florida suburb. It threatened to swallow his motivation, his sense of purpose, and finally his entire being. There was a pervasive sense of utter hopelessness.

Like a dying man making a last ditch effort to save himself, Ty threw back the sheets and rolled onto the floor. He lay there flat, face down on the carpet. His limbs seemed too heavy to move. He could feel the hard concrete floor beneath the carpet, the coolness seeping into his body. He should have been revolted, knowing the kind of contaminants a motel floor might be exposed to. He didn't care, though. Nothing mattered.

He lay there several minutes and somehow found the motivation to crawl in the direction of the bathroom. He didn't bother with the light but slithered over the rim of the tub and turned on the cold water. With his toe, he flipped the diverter and the water pelted his body like a November rain. After several minutes, he was shivering uncontrollably.

It wasn't the experiences of his life that were depressing him. It wasn't like he'd been a drug addict with years of sordid memories he wanted to put behind him. He hadn't been an abused child needing to deal with a whole past of torture and pain. His worst experience was that fiasco in the mud storm. Where did all this come from? These waves of darkness? These demons that tried to steal the light from inside him?

He didn't understand it. He wasn't weak. He was a man who'd trained to power through hardship. He embraced the suck with a grin on his face. He was the guy smiling in the training photos when everyone around him looked exhausted and in pain. He was a tough son of a bitch. Where was that toughness now? Where was that life-long ability to walk through the fire and come out unscathed?

His foot shot out of its own accord and killed the shower, then turned the water off. He sat up, shivering, his arms wrapped around his core. He climbed from the tub and stood there on a shower mat the size of a pizza pan. He yanked a scratchy towel from the rack and dried off. He scrubbed hard, as if he could abrade the oily darkness from his flesh. He imagined it seeping from his skin like some poison on a dark shelf in the basement, long since having leaked through its packaging, and poisonous to anyone who touched it.

He brushed his teeth and combed his hair, not meeting his own eye in the mirror. He couldn't explain why he did that. He didn't know if it was shame or fear of what he'd see there. He dressed, putting on clean clothes, and tucking his others back into his bag. He took a seat on the bed and plugged his laptop into his cellphone. He never trusted shady hotel Wi-Fi, opting for the hotspot on his phone instead.

He checked the text from Jessica again. The tag was registered to a William Barger at an address in Tucson. He frowned at that, realizing he was half a day away from there. He plugged the address into Google maps and found it was in the Barrio Santa Rosa section of the city. Ty was an eastern boy. He'd lived in several states but none of them were in this part of the country. He was familiar with only the basics of the geography and terrain.

The satellite photos showed him that the address was in a fairly congested neighborhood by his standards. All the houses were on little square lots with fences separating them. The yards were dirt. The low houses and sparse trees didn't provide much in the way of concealment. There was definitely no place for setting up a hideout and maintaining surveillance on someone.

He realized that all the elements that made the property hard to surveil should also make it a lousy place to hide a kidnapped child. There were neighbors all over the place. People would see you coming and going. It wasn't impossible, though. He'd seen stories on the news about kids emerging from suburban homes, having been held in captivity for years. None of the neighbors suspected a thing. The kidnappers were always thought of like model citizens. This could be the same kind of situation.

He needed to get on the road before the darkness paralyzed him again. He looked around the room and couldn't imagine much worse than being stuck there for days, lying in bed, the curtains drawn. That would be the end of him. He might not have the strength to pull himself loose next time.

Although Ty had an address, a lot of miles stood between him and that point. He shut his laptop and made sure all his gear was stowed, removed the weapon light from his Glock, and holstered the weapon. Opening the door, he was hit with a blast of heat that transported him overseas, to the sandy misery of the Iraqi desert. He blinked against the light and packed his truck.

24

Tia opened the padlock and pushed the door open. The girl raised up sleepily, framed by the shaft of light coming from the main compartment of the RV.

"Who are you?" Tia asked.

The girl hesitated, looking away before finally responding. "Zarita."

Tia didn't smile and didn't offer praise. "Damn right, you are. I don't want to know what your name was before and I don't want to hear you using it. If anyone asks your name, it's Zarita. Whoever you were before, you ain't never going to be her again."

Tia groped along the wall and flipped the light switch. Dim sconces came to life and Gretchen shielded her eyes. When Tia sat down on the edge of the bed the girl withdrew under the blanket, shrinking away from her. "Give me your arm."

Gretchen's eyes widened in panic. Tia could tell she wanted to ask why, but she didn't. She was learning that noncompliance only brought pain.

Tia held out her hand, waiting for the girl to comply. "Your arm."

Gretchen tentatively extended her arm, flinching when Tia latched onto it with a strong grip. "I'm going to give you a shot."

"Noooooo!" Gretchen screeched. "I hate shots! Please don't."

Tia pulled a bandana from her pocket and started tying off Gretchen's arm. The child was not comfortable with this and twisted, struggling within herself to not fight back, knowing the pain that would invite. Tia used an alcohol wipe to clean Gretchen's arm. When she removed the capped syringe from her shirt pocket, Gretchen could no longer restrain herself. She became hysterical, kicking and screaming like a cat going into a tub of water.

"Stop it!" Tia demanded. She drew back her hand. "I will beat your ass, kid."

Gretchen quit fighting but could not stop whining. She flopped her head back and forth as if she were caught in a nightmare from which she couldn't awake.

"If you move this is going to hurt a lot worse," Tia warned. "Then I'll make you pay for not listening."

Tia used her teeth to tug the cap from the syringe and inserted the needle. Gretchen's eyes widened and her mouth opened in a silent scream. Tia slowly depressed the plunger. When she was done, she pressed the bandana over the injection site. "Hold this in place."

Gretchen didn't respond, eyes wide in horror, tears silently pouring down her face.

"Hold this in place!" Tia barked.

Gretchen's hand shot to the bandana and held it to her arm. Tia got up, snapped off the light, and left the room. She replaced the padlock on the door and threw the syringe in the trash.

She went forward to the passenger seat and settled in. "How much longer?"

"Maybe an hour."

"Her ass will be out cold by then."

"What did you give her?"

"Demerol."

"You know what you're doing, right?" Barger asked. "I mean, she's not going to overdose and die is she?"

"That's why I used Demerol," Tia replied. "There are written guidelines based on weight. I knew exactly how much to give her. Use that shit off the street and you don't know how many times it's been stepped on. Or it could be Fentanyl, and then you're fucked."

Barger nodded.

"What's the matter, old man, you getting a conscience?"

"No. Just don't want her to die after all the trouble we went through. I don't want to blow it at the end."

"Nobody's blowing anything. She'll be fine. At least until she gets where she's going. Then it ain't our problem anymore."

25

Ty pushed through the day with the help of satellite radio and metal playlists on his phone. He tried not to think about Deena and Aiden. His sister was worried he'd take his life in some shabby motel room and he'd been closer to that than he wanted to admit. He also tried to push thoughts of the possible arrest warrant from his head. He expected at any moment the local sheriff's department would call and ask where he was. The way his luck had been going lately, it would probably be one of those condescending assholes he'd bumped heads with the day the Gretchen went missing.

Heading for Tucson, Ty took the opportunity to ditch I-40 and head southwest on the two-lane Route 54. He traveled through flat, scrubby desert past the Mescalero Reservation, turning onto route 70 just before Holloman Air Force Base. At Las Cruces, New Mexico, he hit the interstate again, heading west on I-10 into Arizona.

The landscape was both alien and fascinating. Ty was enthralled by the harsh beauty of it. The terrain was so moving to him that he wondered how he could have been deprived of this for his whole life. It was like he'd been sheltered from some important piece of knowledge, like Luke not knowing that Darth Vader was his father. Why had no one ever shown him this?

He was compelled to stop at a scenic overlook and take in the beauty. He'd been unable to stop himself yet soon experienced a wave of guilt. There was a girl in the hands of strangers and he was gawking at rocks like he didn't have a care in the world. He got back in his truck and hit the road again.

With hours to kill before he hit Tucson, he decided to take a chance and call Cliff Mathis. He was so excited about getting a hit on the RV tag number he'd forgotten Door Kickers International was also based out of Tucson, according to their website. God, he hoped he didn't sound like an idiot. There had been a day when he had the confidence to call anyone and do anything. He didn't feel the same anymore. Most days he felt like he'd been demoted to the rank of Loser. Before he could talk himself out of it, he punched in the number and made the call.

"DKI, how may I help you?" answered a pleasant female voice.

Ty liked the way they used the abbreviation. It gave the name a more professional demeanor and sounded a little less like a professional wrestling alliance. "I wanted to speak to Cliff Mathis please."

"Can I ask who's calling?"

"My name is Tyler Stone. Tell him I'm calling from the Wasteland. He'll probably know what that means."

"One moment please." The receptionist put him on hold and a bland electronic tune filled his ear.

Shortly, a male voice was on the line. *"Cliff Mathis."*

"Hello, Mr. Mathis. You don't know me but my name is Tyler Stone. A friend named Jessica gave me your number. We're active in a social media group called Wasteland For Warriors. She said you used to be part of the group."

"Hey, Tyler, call me Cliff. I actually got an introductory message from Jessica yesterday saying you might call. She gave me a little background on how you two know each other. Always good to meet another Wastelander, fighting the good fight."

Ty gave a chuckle at that. "Not sure that describes my work as much as what you're doing, Cliff. I'm a year post-discharge and still haven't figured out what I want do when I grow up."

"It takes a while to find the new mission sometimes. It took me a while too. Now I feel like this is what I was put here on Earth to do. My time in the military, my time as a cop, all of it was meant to prepare me for what I do now. Jessica said she told you a little about my company?"

"She did."

"If I can cut to the chase, she said you're involved in something I might be able to help with?"

"Possibly. I guess I'm not totally sure at this point."

"I'm not a cop, Tyler. Anything you tell me will be held in confidence as long as someone is not at risk of harm."

"Someone is definitely at risk of harm, Cliff, and the cops are already involved. Law enforcement doesn't agree with my theory, though. They think I'm a crackpot who needs to go on with my life and leave the investigating to the real cops."

"Tyler, are you somewhere you can talk? I might be able to help if I had a little more information to go on."

"I'm driving. No one here but me."

"Then I want you to run me through what you feel comfortable sharing. If I have any insights that might help, I'll speak up."

Ty had an instinct that he could trust this man. His military background, his time in the Wasteland, and his current mission all made him come across like a man of integrity. He took a deep breath and launched into his story. Driving the desert between Las Cruces and Tucson, Ty recounted everything he could remember up to the point that Jessica provided him with the tag number. He even included his firing but left out the possibility that there was a warrant out for his arrest in Virginia.

"So the police had no interest in this tag number?" Cliff asked.

"No," Ty confirmed. "They have that same picture but they disagree with my rationale of why the girl was smiling. They think she was smiling at her dad. I know in my gut I'm right. Besides, the mom confirmed that the girl was obsessed with puppies and would probably not have smiled that same way at her dad."

"I'll be honest, Ty. Random abductions are rare. These crimes of opportunity are usually the work of a serial killer or child killer who commits the crime locally then disposes of the body."

The thought sickened Ty. "If you could see these two pictures in relation to each other, you might see the same thing I'm seeing."

"I'm not saying you're wrong, Tyler, just offering my experience. My wheelhouse is human trafficking and exploitation. There are several channels by which people, primarily young women, are brought in. A lot of them are illegals. Some are forced to work off a debt to the people who smuggled them across the border. There are runaways taken in by pimps and put to work. There are also thousands of traffickers who work social media to manipulate vulnerable young folks into leaving home. The kids think they're gaining freedom but usually end up as drug-addicted sex workers."

"So what you're telling me is the likelihood of this girl being taken to Arizona is pretty slim. If she was indeed snatched as part of some crime of opportunity, then she's probably lying dead back in Virginia, rather than being brought alive into Arizona."

"That's certainly what the typical scenarios would suggest, although there are always exceptions. Could be a trafficker who saw an opportunity and took it."

"I guess I'd prefer that scenario over the idea that we're going to find her dead in the woods somewhere."

"I understand that sentiment, Ty, but I've met hundreds of young women who would argue death is a better end than being trafficked."

"I don't know what to do here, Cliff." Ty was starting to doubt himself again. "I'm not sure what's going on but I feel like I've come too far to let this go. Even if these people didn't take her, they may have seen something."

"Well, what exactly do you intend to do with this address now that you have it? Keep in mind that I'm not a cop. I'll give you my advice, though, if I think you're about to make a mistake."

"I don't have a plan other than to put the address under

surveillance and look for the RV. If I see it, I'll go from there. If nothing else, this woman needs to be asked if she saw Gretchen or saw what happened to her after she exited the store."

"I think you're correct that this is all you can do at this point. If law enforcement isn't buying your theory, you'll just have to collect more evidence and prove them wrong."

"Or bring her back home," Ty countered.

"Don't get ahead of yourself and don't do anything rash. If they really are traffickers, these people can be dangerous. This isn't a business for the soft-hearted. They'll kill both you and the girl without a moment's hesitation."

"Roger that."

"I'm serious, Ty. Violence is an everyday thing for these people."

"For most of my career, it was for me also."

Cliff had no response for that. *"Are you willing to send me the info you have? The two pictures you've mentioned and the address? I'll help out if I can and keep it between us."*

Cliff rattled off his personal cell number and Ty entered it into his phone.

"Got it. I'll send them as soon as we get off here. I'd appreciate any help."

"My job is pretty dynamic, Ty. I don't always know where I'm going to be from day to day. I'd love to catch up with you when you're in Tucson but I can't promise it, though. Depends on my schedule."

"No problem, Cliff. I appreciate your time. If there's anything I can ever do for you, just let me know."

"I'll do that, brother, and I'll add one more thing."

"What's that?"

"Don't invest yourself so heavily that you can't bounce back. You don't have much information to go on. You don't know how this is going to end. Don't put yourself in an emotional place where you can't handle the outcome."

"Got it," Ty said, despite wondering if it was too late for that.

He ended the call and sent Cliff the address associated with the RV tag, then scrolled through his phone and found the two digital pictures which he also forwarded. One was the shot of Gretchen Wells grinning broadly as she exited the Petro Panda, the other of the woman with the gray puppy leaning against the RV, the tag number prominently visible at her side.

He checked his GPS. Two hours until he hit Tucson.

26

W hen he reached Tucson, Ty filled his fuel tank and grabbed some food at a Whataburger. It was afternoon and there was a lot of traffic, certainly more than his sleepy small town had on the worst of days. Besides the stress of the traffic, he was absorbed in the differences between this southwestern town and pretty much everywhere else he'd ever been in his life.

He let his GPS guide him to the address Jessica provided. The neighborhood was old with low adobe houses. Ty couldn't quite figure out the nature of the residents, other than it appeared to be a neighborhood in transition. Where were these people on the income scale? There were houses in disrepair with trashy yards and broken down vehicles. Others were brightly colored with ornate ironwork and period-correct architectural details. Some had expensive cars parked outside and professional landscaping.

The address led him to a home somewhere in between the two extremes. It was a nice house on a decent-sized lot for the area. The house was in good repair, with a tall iron fence to the front and adobe walls surrounding the remainder of the property. While it was not as well-appointed as some of its neighbors, neither was it a crumbling wreck like others. The yard was landscaped with cacti, small stones, and areas of gravel. The roof was terra cotta tile.

It took him several passes to find a decent spot from which to observe the house. There was no place to hide along the street. There were few trees and everywhere he stopped looked like he was parked on someone's property. He finally found a place alongside a pink cinderblock wall that didn't feel too exposed.

There were no cars in the driveway, which made him wonder if he could have beaten the RV home. He'd certainly been driving long hours and pushing himself. Anyone sticking to a more conventional driving schedule wouldn't have covered as many miles. It occurred to him that they could even be days behind him. Perhaps they weren't even headed home at all. He'd never considered that possibility. If that was the case, he was screwed.

Ty studied the satellite map of the neighborhood on his phone. There was a dirt alley that ran along the back of the houses facing this side of the street. He circled the block in his truck, thinking he might be able to cut through the alley and check out the back of the house. No such luck. The alley was overgrown, with tree branches blocking anything but foot traffic. Ty could imagine the residents doing that intentionally to keep cars out.

Since driving through it wasn't a possibility, he parked in the same spot, dug around, and found a legal pad in his laptop case. He got out of the truck and started walking. No one could walk around a neighborhood like this and not be noticed, but he'd learned that a notepad or clipboard gave you an official air. He stopped occasionally to examine the surface of the asphalt street and to check the condition of the sidewalks. He scribbled notes. If anyone asked, he was a contractor preparing a bid for repaving some local streets.

He took a left turn down the side street, and halfway down, turned left again into the alley. The alley looked into the backyards of most of the homes on the block, depending on whether they had fencing or a solid wall. When he got to the home he was interested in, his view onto the property was blocked by a solid wall. There was a wooden door in the wall with a window opening at eye level. The window opening was trimmed with simple ironwork.

Ty glanced around, saw that no one could see him, and peered through the opening. In the yard were stacks of lumber and cinder blocks. A back porch stood incomplete. There was none of the landscaping that was visible in the front yard. Stakes marked an area that might be a planned pool or perhaps a garage. There were no cars and no signs of life.

Turning to walk away, he nearly ran into a short Hispanic woman with braided gray hair. She was only feet away and clearly trying to figure out what he was doing.

"I'm sorry," he said, pointing to his notepad. "I'm a contractor. Getting some measurements."

She appeared skeptical but said nothing as he passed by and continued down the alley. He stopped once more, pretending to make a note, then hurried to his truck.

27

B ill Barger was exhausted by the time he reached Tucson. Each road trip was more taxing than the last. Every time he arrived home he swore he was done and he wasn't going back out on the road again. He wasn't making long trips with that spooky-ass woman and her crazy voodoo gods, or whatever the hell they were. Then he'd get that envelope of cash and it would ease his pain just enough to forget how bad it had been.

It was all about the money for Bill. He'd done well in the late 90s. Loans had been easy to get and easy to pay off. As a contractor with a proven track record for flipping houses, he had an open line of credit. He could buy any house he wanted with the assurance that the bank would cover the loan. The vice-president of the bank had promised it himself. Filling out the paperwork was simply a technicality.

He'd located the offices for his residential construction company in Barrio Santa Rosa because there were existing buildings with large lots that weren't very expensive. Within a few years of locating there, Bill could see that the neighborhood was turning. The kind of people he referred to as *yuppies* were moving into the neighborhood. They wanted houses in quaint historical neighborhoods like Bill's and he wanted to provide them. He began investing all his profits into bank foreclosures and neglected properties in the Barrio Santa Rosa community. It went so well that it was soon the entirety of his business.

He made good money and he lived well. He had an RV, a nice boat, and a vacation home south of the border. Then the recession, specifically the building crunch of 2008 or so, hit him like a brick to the face. Even in this fairly robust market he was caught with eleven properties he couldn't sell and eleven loans that had to be paid. While in the past his properties were under contract before he was even finished with the work, now his properties lingered on the market and the loan payments nibbled away at his savings.

Then, the icing on the cake, his wife became ill. Despite insurance, her illness further eroded their nest egg. In a little over seven months he spent nearly a half million dollars and still lost his wife. The best property in his portfolio was his beautiful home in the El Encanto neighborhood of Tucson. With his children out on their own and his wife deceased, it was just him in the house. Homes in that neighborhood were recession-proof. He put the home on the market at $599,000. In less than a month, he'd sold it for a little more than a half million dollars.

He moved his belongings to his construction company's headquarters and lived in the RV, which he parked on the back lot. Since that time, twelve years of hard work had seen his neighborhood start to come back around. Barger dug his way out of the hole and was now successful again. He had a nice home around the block from his offices and retirement was just around the corner. Soon he would be able to disappear to his house in Mexico and not come back.

The lucrative sideline he'd entered with Tia had come about by accident. When he'd finally moved out of the RV and into his home, one of his employees approached him about borrowing the RV for a few days.

"Why?" Barger asked. "Going camping?"

"No, my aunt wants me to drive her somewhere. She wants to take an RV because it's more comfortable." Barger would later find out that the woman wasn't actually his aunt, she was just known as Tia in the neighborhood. She was everyone's aunt.

"That RV was expensive," Barger said. "I can't let you have it for free. I might rent it, though."

"She has money. She'll pay."

"Tell your aunt to call me."

Barger hadn't expected her to call but she did. She paid up front in cash and assured him that they would cover any damages. Soon they were renting it twice a month. Barger didn't know what they were doing and he didn't ask. The arrangement provided a nice little stream of income, a couple of thousand dollars a month, until Bill's employee didn't show up for work one day and never came back.

A couple of weeks later, Tia was in his office with a stack of cash, asking *him* to drive the RV for her, and she was prepared to pay. After thinking on it overnight, Barger took her up on her offer, and soon learned the nature of their business. Tia went around the country collecting vulnerable young women, then sold them into prostitution.

Barger coped with the morality of what they did by reminding himself he was just the driver. This was not a job he would have taken when he was younger and more capable of hard work. However, in middle age, his body was paying the price for his chosen trade. He was wracked with arthritis, his knees and hips needed replacing, and his discs were deteriorating. As sore as long hours of driving made him, it was easier than hanging drywall and laying tile.

For the most part, Barger had no guilt about this trip. He was over it. His mind was already on getting home. He intended to plant himself in his Jacuzzi tub with a nice cold beer. After a couple of more beers and a hefty dose of ibuprofen, he would call it a night. He'd wake up tomorrow with a clear conscience and go back to work on his latest house.

When he reached his neighborhood, he eased the vehicle into the lot and parked it below the security light. He pocketed his revolver and grabbed the duffel bag with his clothing, locked the RV behind him, and climbed into his pickup for the short drive around the block. Had he not been so tired, he might have walked it.

He was supposed to clean out the RV as soon as he got here. Those were Tia's orders. He didn't like orders, though. He'd do it when he was damn well ready to do it. That would be tomorrow morning at the soonest. He was too tired. Besides, she had a lot of nerve asking him to clean the vehicle when she'd sat on her ass the entire way home. Lazy and crazy, that's what she was.

He circled the block and turned into his driveway. He hadn't installed the automatic opener yet so he was forced to get out and open the iron gate by hand. He got back in the truck and parked, closing the gate back behind him. His little neighborhood was quiet out on the street, with most people settled in for the evening.

In the distance, he could hear the ever-present hum of city traffic. A siren wailed somewhere. None of these sounds would penetrate the thick adobe walls of his home. He failed to notice the pickup across the street with Virginia tags. Had he seen that from his truck, he might have continued driving on past without even going home. He'd have called Tia and told her to check into it. He didn't see it, though, and went inside, glad to be home.

28

W hen the headlights came toward Ty, he dropped his sun visor and slumped in the seat. With his dark clothing, he was hoping he didn't stand out in the interior of the truck. He didn't want to look like a guy sitting in a truck waiting on someone, even though that's exactly what he was. His heartbeat sped up as the pickup headed in his direction, then swung into the entrance of the house he was watching.

A man got out of the truck, opened the gate, and drove on through. Once inside, the truck door swung open again and the man slid out. He threw a duffel bag over his shoulder and closed the gate. He paused there a moment, looking out onto the street. He didn't appear to have noticed Ty in particular. It was like he was just checking out his neighborhood, taking the temperature of his surroundings. When he was satisfied, he turned away and limped inside.

None of the video footage from the Petro Panda or any of the social media pictures showed the driver of the RV. Ty couldn't be certain if this was him or not. If it was, where was the RV? More importantly, where was Gretchen?

Ty didn't know what to do. He had a man he didn't recognize and no RV. The woman he wanted to speak with was nowhere in sight. Was she already inside the house or was she with the RV somewhere? He noticed the truck had a logo on the side of the driver's door. It was faint, no doubt faded by the harsh desert sun. He rooted around in the back seat to find his binoculars and studied the logo. He was initially pleased to see the name on the logo read Barger Properties. The name was right, but how did that help him? He still didn't have any answers.

He put the binoculars on the passenger seat and picked up his phone from the center console. He was going to do a quick search on Barger Properties and see what he came up with. No sooner had he typed in his search query than he noticed more headlights coming toward him. He clicked off his phone, not wanting to glow of his screen to give away his presence in the parked vehicle. As the vehicle passed, he looked out his window and saw the outline of emergency lights on the roof.

Shit. It was a cop.

Even worse, he was looking directly at Ty.

They made eye contact and Ty didn't know what to do. Should he give a casual wave, like he was just hanging out waiting on someone? Was this the kind of neighborhood where people sat in cars late at night or was Ty's presence something that would be of concern to the officer? If he was suspicious, he might circle around the block and come back to check Ty's identification.

He couldn't allow that. If the police discovered he had an assault warrant in Virginia they might lock him up. He didn't know exactly how that worked. He didn't know if he'd be extradited but it was better to not take the chance. He dropped the phone back in the console, started his truck, and headed down the street.

Ty didn't know where he was going at this point. He was simply focused on putting distance between him and the cop. At the end of Barger's block he hung a left, keeping to the speed limit. His mind was already steps ahead, assuming the safest thing to do at this point was to get a hotel room for the night. He could settle down and regroup. Then his headlights reflected off the shiny sidewall of an RV parked in a lot to his left.

He hit the brakes and slowed to a stop in the road. There were no lights along the street and Ty couldn't make out the license tag in the darkness. He could, however, make out the peeling sign fastened to the front of the cinderblock building and illuminated by the amber glow of the sodium security light fastened to the front of the building.

Barger Properties.

As he considered turning into the parking lot, another set of headlights flashed in his rearview mirror. He glanced up and saw that a car several blocks back had turned in his direction. While he didn't know for certain it was the cop, he couldn't take a chance. If it was, he'd just given the officer probable cause to pull him over. There he was, idling in the middle of the public street, directly in front of a closed business. If Ty was a cop, things like that would certainly get his attention.

He held his breath and accelerated to the speed limit. He checked his truck's navigation system, searching for the closest busy thoroughfare and heading in that direction. The vehicle behind him soon closed the distance and was on his bumper, lights on bright. Ty's Virginia tag boldly announced that he didn't belong here.

They passed below a streetlight and Ty chanced a quick look at his rearview mirror. The vehicle behind him was indeed a white Impala but there were no emergency flashers on the roof of this one. He let out a sigh of relief, then signaled and turned into a parking place. The other driver punched the gas and shot around him. When the vehicle was past, Ty raised his shirttail and wiped the sweat from his forehead.

He sat in the unfamiliar neighborhood for nearly thirty minutes trying to decide what to do. He constantly monitored his mirrors, watching for cops. At no point did he see the police car that had passed him earlier. He needed to relax. He wasn't even certain that the warrant in Virginia had materialized. Other than Lieutenant Whitt, no one had notified him of anything. Without a warrant hanging over his head, he could be a lost traveler who'd wandered into this neighborhood by mistake.

The smart thing to do would be to find a hotel room and call Cliff Mathis in the morning. He could tell him he'd located the RV and see if Cliff could help him figure out the next step. That would have been the smart thing.

Instead, Ty made a U-turn and headed back in the direction of Barger Properties. He parked along the street a short distance from the business and killed his engine. When he was certain there were no cars coming from either direction he slipped out of the truck. As casually as one could do such things, he approached the closed business. He pulled a short Streamlight flashlight from his shirt pocket, thumbed the button on the back, and flashed a beam of light onto the tag. It was the same RV.

He circled the vehicle. The curtains weren't drawn around the windshield, something people often did when they were sleeping inside. He listened for any sounds–the television, talking, or snoring. He climbed the single step leading to the side door and peered through the window. Seeing nothing of interest, he got brave and flashed his light around the inside. He didn't see anyone.

On the inside it pretty much looked like any other RV. There was no personalization or decorating of any kind. There was nothing to make him think the woman from the photo might be inside. The front of the RV, facing the business, was secluded from the street. Ty climbed up onto the bumper and flattened his face against the windshield. He clicked his flashlight on, peered through a gap in the curtains, and gave the interior a more thorough examination. Aside from a little trash, there was nothing that caught his attention. Then something near the bedroom door reflected his light back at him.

Ty turned the light back in that direction and squinted, trying to make out what he was looking at. It was too far away and too small. He moved back to the side and climbed onto the single step leading to the entrance door. He flattened his face against the door glass and angled the beam of his light toward the back. He could clearly see what the object was now. It was a padlock hanging from a hasp. The disturbing thing was that the placement of the padlock meant it was intended for locking someone in the back bedroom.

Could Gretchen be locked in there?

Throwing caution to the wind, he searched the area around him and found a fist-sized rock in the abandoned landscaping. Returning to the door, he hesitated only a second before throwing the rock through the glass. The safety glass shattered but did not fall from the frame. Ty scanned the area and found a foot-long section of rebar with an orange ribbon tied around one end. He used the steel rod to punch the remaining glass from the opening.

When he had a hole he could safely get his arm through, he reached inside and unlatched the door. He backed up and it swung open, shards of glass raining out at his feet. Only then did it occur to him that he was probably making way too much noise. It was too late to worry about it now. He bounded up the steps and headed toward the back room.

"Gretchen!" he whispered. "Are you in there?"

He paused and listened. There was no answer. He closed the distance to the door and placed his ear against it. He pulled the padlock and found it locked securely.

"Gretchen!" he hissed louder.

With no reply, he shined the light around the room while he considered what to do. He spotted a garbage bag sitting in one of the dinette seats and picked it up. He opened it and flashed the light inside, spotting a ball of blue cloth in the bottom. He pulled it out and the sight of it was like a punch to the gut. It was a shirt he recalled from a memorized photo. Blue with a yellow frog.

Gretchen's shirt.

It was damp and he soon discovered a pair of damp shorts in the bag with it, everything covered with strands of hair, and he wondered if it was Gretchen's. He couldn't tell for sure, though the shirt told the story. There could be no doubt Gretchen had been in here. He closed the bag and barreled toward the locked door, raised a foot, and stomped. Wood splintered and the doorframe gave a loud crack, the flimsy door falling into the back bedroom.

He stepped onto the flattened door and it gave way beneath his feet. It was obvious in a split second that there was no one in the tiny room. Shining his light around, he spotted a narrow doorway to his left. A closet? Bathroom?

He tried pulling on the door but there was no room for it to swing open with the broken door taking up all the floor space. He went back into the main living area and grabbed the end of the broken door. He started tugging it backward, trying to get it clear of the other door.

Ty bumped into something. Before he could turn to see what he'd run into, he heard the arc of a stun gun. He was familiar with that sound but there was no time to react. His muscles went rigid and he toppled to the floor. As he dropped, he was certain he'd been busted. He'd drawn too much attention by parking so obviously on the street. He'd moved around the neighborhood the same way a criminal would when he was staking out a business.

A powerful flashlight beam hit him in the face. Ty squinted against it, waiting for a Tucson police officer to slap the cuffs on him. The light turned away for a moment and Ty saw that it was not a police officer but William Barger, the flashlight now held like a club. Ty crushed his eyes shut as the heavy Maglite came crashing down on his skull.

29

B arger's loud ranting roused Ty to consciousness. He had no idea how long he'd been out but his head was splitting. Though he suspected he had a concussion, that only mattered if he was going to survive, which remained to be determined. One eye was matted shut with dried blood. He cracked the other and could see light coming from somewhere around the front of the RV. There was a bulky shape, presumably Barger, crammed into the dining area with his back to Ty. He was shouting into his phone.

"I told you it's a fucking Virginia driver's license! That can't be a coincidence."

In the silence after Barger spoke, in the insular bubble of the RV, Ty could hear a voice through the speaker of Barger's phone. He couldn't make out the words but the tone was calmer than Barger's.

"I don't know how he found me," Barger snapped. "Maybe he's been following us for days."

Ty held his breath and strained to hear. He could make out a voice now, hoarse and female.

"That makes no sense," replied the voice. *"Why would someone follow*

*us from Virginia? If they knew anything, they'd have called the cops. You
need to calm down."*

"Then why the hell is he in my RV!" Barger demanded. "Somebody needs to figure this shit out! This isn't my job. I did my part."

"You need to calm down..." the voice began before becoming so
quiet that Ty couldn't hear it any longer.

"He trashed the place," Barger said. "He busted out one of the
windows and kicked down the bedroom door. Damages are supposed
to come out of your end, not mine. That's always been the deal."

Taking advantage of his distraction, Ty explored his circumstance.
He didn't want to give away the fact he was conscious so he made
small adjustments to his body to see what had been done to him. He
shifted his fingers, groped around, and determined that thick zip ties
bound his wrists. They weren't proper flex-cuffs, though, and not
handcuffs. His feet were not bound. He was lying on his right side
and the void beneath his hip told him that his Glock had been taken.
He wasn't certain about the knives he carried but he couldn't imagine
someone taking the Glock and leaving them. With his hands behind
his back he couldn't check for them.

"Yeah, I know where that is," Barger said. "Why don't they come
here and pick him up? I've been driving all damn day and the last
thing I want to do is run all the way out there."

There was a low response, more murmuring that Ty couldn't
make out.

Barger let out a long sigh. "Yes, I *do* want you to deal with this," he
conceded. "I'll be there in about thirty minutes."

Ty heard the clatter of a phone being tossed onto the table.

"Fuck!" Barger bellowed, slamming his fist down.

Ty waited for that rage to be directed at him in the form of a kick
or punch but it didn't happen. Barger continued to mumble curses.
He made threats he'd not had the stones to make when he was actually on the phone with whoever he was talking to. When he had it out
of his system, he squeezed out of the tight booth and stood. Ty sensed
the man staring at him. He continued to breathe slowly, not moving,
trying to give the impression he was out for the count.

Apparently coming to the conclusion that Ty needed to be secured further, Barger drew another zip tie from a drawer. Ty forced his body to relax as Barger looped the zip tie through his restraints, then through a cabinet door handle, yanking the zip tie tight with a ratcheting sound. Ty considered whether he should take this opportunity to launch an attack. Barger put himself in an extremely vulnerable position when he was crouched over Ty. Had his hands been bound in front of him, Ty might have been able to pull it off. With his hands behind his back, however, it was a losing proposition no matter how tough someone claimed to be. He might threaten he could kick someone's ass with his hands tied behind his back, but could he really? He'd be reduced to footwork. No grappling, no punching, and no blocking.

Satisfied that Ty was wasn't going anywhere, Barger went to the cab area. He cursed and grumbled a few more times before starting the RV. He let the engine run for a little bit before putting it in reverse and backing out of the Barger Properties parking lot.

While Barger drove the large vehicle out of the neighborhood, Ty realized he had no idea what lay ahead of him. Strangely, there was no fear. Instead, he experienced the exhilaration of redemption. He'd been right. Of course, that did him no good if he ended up dead. No one would know where Gretchen was and his sister would probably assume he'd committed suicide somewhere in the desert. Being right wasn't enough. He had to turn this around. He had to survive.

From his time in the military, Ty was SERE obsessed. SERE stood for Survival, Evasion, Resistance, and Escape. It was the art of trying to avoid capture or escaping if you were unfortunate enough to be captured. That obsession with SERE training did not leave him in civilian life. While the odds of someone abducting him at this point in his life were pretty slim, they were obviously not zero because there he was, bound and abducted.

As part of his paranoid fixation, Ty carried a SERE kit integrated into his everyday clothing. The Levi's jeans he wore had a distinctive leather patch on the back with the Levi Strauss logo. Ty had unstitched that logo when he first bought the jeans and replaced the patch using Velcro instead of stitching. He could remove it if he needed access to the area underneath, where he stored a ceramic razor blade, a handcuff key, and a short section of jigsaw blade. He had a section of abrasive Kevlar cord threaded through the hem of his jeans along with a second non-metallic handcuff key.

With Barger distracted by driving and the sound of the engine covering his actions, Ty slipped a thumb under the patch and raised one end of it. He probed beneath it and discovered the saw blade, careful not to lose the remaining items. He pinched the thin blade between his thumb and finger, then began sawing through the zip ties. The blade's teeth were coarse and it required a lot of force to cut the thick plastic. His fingers cramped and he was terrified of dropping the blade. He held onto it, though, and soon the plastic ties sprang free.

He laid there considering his next course of action. Should he subdue Barger and then call the cops? After all, he'd found evidence of Gretchen's presence in the RV now. Surely the cops would listen to him. He was no closer to the woman, though. Had that been her on the phone? If he took out Barger and called the cops, would they find the woman? Would there be some thread that led them to Gretchen? He had no way of knowing.

On the other hand, they were headed toward a meetup with someone. That woman might be there. Gretchen might even be there. Certainly someone with deeper involvement than Barger would be there. He said over the phone that he'd done his part. Was he simply the driver? What did it make this other person?

Ty decided he needed to wait this out. As hard as it was to sit there, he needed to see who was at the end of the line. He wrapped the zip ties back around his wrists, making it appear as if his hands were bound. When the time came, if the right opportunity presented itself, he could free them and attack.

30

T y lost track of time, but at some point they turned onto a dirt road. The sound of the terrain beneath their tires changed from the hypnotic hum of asphalt, and gravel pinged off the undercarriage. Ty heard Barger grumbling about chipped paint and tire alignment. After ten minutes on the rough road, the RV eased to a stop. Barger sat idling for a moment before turning the vehicle to face the way they'd come in. Once that was done, he killed the engine and they sat there in the dark.

"You awake back there?" Barger asked, breaking the silence.

Ty didn't respond, feeling that nothing good would come from responding. It would invite Barger to begin interrogating him.

"Hope I didn't kill you," Barger mumbled.

They sat there in the dark for a long time. Barger complained, wondering if he'd been stood up. At one point, when he stepped outside to take a leak, Ty resisted the urge to take action and subdue him then. Whoever was coming would be expecting Barger. If he failed to greet them, they might leave without even getting out of their vehicle. That wouldn't help Ty at all. When Barger came back inside, he sat in a leather recliner and stretched out. Ty wondered if he was going to sleep.

The first indication they had company came in the form of a low rumble from a powerful engine. As it got closer, Ty recognized it as the distinctive sound of a modified diesel pickup, probably a Dodge. He could hear the whine of a powerful turbo and the growl of the oversized exhaust. As it got closer, Barger got up from the recliner and moved to the window, nervously watching the vehicle approach through a gap in the curtains.

The vehicle did not pull alongside them but stopped a short distance away. The driver killed the engine but left the headlights on, spotlighting the RV. With the engine off, Ty could hear the thump of music. It got louder for a moment when the truck doors swung open, then someone turned it off. Ty heard two doors shut. At least two men.

Barger opened the side door and clambered out of the RV. He called a greeting to the men. The tone of his voice was different. He was trying to sound loud and authoritative but Ty could hear the undercurrent of fear. These people scared him.

The men addressed him in Spanish.

"He's inside," Barger responded. "Got him tied up on the floor. The sooner you get him, the sooner I can get the hell out of here, so let's *vamanos.*"

The response came in the form of three rapid gunshots. Ty sat bolt upright. Was this what the men had in mind for him? If so, it was time for a new strategy.

He yanked himself loose from his severed zip ties and rolled smoothly to his feet. He stepped to the nearest window, trying not to make any noise. Outside, he saw a man nudging Barger's body with his toe to confirm he was out of the fight. The interior of the RV was illuminated by the pickup's headlights shining through the open door and gaps in the curtains. Ty frantically looked around for his missing Glock but didn't see it. Barger probably had it on him, not that it did him any good. Ty checked the window again and spotted one of the men headed toward the RV. He had seconds before the guy was inside with him.

He stepped toward the side door and pulled it shut, locking it. It wasn't going to buy him much time since he'd broken the window out at Barger's shop. One of the men spotted the swinging door and called out. They knew something was up now. Ty had lost any element of surprise.

Two gunshots punched through the door, one through the bottom half and a second through the empty window opening. There was no way he was escaping out that door. Ty knew that most RVs this size had escape hatches in the roof in case they turned over in an accident. He scanned the ceiling and spotted the escape hatch in the kitchen area. He checked his shirt pocket and found the small flashlight he carried there. He played it over the hatch and found the crank that opened it.

The men cut loose with a barrage of random gunfire. Rounds punched through the side wall of the RV. With each new hole, a tiny beam of headlights carved through the interior like a laser beam. Dust and tufts of insulation floated in the shafts of light. Ty scrambled onto the countertop and furiously cranked open the hatch. He got it partially open but couldn't find the release to swing the hatch door completely out of the way.

A round shattered a cabinet door beside him and splinters sprayed the leg of his jeans. Two rounds punched through the refrigerator. Ty heard a carbonated drink give up the ghost and start spewing as it rolled around.

In a panic, he wrenched the entire hatch assembly loose, shoving it through onto the roof. He hooked a hand over the lip and started pulling himself out. The RV door swung open, banging against the exterior wall. Someone was shouting in Spanish. Ty placed his feet on the cabinets, desperate for traction, and forced his body through the opening.

Then he was out in the cool night air. He got to his knees and laid the hatch lid back in place. Ty figured he had less than thirty seconds before the gunmen searched the RV and realized he wasn't inside. If they trapped him on the roof, it would be like shooting fish in a barrel. He couldn't let that happen.

He sprang to his feet and peered over the edge. In the harsh glare of headlights, he could make out one gunman outside, perhaps eight feet from the RV. His attention was focused on the door opening, a pistol held ready in two hands. Ty launched himself into the air, coming down across the man like a wrestler jumping from the top rope. He must have had a finger hooked around the trigger because the impact caused him to send a round into the RV.

Ty heard yelling in response, cursing in Spanish directed toward the *fucking pendejo* who'd fired the shot. The man beneath Ty was too stunned to cry out, the wind knocked from him by the impact. Ty didn't waste the opportunity, raining powerful elbows onto the man's head and face, one after another. The man quit moving and Ty spotted his chrome 1911 laying in the dirt beside him. He swept it up, got to his feet, and paced backwards, aiming at the door. He didn't know how many rounds remained in the magazine and had no time to check. He wanted to put some distance between himself and the remaining gunmen.

There was another yell from inside, then loud steps. The man stomped out the door, ready to curse his partner for the errant round. Blinded by the headlights, he didn't notice the body on the ground until it was too late.

Ty halted his retreat, aiming at the gunman spotlighted against the RV. "Drop your fucking gun! Do it now!"

He didn't listen. His face crunched in a tight ball of hate, he swung his lowered gun toward Ty, but he was not fast enough. Ty sent a .45 slug into the man's body then his slide locked open.

Empty.

The gunman twisted and took a single, lurching step. He tried to raise his gun but his arm wasn't cooperating.

Ty launched himself toward Barger's body, hoping that was where he'd find his Glock. He yanked the man's jacket up to his chest and spotted the familiar grip protruding from his waistband. He yanked the gun free and leveled it on his attacker.

Ty hesitated, not wanting to kill the man if he didn't have to. He could have information they needed. He could know where Gretchen was. The gunman shifted his pistol to his offhand and swung it upward. The barrel wavered as he searched for Ty in the darkness.

"Drop it!" Ty barked.

The gunman zeroed in on Ty's voice and left him no options. Ty fired and the round punched the man in the sternum, staggering him. He arched backward, the gun dropping from his hand. Ty rushed toward him and kicked the gun away. The man was conscious, his eyes open, but the fight gone.

Ty shoved him back against the RV and searched him for weapons. He found a backup .380, some spare mags, and a fixed blade knife, which he tossed off into the darkness. Ty lowered the man to the ground, then climbed into the RV, and found the drawer where Barger kept the zip ties. He grabbed the entire pack and hurried outside.

He secured the man he'd knocked unconscious, binding his hands and ankles tightly. The man with two bullets in him had rolled onto his belly and was trying to crawl away on his elbows. There was no surrender in that one.

Ty hauled him backwards, zip tying his ankles together and securing his hands. He rolled him onto his back and examined his wounds. The round from the .45 had ripped out a chunk of the man's left pectoral. It was an ugly wound but probably not fatal if he could control the bleeding. The second wound, from Ty's Glock, had created a sucking chest wound. That was serious.

Ty raced back inside and started pawing through cabinets. He found a stack of dishtowels in a drawer and tucked them under his arm. He looked for something to seal the chest wound with, praying for some saran wrap or something, but turned up empty. Then he recalled something he'd seen in the drawer with the zip ties. He grabbed it and returned to the injured man.

He tore open the gunman's shirt, exposing the wounds, and packed the bicep wound with two towels, using duct tape to secure it. He used another to wipe down the man's chest, removing all the blood and fluid from the area around the lung shot.

He held the glue trap in the beam of the headlights and opened it.

It was a square of paper approximately five inches by seven inches and coated with a powerful adhesive. It was used to catch mice, rats, and spiders. When they walked across it, they became stuck, and couldn't free themselves. Ty had read about them being used as chest seals in extreme conditions. It wasn't optimal but it was what he had. He placed it over the man's wound and pressed down hard, gluing it to his flesh. The man gave a cough, a spray of blood flecking his lips and cheeks. He was breathing for now.

Ty was shaking, the aftereffects of the adrenaline dump. Sweat soaked his clothing and his heart raced. He took a deep breath and tried to calm himself. He needed to get his head together. What the hell was he supposed to do now? The responsible voice inside warned that he'd pursued this thread as far as he could chase it alone. He was in deep now and he was going to need help.

He got to his feet and searched the RV, finding his phone in the driver's cup holder. He sat down at the kitchen dinette. A stray bullet had shredded one of the cushions and foam rubber chunks were everywhere. Ty brushed them to the side with his forearm and unlocked his phone, pleased to see that he had signal. He scrolled through his recent calls and punched the last number he expected to be calling.

Only as it was ringing did he notice the hour. Back in Virginia it would be the middle of the night. He hoped she answered, and on the third ring she did so.

"Lieutenant Whitt." It was a sleepy voice trying to sound alert and official but failing.

"Lieutenant Whitt, this is Tyler Stone and I need your help. I'm in trouble."

There was a sleepy sigh on the other end. *"Mr. Stone, if this is about those assault allegations, I suggest you get an attorney. There's nothing I can do for you."*

"Please listen carefully. I'm outside of Tucson, Arizona. I have no idea exactly where I am but I have two men in custody and another dead. I found that RV that I told you about."

"*I told you that we weren't interested in that fucking RV! What have you gone and done?*"

He did not let her outburst deter him. "And I found a garbage bag with Gretchen Wells' clothing inside it."

Her silence told him that she was suddenly a lot more interested in that fucking RV.

31

Ty was aware that his current situation was outside of Lieutenant Whitt's jurisdiction. He'd considered calling 9-1-1 himself but was concerned about how the scene would be handled. If he told the dispatcher, then the officers on the scene, about a kidnapping in Virginia would they even believe him? They would probably think this was a drug deal gone bad. He'd end up in jail and they'd lose even more precious time. Evidence would be mishandled.

He knew he was going to be treated like a suspect either way, but he didn't want evidence of Gretchen's abduction to be lost. He determined that the only way he could assure they'd take him seriously was to have Lieutenant Whitt make the call. He could only hope she'd been able to get through to a detective on duty so they would take charge of the scene. Presumably the FBI would also show up, if the crap he saw on crime shows was at all accurate.

In this flat terrain, he saw the flashing lights of emergency vehicles approaching from a long way off. He had no clue where he was in relation to the city but the GPS app on the phone had given him coordinates for his location, which he'd provided to Lieutenant

Whitt. Sirens cut through the night, echoing off the hard surfaces of the cool, rocky desert. Although the truck headlights were on, Ty waved his flashlight in their direction like he was directing aircraft to the runway. When they were closing in on him, he turned his back to them. He spread his feet and laced his fingers together behind his head. He would wait on them in that manner until they instructed him to do otherwise.

There were at least a dozen vehicles strung out in a loose caravan. They skidded to a stop in a cloud of red dust. Motes of it floated in the sharp beams of powerful headlights. Men sprang from their cars, leveling guns over the top of the doors. They barked orders at Ty, having him back up toward them before dropping to his knees and crossing his ankles. They'd all been instructed that he was likely the good guy in this scenario, but they needed to confirm that for themselves. They weren't taking any chances.

In a matter of minutes he was cuffed and stuffed, sitting in the back of a police car while officers and men in lettered windbreakers combed the scene. An ambulance rolled up and EMTs began treating the two gunmen. The fact that none were attending to Barger confirmed Ty's initial assessment that the man was dead from multiple gunshot wounds. While he patiently watched the actions of the officers, two men approached the vehicle and opened the rear door. They studied him in the beam of a flashlight before speaking.

"I'm Agent Esposito and this is Agent Cornell from the Tucson field office. I've been on the phone with a Lieutenant Whitt from the Virginia State Police. She's been trying to explain to me what the hell is going on here, but I want to hear it from you."

"My name is Tyler Stone. I was working as a security guard at the Petro Panda, a truck stop in Virginia, when a girl named Gretchen Wells was abducted." Ty explained a summarized version of the chain of events that led him to Arizona. With the agent's assistance, he unlocked his phone and showed them the pictures that convinced him the state police investigators were headed in the wrong direction.

"So you're alleging that the clothing in that garbage bag is the same clothing visible in this image taken by the security camera?" Agent Esposito asked.

Ty nodded. "The bag is also full of hair. I would bet anything it's Gretchen's hair."

The two agents exchanged a look.

"Sometimes kidnappers alter the appearance to make the kid harder to spot," Agent Cornell offered.

"The problem was that the child's parents were in the middle of a divorce," Ty said. "The dad is missing right now, so the investigators in Virginia assumed he was responsible. They weren't interested in my theories."

"And you assumed it was your duty as a security guard to look into this?" Cornell asked, a sarcastic eyebrow raised.

Ty stared hard at the man. "No, asshole. I lost my job because management didn't approve of me locking down the station when we couldn't find the little girl. I decided to look into it myself because no one was listening to me."

"How did you trace the tag?" Agent Esposito asked. "How did you find these people?"

Ty needed to keep Jessica out of this as he'd promised. "My background was in special operations in the military. I called in a favor from an old Army buddy who has access to that information."

"The name of this friend?" Agent Cornell asked.

Ty shrugged. "I don't feel comfortable sharing that at this time."

Cornell frowned at him.

"Was this part of your plan?" Agent Esposito asked. "A gunfight? Vigilante justice?"

"I think you know better than that. I'm trying to find the girl. A friend gave me the number for a guy named Cliff Mathis who works with human trafficking cases. I've been in contact with him. I was hoping he might give me some idea of how to proceed after I found the RV. Things went south before I got a chance to follow up on that."

The two agents exchanged another glance. "We know Mr. Mathis," Agent Cornell said.

"I was going to call him in the morning. I assumed he would advise me to bring law enforcement in at that point."

Agent Cornell nodded at the RV. "Yeah, it might have been advisable to bring us in before it reached *this* point."

Ty conceded that. "I didn't feel like I had enough evidence, especially since the Virginia investigators didn't believe my theory. I figured no one would listen. The FBI wouldn't even talk to me. Then when I talked with Cliff Mathis, he said this didn't sound right. I was beginning to doubt myself."

"Well, if what you said about the child's clothing pans out then I would say you have a strong case. People will listen to you now. Your friend Lieutenant Whitt is flying out here in the morning to bring us up to speed on the Virginia end of the investigation. She's also collecting a hair sample from the child's home and delivering that to us for comparison with what's in the garbage bag."

"Am I under arrest?" Ty asked. His tone was neither scared nor accusatory, only curious.

Agent Esposito shook his head. "You're not under arrest. You're not a suspect but we'd prefer you not leave yet. Do you have a hotel room?"

"I haven't found one yet," Ty replied. "I got sidetracked."

"Obviously. Well, when we're done here, we'll get you settled into a hotel room," Agent Esposito replied. "You'll need to stick around for a couple of days in case we have questions."

"Trust me, I don't plan on going anywhere until Gretchen Wells is found."

"You do realize you're out of this now, right?" Agent Cornell said. "You proved your point. You have law enforcement's attention and we're looking in the right direction. This is where you back up and let us do our job."

"I'm fine with that. That's all I ever wanted."

Agent Esposito leaned forward and removed Ty's handcuffs. "You stay over here. Stay out of the way until we're done."

"No problem," Ty said. "I do need to point out that the Glock 19 over there is mine. I have a concealed carry permit from Virginia and had it on me when Barger bashed me in the head."

"It's evidence now," Agent Cornell said. "You'll get it back when the investigation is completed. Maybe."

"We'll get somebody to look at your head," Agent Esposito said. "You might need some stitches."

32

W hen the sicarios didn't answer Tia's calls, she became concerned. These were loyal men, associates of her son, and they'd worked for her before. They didn't quit until the mission was complete unless something went very wrong. When she finally gave up trying to reach them, she went to the carport, removing the battery from the phone as she walked. She placed the burner phone on the concrete and pounded it with a rusty claw hammer until nothing remained but shards of plastic. She swept the pieces into a dustpan then dumped them into the garbage.

Everything in life meant something. Everything was a sign. She wondered if this most recent turn of events was a sign. Perhaps she was entering a downward cycle in her life. First, the girl they were supposed to pick up in Richmond, Virginia, had not shown up. Then, after her prayers, Holy Death provided them with a new girl and everything was looking up again. Now things were weird. Some guy from Virginia showed up out of the blue and the men she sent to deal with him were not answering her calls. That was not a good sign.

Tia was no stranger to the ups and downs of life. She'd come into this world at the bottom. Her childhood had been miserable. They were poor and entered the country illegally. Her father was a hard worker who always found jobs, but couldn't keep them because he drank too much. He was a mean drunk, abusing everyone in the family when he was in the bottle. Her mother died when she was ten and Tia distinctly remembered thinking how lucky her mother was that she'd found a way to escape the misery.

Tia escaped her father's house by selling that thing all men wanted. On the street, she was a renegade, working without a pimp. They called it working "out of pocket" and the local pimps didn't like it. They tried to make her choose up. When they forced the issue, trapping her in a pimp circle, she fought back. She drew a gun and opened fire on them.

The looks on their faces. She smiled at the memory of it. They had not expected that. She made no threats, just whipped out a gun and started blasting. She didn't kill any of them but she'd hit a couple. No one went to the cops. That was not how they did things in the neighborhood. Some of them tried to get revenge over the years but she always came out on top.

She developed a reputation for her willingness to kill any man who laid a hand on her. In fact, she became so powerful it led to other girls wanting to come work for her. Soon she was a madam, and the proceeds from that enterprise were how she started her crew.

From the mid-1980s up through the late 1990s, Tia became a boss in Barrio Libre through ruthlessness and sheer force of will. She grew her stable of prostitutes into other lines of revenue. She ran drugs and robbed houses. She had crews chopping cars and selling the parts in California and Mexico. She ran all of it from a decrepit home in Barrio Libre with an enormous satellite dish in a bare dirt yard. Even as technology evolved and satellite dishes got smaller, she kept hers. In Mexico, those large dishes had been status symbols. No matter the condition of your home, that dish meant you were a person of resources. You were somebody, and Tia was definitely somebody.

Things changed though. The cartels began to exert more influence north of the border. People moved in on her territory, bringing more firepower to the fight than she could ever muster. She was faced with a simple choice. She could fight and die, or she could retire. So that was what she did. She surrendered her territory.

It was a hard pill to swallow. She had money stashed away but it was hard to give up the life. *La vida*. It was all she'd ever known. These days, she had no dreams of becoming a gang leader again. Her time had come and gone. She was a fat old woman. She needed to feel alive, though, and she needed to earn. You didn't spend your entire life in the game then start knitting old lady shit when you turned fifty. That wasn't how it worked, and that wasn't who she was.

When she surrendered her territory to the cartel, she had a crisis of faith that eventually led her to discover Santa Muerte. Like tens of millions of other Mexicans, she began to pray to the saint affectionately called Holy Death or The Bony Lady. She built an elaborate shrine to Santa Muerte in her home. From the neighborhood botanica, she purchased an effigy of the saint, a skeleton in a beautiful hooded robe, with jewels for eyes. She carried a scythe in one hand, like the grim reaper, and held a globe in the other. Tia surrounded it with votive candles to light in prayer, with different colored candles having different meanings.

She learned more about the religion from the folks who were fresh over the border. There were no books, bibles, or churches to Santa Muerte. It was a people's religion, spreading from person to person like wildfire. People told her about shrines that sprang up in villages and drew steady streams of pilgrims. They brought offerings of cigarettes, marijuana, money, and tequila. Some crawled for miles on bloody knees to show their devotion.

Some in her neighborhood told her about the dark offerings that could bring favor with Santa Muerte. Black candles, animal skulls, and blood were offered for those requests that the other saints wouldn't hear. It was said there were cannibals in Mexico who ate flesh in an attempt to earn her favor. After all, only she would offer protection for your illegal cargos. Only she would help you retain your criminal power. Only she would help you kill your enemies.

This was part of why the Catholic church didn't recognize Santa

Muerte as a saint. As far as they were concerned, she was public enemy number one. As people left the church, the ranks of Santa Muerte worshippers grew steadily.

One night, when the wound of losing her territory was still fresh, she lamented her loss of power. The loss of status in the community stung. People no longer feared or respected her in the same way. She wondered if Santa Muerte might be able to help her, as she had helped others. Rumors of Holy Death's taste for those dark offerings made Tia think of the child she'd lost. She had six sons by six different men over the years. One child had died at birth and four others had since died in the life. Only one, Luis, remained alive.

The dead child had been delivered at home, stillborn because Tia was too old and drank too much to be having children. Her body swollen by alcohol, she hadn't even known she was pregnant until it was too late. There was no record of the birth and the body was buried beneath a dead bush in the back yard.

Desperate for her life to change, for the blessing of Holy Death, she'd stumbled drunk into the backyard in search of a powerful offering. She wanted to honor the saint and ask for her help. With a butter knife, she scratched at the baked soil until she found all that remained of her child–a tiny skeleton held together by blackened strips of desiccated flesh. Tia carried it to her bedroom, where she placed it on her shrine with a flurry of frantic prayers.

Santa Muerte listened.

In just a few months, she was back in the life again. This time she wasn't a madam or a drug dealer. She wasn't running a gang. She was a trafficker, working with the cartel instead of against them. She found the girls, she groomed them, and then she delivered them to El Clavo. The arrangement came about because of her son, Luis, who introduced her to the business. While Tia had been shut down by the cartel, Luis had risen within the ranks of the Jalisco New Generation Cartel. Although it was a sore spot for Tia she kept her mouth shut about it.

The girls became a lucrative sideline. For nearly twenty years now, Tia had been working her special kind of magic with the young girls. She drew on skills she learned as a madam, befriending those who appeared to have no one else in the world. If they needed a mother, she mothered them. If they needed a hug, she hugged them.

Eventually, when she earned their trust, she offered to let them come live with her. They could do what they wanted. There would be no rules. They wouldn't have to go to school. They could live like adults. She promised to give them everything their current lives denied them. For a certain kind of girl, those promises were a dream come true.

It was all a lie. As soon as they were in Arizona, she got them addicted to heroin, meth, crack, or pain pills, then turned them over to El Clavo. Through his network of pimps, he put them to work on the streets. He had a circuit of girls working Seattle, Portland, Las Vegas, Los Angeles, and San Diego. He paid Tia a certain amount for each girl, based on what he expected to earn from them. It was a simple deal for Tia and worked like clockwork for twenty years.

Until the trip to Virginia.

There was a cold, sinking feeling within her. Things were flying apart. Like she might be returning to that gloomy, helpless place she was when the cartels ran her out of business and took her territory. Had she screwed up by taking the girl at the truck stop? Had that been a mistake? It wasn't the way they normally did things but the child was like a gift from Holy Death. Like a prayer answered. Had she been wrong?

In her bedroom, she removed a cheap Nokia cell phone from her nightstand. It wasn't a smart phone. It didn't do anything fancy. It was just an LCD display and some clunky plastic buttons. She dialed Luis. When he answered, she addressed him in Spanish.

"Those sicarios are not answering. I think something might be wrong. I should probably get out of the house."

Luis sighed. *"I guess I can let you stay here for a few days. My wife will not like it."*

Tia ignored that comment. She didn't care for Luis's wife. "I have a guest here that will need to come with me. Her ride is supposed to pick her up next week."

"*Jesus, Tia, what kind of trouble are you in?*"

"No trouble. I just missed the pickup."

"*Will this bring trouble down on me, Mother?*"

"No, Luis. I just need to stay low until my guest is gone."

"*What about this business you sent the sicarios to deal with? Can it be traced back to you?*"

"I don't think so. I just needed some help with Barger. He was becoming a whiny bitch." She had no interest in telling Luis about the man from Virginia. If she did, he might not help her.

"*Can you drive yourself to my house?*"

"No. I don't drive at night any longer. My eyes are old."

Luis sighed. "*Your eyes are probably drunk. I can have a car there in an hour. You be ready. Is your guest cooperative? Will she be a problem?*"

"She's young and sleepy. There's no fight in her."

"*Then make sure your shit is packed and you're ready to go. An hour, Mother. If you're not ready, we leave you.*"

"I'll be ready."

Tia ended the call and placed the phone on the nightstand. She went to the closet and got out a large suitcase. It'd been a gift from one of her sons but she'd never used it. People like her didn't go on vacation. They didn't take cruises and go to Disney World. She spread the suitcase open on the bed and began piling in some cheap clothing, several handguns, an AK-47 with a folding stock, and several rubber-banded stacks of cash.

She went to the spare room where Gretchen lay handcuffed to the bed. She was conscious but groggy from the dose of Demerol Tia had given her in the RV. Tia gave her another injection for the road. She needed her to be cooperative during the move. When she was done, she stashed the Demerol in the suitcase with a box of syringes. She made a last pass through the house but there was nothing she wanted.

She returned to the bedroom and struggled to kneel in front of her altar. She kept a thin pillow there for such moments. "Holy Death, I have tried to honor you. I pray to you many times each day. You have saved me more times than I can count. You gave me purpose when I had nothing. What have I done that you have turned your back on me?"

Tia leaned forward and used a long match to light the two candles. One showed Santa Muerte in a long brown robe, like a monk. The other showed her in a white gown like the Virgin Mary. Both showed the same skull face with its wide eyes and shining teeth. When she attempted to return to kneeling, her elbow struck the skeleton of the child she'd offered all those years ago and it fell to the ground. The sinews and leathery flesh were no longer enough to keep it intact. It collapsed into dozens of pieces, the tiny skull rolling across the floor until it landed on its side, facing her.

Accusing her.

In those blackened sockets Tia suddenly saw the problem. Though she prayed several times a day, when had she last offered Santa Muerte anything of true value to her? When had she last made an offering of significance? Had it been that long ago? Was it truly twenty years since she unearthed her dead child and placed her there?

Over the years, Tia had killed people who wronged her. It was part of doing business. Had she offered anything to her godmother? Had she brought Holy Death even a taste of the blood she spilled?

No.

She'd been selfish and now she was paying the price. She understood now what she had to do.

She went to the kitchen and found her largest, sharpest knife. She returned to her spare bedroom and stared at the sleeping Gretchen. It had been several years since she'd removed a head. It was not as easy as they made it look in the movies. It was nasty work and even the sound of it turned the stomach. The hacking and chopping. The splashing. The spine.

Lights swept her window as a car turned into her driveway. Had she spent that long in prayer? Had an hour passed already? She placed the knife on the dresser and went to the door. The child could wait. At least she knew what she needed to do now.

"I'm sorry, Holy Death," she whispered. "I will make this up to you."

33

J ust before sunup, two armored vehicles from the Tucson Police Department's SWAT Unit rolled into the Barrio Libre neighborhood. Masked men in armor and tactical gear rode on running boards, hands locked around grab handles, weapons dangling from slings. The vehicles rolled to a stop in front of a nondescript house and the officers swarmed in efficient, practiced movements.

While one team covered the side entrance, the primary element used a battering ram to take out the front door. Black-clad teams flooded into the house, weapons raised. Tactical lights bathed the interior in bright light.

"Police!" an officer bellowed. "*Policia!*"

In seconds they'd cleared the house.

"*All clear!*" reported team leader said over his radio. "*There's no one in the house.*"

Two detectives in police windbreakers entered the cramped house. Detective Terry Smith played a flashlight around the interior of the living room. He flipped a wall switch and turned on the overhead light, frowning at the decor. "I thought this lady was some kind of big shot. This place is tacky as hell."

Detective Janet Paye was shining her own light around, taking in the gaudy artwork and the shelves of knick-knacks. "Big fish in a small pond."

In the kitchen, Detective Smith opened the refrigerator and sniffed the milk. He laid a hand on the stove top and checked the grounds in the coffee maker. He hit the garbage can with his light and flipped through some of the contents with a gloved hand.

"Terry!" Detective Paye called from further back in the house. "You have to see this."

Detective Smith left the kitchen, eased by a couple of retreating SWAT Team members, and found Paye in the bedroom. She was staring at an altar against the bedroom wall.

"Jesus Christ," Smith mumbled.

"Not Jesus. Santa Muerte."

The statue of the skeletal saint stood on a wooden table, placing her head at roughly eye-level with Detective Smith. The base of the statue was surrounded by burned candles, incense burners, and food offerings on plates. A dead gray puppy lay draped across the statue's feet.

Detective Smith touched it carefully, examined the eyes and the mouth. "I don't think this puppy has been dead for more than a few hours. What the hell kind of people do this shit?"

"Someone who needs a blessing real bad," Detective Paye said. "This is dark shit."

Detective Smith started toward the altar, wanting to more closely examine the items laid out as offerings. He heard a crackle beneath his foot and stepped back, shining his light onto the floor. "Is that a chicken bone?"

Detective Paye moved her light around the floor, stopping on what was laying beneath the edge of a dresser. "Oh shit."

"What?" Smith asked, craning his neck to see where she was pointing her light.

"That's human," Paye asked. "I think it's real."

Then Smith saw it. "It's a baby."

34

Ty was asleep in his hotel room when a knock at the door woke him up. He checked the peephole and found a man in a suit holding a badge up for him to see. Ty opened the door and peered out.

"I'm Agent Banner. I need you to get dressed and come with me. We've got a task force meeting in thirty minutes and they want you there."

Ty gave a groggy nod. "Give me ten minutes."

"I'll be waiting downstairs."

Before the agents had delivered him to the hotel the night before, they'd let him pick up his truck from Barger's neighborhood. When he reached the hotel, he'd changed into clean clothes, and the agents took his dirty, blood-stained clothing into evidence. After they left him, he didn't even have the energy to check his Facebook account or reply to any messages. He was out like a light.

He took a quick shower, dressed, and delivered his duffel bag to the truck before meeting up with the agent. He didn't know if he'd be staying in the hotel another night or not so he wanted to stow his gear. He grabbed a cup of coffee in the lobby, and rode with the agent to the Tucson field office.

He was ushered upstairs to a conference room where the meeting was already underway. Ty recognized Agents Esposito and Cornell. Lieutenant Whitt was sitting there with an expression on her face that was nowhere in the range of friendly. She acknowledged his presence with a curt nod. The remaining dozen or so men were unknown to him, though one looked vaguely familiar.

Agent Esposito was conducting the meeting. He gestured for Ty to take a seat to his right. "This is Tyler Stone. He was the security guard on duty at the truck stop where Gretchen Wells was abducted. As I learned last night, Mr. Stone had a fourteen year career with U.S. Special Forces before receiving a medical discharge. I asked Mr. Stone to attend this meeting so he could explain how he ended up at our crime scene last night. I think we all know each other but I'm going to go around the room and have you introduce yourself for the benefit of our guests from Virginia."

The introductions were brief but demonstrated that the group represented a broad range of law enforcement divisions. There was local law enforcement as well as FBI, and representatives from departments investigating everything from gangs to crimes against children. It turned out the person Ty found vaguely familiar was Cliff Mathis from Door Kickers International. Ty figured he recognized him from one of the pictures he'd seen on the website.

"With no offense intended toward Lieutenant Whitt of the Virginia State Police, Mr. Stone's intuitive conclusions led him here when everyone else was going in another direction," Agent Esposito began. "I also asked Cliff Mathis of Door Kickers International to be part of this meeting because Mr. Stone reached out to him during his 'investigation', if that's what you want to call it. Most of you are familiar with his expertise in the field of child trafficking and exploitation."

Esposito continued down a checklist written on a yellow legal pad. "Just to bring everyone up to speed, we obtained a search warrant for Mr. Barger's residence, which turned up nothing. Mr. Barger has security cameras at his home and we've reviewed the footage. We found no evidence of the missing girl being taken to that address. I have more information along that line that may be of interest to you, but first I want to hear from Mr. Stone. Tyler, can you give us a detailed account of how you ended up in our state?"

Ty recounted his experience at the Petro Panda on the day of Gretchen's abduction. He mentioned his lockdown of the business and how that led to his firing. He discussed how he and Lieutenant Whitt had been unable to understand the excited expression on Gretchen's face, seen in the security camera footage as she exited the store. When he mentioned that image, Agent Esposito projected it onto a screen in the conference room so the others could see what he was describing.

"This was all playing through my mind when I got home from work on the night of the abduction. I remembered seeing a softball team taking a lot of pictures while they were there and I started wondering if some of those pictures got posted to social media. If they had, they might have picked up something that the security cameras missed. I printed everything I found and ended up with a big stack of pictures that didn't make sense to me until the next day. I was at my sister's house and noticed the reaction on my niece's face when a neighbor brought over a puppy. It was the exact same look Gretchen had as she was leaving the store. When I left my sister's house, I started going through those images again. That's when I found the picture of the woman hanging out by an RV with a puppy. I came to the conclusion that Gretchen's expression had to be related to that woman and that puppy. I didn't find any pictures that showed them together, but that was my conclusion based strictly on her expression. It was just a gut feeling. I was frustrated that law enforcement wasn't interested in my theory, but I understand there was no evidence to back it up."

Agent Esposito clicked a button on his laptop and the image on the projection screen changed to that of the woman with the puppy. "So, if I can just interrupt you here for a moment, I think Detective Johnson from the gang unit has some information on the lady in this picture."

A man in plain clothes cleared his throat and spoke up. "The woman in the picture is Fidelia Mendoza. She's known on the streets as Tia, which is a nickname meaning 'aunt.' The name goes back to her early days as a madam. She was a major player in the Barrio Libre gang scene in the 80s and 90s, but basically retired when the cartels pushed in. She didn't have the manpower to take them on."

"So if I can jump in here," Agent Esposito interrupted, "Mr. Stone provided us with this picture last night. With assistance from some of the old timers in the gang unit and facial recognition software, we were able to identify Miss Mendoza. We obtained a warrant to search her home, based on this photo connecting her to the RV where Gretchen Wells' clothing was found. That warrant was served around 5 AM this morning."

Ty looked excitedly from Lieutenant Whitt to Agent Esposito. He'd had no clue of this development. The agent who delivered him to the meeting hadn't mentioned it. "Did you find her?"

"No," Esposito replied, "she wasn't there. Detective Smith's unit ran the operation and I'll let him go over the details."

A pale man in his fifties with white hair picked up the story. "Despite Miss Mendoza looking like a little old lady, she has a very violent history. She's one of the few female gangsters in our city to run her own crew. She rose to power because of her willingness to inflict violence against anyone who messed with her. She never pulled hard time but she was a suspect in several murders. For that reason, we obtained a no-knock warrant and served it with SWAT support. A breaching team took down the door and made entry. Detective Paye and I entered behind them. A thorough search of the house didn't turn up the missing girl but several items of interest were found, including weapons and a small amount of drugs. The closet and the dressers were left open as if someone had recently packed up and cleared out. The most unusual item we turned up in the search was an altar in Mendoza's bedroom."

"Altar?" Ty asked. "Is that a Catholic thing?"

Detective Smith shook his head. "Not quite Catholic. Santa Muerte."

"I don't mean to derail the conversation here," Ty said, throwing a glance at agent Esposito, "but I'm not familiar with Santa Muerte. What is it?"

The way that they all looked at each other told Ty the term was familiar to everyone else in the room, except perhaps Lieutenant Whitt.

"It's like a blend of Catholicism and some kind of ancient death cult," Agent Cornell explained. "They worship this saint called Santa Muerte, or Holy Death. She's depicted as a skeleton in fancy robes, like a decked-out grim reaper."

"So it's a cult?" Lieutenant Whitt asked.

"Not a cult," Agent Esposito said. "It's much more than that. It's a religion with tens of millions of adherents. Anytime you read about some weird occult shit going on in Mexico with the cartels, Santa Muerte is involved. I could talk about this all day but we need to keep moving. Detective Smith, can you explain the significance of the shrine?"

"There was a child's skeleton located on the floor in front of the shrine. An infant. It could've been a stillborn baby. It's in the Medical Examiner's hands now and they're conducting DNA analysis to see what they can figure out. There was also a dead puppy but it was fresher. Maybe a day or two old. As a matter of fact, it looked very much like that puppy we saw in the picture with Fidelia Mendoza."

There were some looks of disgust around the room.

"So this skeleton was like an offering or something?" Ty asked.

There were nods around the room.

"That's what it appeared to be," Detective Smith said. "It was old and dried out."

"Santa Muerte can be a dark religion," said Agent Esposito. "There are a lot of stories of cannibalism and human sacrifice."

Ty had never heard of this.

"Detective Smith, you said Fidelia Mendoza was once a madam. Do we have any recent evidence of her being involved in trafficking activities?" Agent Esposito asked.

The detective settled back in his chair, tapping his ink pen on his legal pad. "None at all. Her name has not been linked to an active investigation since the 90s. She's been flying under the radar for two decades now. We assume she's been living on the money she squirreled away when she was in the life. She has connections though. An associate who goes by the name Luis, reported to be her son, is active in the JNGC. We're not sure if that's his real name or an alias."

Agent Esposito looked toward Lieutenant Whitt. "JNGC stands for the Jalisco New Generation Cartel."

The lieutenant nodded. "You guys keep using this word *trafficking* but there's no actual evidence of that, right? At the risk of sounding defensive, I'd like to point out that the reason we were not interested in Mr. Stone's theory about this kidnapping was because it was so unlikely. You all know as well as I do that these types of abductions almost always occur as the result of a custody dispute. This clearly fit the profile. The parents of this child had recently separated and both were fighting for custody. The husband couldn't be reached to notify him about his missing daughter. This was initially attributed to him being on a backcountry four-wheeling trip in Utah. We eventually found out that he was house shopping in Mexico with his mistress and made up the story about Utah so his wife wouldn't find out."

There were nods around the room.

"Your conclusions were completely logical, Lieutenant Whitt," Agent Esposito said. "They were supported by our agents on the scene. To be clear, we have no evidence that the child was picked up with the intention of trafficking her. We're just trying to put the pieces together. We're trying to understand why the paths of this woman, Fidelia Mendoza, and this girl, Gretchen Wells, intersected."

"I support your conclusions," Cliff Mathis said to Lieutenant Whitt. "I would have gone in the same direction. Despite the public's fear of random child abduction, it's extremely rare. We understand now that most people who end up being trafficked are either groomed into it, owe a debt to the traffickers they are being forced to repay, or suffer from an addiction that makes them easy to manipulate. A random abduction is much more likely to be the work of a child killer. As I told Mr. Stone when we first spoke, I don't know what to make of this. It doesn't fit the pattern for any of the most likely scenarios."

"I still don't know how Mr. Stone ran that tag," Lieutenant Whitt said. "He did *not* get that information from us and couldn't have obtained it through customary channels." She glared at Ty.

"He declined to provide us with that information," Esposito noted. "I'm not sure that's relevant at this point, though. So what about this contractor? What do we know about Barger?"

A female detective spoke up, referring to her notes. "We're waiting on the subpoena for his bank records, but there's no obvious link between him and Mendoza, other than the picture obtained by Mr. Stone. We're checking the RV for prints. We're analyzing Barger's phone and waiting for billing records so we can see if those two have communicated in the past. Preliminary inspection of the contents of the trash bag found at the scene indicates that the clothing appears similar to what Gretchen Wells was wearing when she was abducted. We have the hair sample Lieutenant Whitt provided from the girl's home and we're waiting on that analysis now."

"And the gunmen?" Esposito asked.

"Sicarios," replied the detective from the gang unit. "Long history of cartel-related arrests. Fancy clothes, fancy truck, and fancy guns. Both alive at this point, thanks to Mr. Stone stabilizing the one with gunshot wounds. He's not able to talk. The one with the concussion is stable but won't say anything."

"Again, pardon my ignorance here, but what exactly is a sicario?" Ty asked. "I've heard the word on TV shows but have no idea."

"Cartel assassin," Cornell offered. "A hitman."

"Looks like somebody wanted all this to go away," Detective Smith said. "Some stranger from Virginia shows up and Mendoza panics. The most obvious solution is to kill Barger and kill the stranger. Wrap up any loose ends and get the hell out of town."

"Loose ends from what?" Mathis asked. "That's the question. Is this a kidnapping for ransom? It makes no sense."

"Do you have anything connecting the sicarios to Mendoza?" Esposito asked.

There were several shaking heads but a female detective, Moldonado, replied. "Nothing yet. No phones, other than Barger's, were located on the scene. We don't know how they got their orders."

Esposito sat back in his chair. "Well, what we have makes absolutely no sense at all. You're all here, though, because I've asked that you be part of a task force assigned to this case. You know we've missed the critical window. The first forty-eight hours have come and gone. This is going to be a tough one. Besides the victim being a child, we don't have a motive. As we've said a hundred times now, nothing about this case makes sense."

Cliff Mathis was nodding in agreement.

"What about the Mexican connection?" Detective Smith asked. "If the dad was in Mexico shopping for a house, could he have hired Mendoza or the cartel to kidnap his child? If they delivered her to Mexico, he wouldn't have to deal with a court battle for custody. He could hide her."

"It's possible," Esposito said.

"We still haven't spoken with the father," Lieutenant Whitt commented. "The FBI is working with Mexican authorities, but we've not located him yet."

As Esposito continued to talk, Ty was suddenly hit with a wave of anxiety. He experienced a dissociative state, sinking further and further inside himself. Deeper and deeper into a hole.

Why was he here? He'd done all this for nothing. His routine back in Virginia was all that held him together and he'd broken that. It was inevitable he was going to fall apart. How had he been so stupid to think he could help that little girl? He'd never been able to help anyone. He couldn't even help himself.

His mind went to the face of that dead Pakistani child in the van in Afghanistan, the operation that ended his career. Gretchen was going to end up dead too. He'd failed to protect her at the truck stop and he'd failed to find her here. It was his fault. Two dead children. How could he live with that? He was a failure.

"Please excuse me," Ty said, shoving his chair back suddenly and standing up.

"Are you okay?" Agent Esposito asked.

Ty nodded, sweat beading on his forehead. "I just need some fresh air."

He sensed the eyes on him as he hurried from the room. Outside the conference room he found a pool of desks. A young lady seated at one met his eye.

"The restroom?" Ty asked.

She smiled and pointed down a hallway.

Ty rushed in that direction, feeling the world closing in on him. Every sound, from ringing phones to dinging elevators, sounded unnaturally loud. The angles of the walls around him leaned in toward him, converging, attempting to close around him. He was hyperventilating. He spotted the restroom and ducked inside like it was the final refuge.

It was empty and he went directly to the sink. He ran cold water, cupped it in his hands, and splashed it on his face. His heart was pounding and his chest was tight when he tried to suck in air. He had to be having some kind of panic attack. Where the fuck had it come from?

He grabbed a stack of paper towels and dried his face, went into a stall, and locked the door behind him. He sagged against the wall, resting his head on his forearm, trying to get control of himself. After several minutes, the feelings subsided and he began to calm down. He could breathe again.

He rinsed his face and went back into the hall. Everything was almost normal now though his heart rate was up. He grew self-conscious, as if everyone had seen him rushing off. They probably thought he was crazy, and they might have been right. As he neared the pool of desks, he ducked into an alcove to get a long drink from a water fountain. He could hear the lady who directed him toward the restroom talking on the phone.

"Agent Esposito, I'm sorry to interrupt you but I wasn't sure if you'd see a text or not. Could you let the lieutenant from Virginia know that her extradition paperwork just came through? After the conference, have one of the city detectives make the arrest. Mr. Stone can then be transferred to the lieutenant's custody for return to Virginia. The paperwork is on my desk when you're ready."

Ty stood there bent over the fountain, mouth agape. He released the button and stood up. He couldn't believe what he'd just heard. He headed for the stairs.

He could trust no one.

35

T y bounded down the stairs two at a time. Catching a glimpse of a security camera on a landing, he forced himself to slow down. While he might be on the run from the cops, he certainly didn't need to look like it. He reached the ground floor of the low building in no time. He ran a sleeve across his forehead, wiping away the sweat, and stepped out into the lobby. He was just a casual guy walking casually to the exit. He figured he had a couple of minutes before someone from the conference room went looking for him but they wouldn't have any reason to think he would run. It had been sheer, dumb luck that he'd even found out about their plan to arrest him.

Once he was out of the building, he breathed a little easier. The Tucson field office was off Interstate 10 in a jumble of residential, industrial, and commercial properties. He needed to get to his hotel and his vehicle, but he wasn't sure where it was in relation to his current location. Once they figured out he was missing, he assumed that was where they would start looking for him. He needed to get there first.

He opened his phone and used the map to orient himself, pleased to find that his hotel was relatively close to the field office. This was probably something they had to do on a regular basis, putting a witness up for the night. It only made sense they would use a place nearby. Ignoring the streets and sidewalks on his map, he tried to plot a direct course to his hotel. The route, which had taken them fifteen minutes to drive, could be reached on foot by a much more direct path.

Looking around the parking lot, he realized he was getting ahead of himself. He was fenced in and needed to find a way out of here first. The entire property was surrounded by a low brick wall and topped with steel fencing. Doing his best to appear casual, he walked toward the rear of the property, away from the manned entry and exit gates. The back parking lot adjoined a residential neighborhood. Ty held his phone to his ear as he walked, trying to look like a man deep in conversation. He worked his way to a section of fence concealed by low trees, did a quick check and saw that no one was around, and scaled the fence. He landed in the parking lot of a hair salon and hurried off.

Following the map on his phone, Ty made his way to West Alameda Street and then onto a running and biking trail called the Diamond Street Loop where, despite his street clothes, a running man might draw less attention. He was somewhat screened from the road by trees and the terrain, so he picked up the pace. He ran south toward his hotel, pushing hard on the paved trail. He ran through a little park called the Garden of Gethsemane, crossed the bridge on West Congress Street where his map showed a river but he saw nothing but a dusty, dry ravine, and once across the bridge, his hotel was on the right.

He swung into the parking lot of the Carl Junior's that was adjacent to his hotel, sliding his phone into his shirt pocket as he dug for his truck key. He scanned the parking lot. He had no idea how much his arrest meant to them. Would they even bother coming after him? Certainly Lieutenant Whitt would if it was left to her, but was he the real goal there? No, it was Gretchen. Surely they would focus on her. There was no guarantee of that, though.

As he neared his truck, he began to imagine a squad of vehicles screeching to a halt around him. Would there be snipers? Air assets? He decided to spend a precious two minutes checking the parking lot before approaching his truck. He made a hurried circuit of the lot, making sure there were no suspicious men sitting in cars. When he finally confirmed he was the only suspicious guy in the parking lot, he jogged to his truck.

He unlocked the door and hopped inside, started the engine, and wasted no time getting out of there. He drove carefully, not wanting to draw any attention or, even worse, get pulled over by the cops. His mind raced. Where was he going to go? What was he going to do? How was he going to find this little girl in this big city?

There was no retreat at this point. There was no running away. The only thing waiting on him at home was the same battle he'd been fighting before he left. He would try to put on a happy face for Aiden and Deena but he would continue to fail miserably. He would try to find another crappy job and it would only make his depression worse. He would spend his nights in the Wasteland For Warriors, trying to help folks who were having a harder go of it than he was.

He could imagine how it would end. He'd seen it over and over again. Eventually the same demons that had shaken him in that conference room would wear him down. They would make his symptoms so ever-present that he would alienate everyone in his life. Once they had him isolated from the herd, they would pick him off.

Ty pulled into the parking lot of an immense shopping center. There was a Target, a pet store, an electronics store, and an office supply store. He parked in a congested area where his vehicle would be less noticeable. The conclusion he'd reached on his drive was that he had absolutely nothing to lose. The worst the kidnappers could do would be to kill him and, at this point, that simply saved him the anguish of doing it himself. He reached into the cooler in the back and removed a lukewarm bottle of water.

He took a long drink while he thought about what he'd heard in that conference room. He had a name for the woman in the picture now. Fidelia Mendoza. She'd been well-known in a neighborhood named Barrio Libre where she'd once been a player. She'd lived there until last night when she bolted for an unknown reason, likely related to Ty's appearance at Barger's RV. She was a follower of a religion called Santa Muerte. And she had a son who was possibly cartel-affiliated.

Had he been back home, this might have been enough information to provide a lead. Here, he didn't know anything about the people and the neighborhoods. He didn't know the customs and he didn't know how you went about obtaining information. He had the sudden insight that this was exactly the same battle they'd fought to obtain information in Iraq and Afghanistan. They were strangers trying to question locals who often had no good reason to comply with their requests. It could be like throwing a hook with no bait into the ocean and expecting to catch a fish. It was often a frustrating and futile effort.

Ty had a secret weapon, though. He had no fear. He wasn't scared of dying, he wasn't scared of the cartel, and he wasn't scared of being tortured because he was tortured now. His only focus was getting Gretchen back. Every man had to make a stand and this was where he would make his. He was bringing Gretchen Wells home or he would die trying.

He used his phone to search for the location of the Barrio Libre neighborhood. He was pleased to discover it was not very far at all from where he'd stayed the previous night. When he was done, he turned his phone off and retrieved a Ziploc bag from his food box. It had Pop Tarts in it, which he dumped into the seat beside him. He sealed the phone into the bag and drove to a less-trafficked area of the parking lot. Positioning his truck to block him from public view, he buried his phone in one of the landscaped islands of mulch and hedges.

He didn't wanted to carry it with him on the off-chance the FBI thought he was important enough to track. He'd even considered throwing it into the trash but there was something too final about that gesture. It was like opening a bottle of liquor and throwing the cap in the garbage. You were making a commitment. For Ty, throwing his phone in the garbage or out the window would have implied that he would not be coming back from this. While he fully accepted that possibility, he did not want to give the impression of surrender. That would only embolden the demons and he didn't need that distraction. He had to fight. If not for himself, for Gretchen.

36

T he detective from the gang unit was laying out Fidelia Mendoza's complex criminal history when Lieutenant Whitt interrupted.

"Excuse me, but should we check on Mr. Stone? He's been gone a long time."

"He's a big boy," Agent Cornell said. "He'll be fine."

Addressing the entire task force, Agent Esposito explained, "The lieutenant has an arrest warrant from Virginia. We were supposed to arrest Mr. Stone after the meeting and transfer custody to her."

Cornell looked shocked. "For what?"

Lieutenant Whitt sighed. She hadn't wanted to get into this. "Apparently Mr. Stone has severe PTSD. He was in a movie theater and a stranger put his hands on him. He kind of flipped out and took the guy to the floor."

"How badly was he injured?" Cliff Mathis asked.

"He wasn't injured," the lieutenant replied. "Mr. Stone stopped himself before he hurt the guy. The man still pressed charges."

"That's a bunch of bullshit," Mathis spat. "Stone gave you your biggest lead. He came all the way across the country on his own dime to try and find this girl *while* he's dealing with his own personal issues. How dare you ambush him like that?" He leaned back in his chair and glared at Lieutenant Whitt with disgust.

"We've all got a job to do," said Whitt.

Cliff Mathis shoved his chair back from the table. "I'm done here. I don't want any part of this. You've got a little girl out there in danger. We shouldn't even be wasting time on this conversation."

Cornell was reclined back in his chair, arms folded across his stomach. "I agree with Mathis. This is bullshit."

"Can we take a five minute break?" Agent Esposito suggested, trying to defuse the situation. "We'll check on Mr. Stone and go from there."

"This is bullshit!" Cornell called to their backs as Esposito and Whitt left the room.

"Real supportive group you have there," Whitt remarked.

"They're right, you know," Esposito replied. "This is vindictive and petty."

They hurried down the hall to the restroom. Esposito went inside and found it empty. "He's not in there."

"Damn," Whitt mumbled.

Esposito walked back to the pool of desks outside the conference room. "Did you see what happened to the guy who came out during our meeting?"

"He asked about the restrooms," the young lady replied. "Didn't see him again after that."

"Thank you."

"You've got cameras all over the place," Whitt said, pointing them out along the walls. "Can we run the footage?"

Esposito raised an eyebrow. "You really want to go to all that trouble now? These guys are right. That's *not* where we should be putting our resources."

Whitt hooked her thumbs onto her belt and stewed.

"Are you sure this isn't a little retaliation?" Esposito asked. "You're pissed because Stone was right and you guys were chasing your tails?"

"It wasn't just me!" Whitt snapped. "The FBI was in agreement with our conclusions."

Esposito held up a conciliatory hand. "I'm just saying that I think we should leave this alone. Sure, we could track his phone and the navigation system in his vehicle. We could send out a bulletin to be on the lookout for him. Where's the real crime here, though? It's not with him. It's with Gretchen Wells. Let's find her."

Esposito put a hand on Whitt's shoulder, ushering her back toward the conference room. Whitt relented. She understood she had no support here.

"Stone will turn up," Esposito said as they walked. "He's not the kind of guy who's going to run from this. He's probably out there right now trying to pick up the trail. He's on a mission."

fter burying his phone, Ty went into a discount store and used cash to buy a burner phone. He activated it in the parking lot while listening to Motorhead. He and his fellow soldiers had done this while deployed to psych themselves up for missions. There was nothing like loud metal to make you think you were invincible.

When he had the burner phone working, he got back on the road and drove to Barrio Libre, a short drive from his current location. Cruising the quiet streets, it didn't take him long to figure out which house had belonged to Fidelia Mendoza. It was wrapped with crime scene tape, an evidence van was parked in the driveway, and a half-dozen police cars were parked along the street. Ty wondered if there was a similar scene at Barger's house and at the spot in the desert where Barger had been killed.

He kept his head down, his sun visor blocking his face, and rolled on by. He had no intention of trying to get into that house but he wanted to see the neighborhood. That crime scene was the epicenter of this whole thing. It was the only connection he had right now to the woman who'd taken Gretchen.

Around the corner, he pulled to the curb in front of a corner store made of yellow cinderblocks. The heat was sweltering and the window air conditioner was the loudest sound around. Ty went inside and glanced around the place. It was a tiny square building with few offerings. Basically just cigarettes, snacks, drinks, and beer. He grabbed an energy drink from the cooler and walked to the counter. The cashier, too cool to be pulled from his phone, made Ty wait for a while before he stood. Ty tolerated it because he wanted information.

"What's going on with all the cops?" Ty asked as the guy strolled the three steps to the counter and rang up his drink on the cash register.

The cashier studied Ty, didn't recognize him, and shrugged. "Who knows?"

Not the talkative sort. Ty tried again. "Can you tell me where I might find the closest botanica?"

The cashier raised an eyebrow at him. This didn't look right. "What do *you* want a botanica for, *amigo*?"

Ty passed his money across the counter, struggling to appear casual when he was anything but. He was working to give a touristy vibe, but with his physical stature and cop haircut he probably came off more like a detective than a tourist. Either way, not the kind of guy who would be asking about a botanica. "My grandmother has been getting involved in something called Santa Muerte. I wanted to find out more about it. She's been getting a little weird over it."

The cashier gave Ty his change and retook a seat on a stool. He looked out the window toward the street and didn't make eye contact with Ty. "You don't want no part of that, man."

"You don't believe in it?"

"I ain't gonna say I don't believe, you know what I'm saying? My grandma's into it too. My sister burns candles to her."

"So where does your grandmother go to get her...stuff? You know, candles and shit. For her...shrine." He kept throwing out what little information he had, hoping it would make his request sound authentic.

"Little botanica down in Wakefield. You know where that's at?"

Ty shook his head.

"You can Google it. I took her there once. Tiny place."

"Do you mind to look it up for me?" Ty asked. "My phone is a piece of shit."

The guy sighed, rolled his eyes, and gave a pretty good show of just how much Ty had inconvenienced him. He looked up the directions and scribbled them down on a scrap of paper. He slid them across the counter with a "will that be all?" look.

It wasn't.

Ty held up a printed copy of the picture of Fidelia Mendoza leaning on the back of the RV with the puppy in her arms. "You ever seen this woman before?" He assumed that she had to come into this store sometimes because it was the closest one to her home. Surely she'd wandered up here for something.

"You a cop?"

Ty wanted to deliver some badass line. *No, I'm not a cop, I'm your worst fucking nightmare* or *You're going to wish I was a cop when I'm done with you.* He didn't think fast enough.

The cashier moved his eyes from the picture to Ty. "Get the fuck out of here."

They were the only people in there. Ty reached across the counter and grabbed the cashier by the wrist before he could yank it away. The young man struggled but Ty held him like a vise. If he couldn't find Tia, he was going to make her come to him.

"Listen, I know a punk bitch like you probably doesn't know Tia personally but you know people who do. You let her know that Tyler, a friend from Virginia, wants to speak to her."

Ty released his wrist and the young man snatched it back, rubbing the place where Ty's iron grip had held him. Ty tore off a scrap of paper from the directions to the botanica and wrote down the number to his new phone. He shoved it across the counter.

"You throw this away and it won't go well for you. Tia's going to want to talk to me. She finds out you didn't relay the message and you can probably guess what her people will do to you. That son of hers, he'll fuck you up."

Ty left the store, a dangling bell ringing as he exited. When he got in his truck, he turned back to the store and saw the kid glaring at him. He raised his phone and shot a picture of Ty, then of his license tag.

That was okay with Ty. He was all in now. There was no turning back.

38

T he botanica was a squat block building not significantly
different from the corner store Ty had just visited. It was
painted bright green with the name of the business hand-
painted in purple letters on the side. There were no hours listed but
there was a phone number to call if no one was there and you had an
emergency. He wondered what kind of emergencies they got called
out for.

Ty parked next to the building and noted there were no windows.
An air conditioning unit was fit into a hole in the wall. Condensation
dripped from the back corner. The ground beneath it was so parched
that the moisture evaporated nearly as fast as it fell. At the window-
less front door, Ty hesitated, uncertain of the protocol. Did you just
go in? Did you knock?

He decided to do both, tapping on the door with his knuckles as
he twisted the handle.

"Come in," called a voice from inside.

Ty wasn't sure what he expected but this was certainly not it. He
was anticipating an old crone in some dark room, lit with candles,
and smelling of bitter potions. Instead he found a brightly-lit and
clean interior. The walls were decorated with folk paintings and

draped with bright cloth. Several tables and shelves displayed a variety of items, from jewelry to candles. Some held items Ty didn't recognize. If there was a theme to the room, it was that nearly every item featured the image of that robed, grim reaper figure.

He shut the door behind himself and stood there. He was mesmerized by one display in particular that took up an entire corner of the small room. A life-size skeleton stood there draped in an elegant hooded robe of embroidered white silk. One hand was extended, a small globe clutched in the bony fingers. A scythe lay against the other shoulder. Red plastic jewels were set into the eye sockets, giving the statue a menacing presence. Ty couldn't pry his eyes from it.

"Can I help you?"

Ty had been experiencing sensory overload since opening the door. The interior was disorienting, like a magical room that was larger inside than the outside led you to believe. He'd been so taken by the skeleton that he'd failed to observe the proprietor. Behind a small counter, his eyes landed on a Latina who must have been in her late twenties. She was far from the hunched crone Ty was expecting. Her hair was blonde with pink streaks, she wore black lipstick, and her face was painted in what Ty assumed to be magical symbols. She almost resembled those sugar skulls that Ty had seen tattooed on people. She was both beautiful and a little scary at the same time.

"Are you okay?" she asked, smiling at his befuddlement.

"Yes, thank you." He gestured at the skeleton in the corner. "Is this Santa Muerte?"

She leaned forward, resting her elbows on the counter. "It's a shrine to Santa Muerte. People who don't have shrines at home come to make offerings to her. People who cannot come here in person pay me to burn candles to her. I also sell smaller statues and candles for folks who want a shrine at home but don't need something so..."

"Dramatic?" he offered.

"Exactly."

"So, is this your place? I was expecting someone more..."

"Witchy?"

"No, *ancient*, actually. I guess I was expecting a little old crone."

"Maybe I'm an old crone who can alter my appearance?" she said. "I might appear differently to the next person."

He stared at her, unsure of what to say.

She laughed into her hand. "I'm teasing. You'll find old women at some botanicas. If that's your preference, I can give you some addresses. They won't have pointy hats and brooms, though."

He waved a hand. "No, that's not necessary. You're fine."

She frowned but the expression went over his head. Like a lot of guys, he didn't get that being "fine" was not complimentary. It was the equivalent of "you'll do."

"What can I do for you, Señor?"

"I'd like to learn more about Santa Muerte," he said. It was the only place he knew to start.

She nodded at his request. "I can do that. I am a business, though. I charge for my time. I offer consultations and Tarot readings. I do spells, cleansings, and even personal rituals. Thirty minutes of my time is fifty dollars."

Ty was a little taken aback by her abrupt, businesslike manner. It could be because he was a Southerner, used to a different ritual where commerce was involved. In his region, people were not quite so blunt about demanding money for their time. People went into barber shops, gun shops, and garages and spent all day flapping their jaws without spending a dime.

Yet it made sense. It wasn't like there was a line stretching out the door. He was sure she had bills to pay. He counted out fifty dollars in cash and slid the bills across the counter. She deftly folded them and tucked them into a low-cut shirt.

She pulled a small whiteboard from beneath the counter and scribbled on it in marker: *Consultation in progress. Come back in thirty minutes.*

With the sign hung on the door, she gestured for him to take a seat at a tiny round table with two chairs. A deck of tarot cards sat in the center. Ty sat down carefully, afraid he might break the flimsy wooden chair. He was not a little guy. He nervously laced his fingers in his lap and tried not to move.

She sat down across from him and placed her hands on the table in front of her, palms down. "I'm Lucia. What should I call you?"

He found it interesting that she didn't ask for his name, as if she came from a world where the use of aliases was customary. "I'm Ty."

"Okay, Ty, what can I do for you? What is it you want to know about Santa Muerte?"

He fell back to the story he'd used at the bodega. "My grandmother has become interested in Santa Muerte. Very deeply involved, actually. It's all she talks about. I want to know more about it."

Lucia raised a thin eyebrow at him. "Your grandmother?"

Ty found himself captivated by her beauty, despite the bizarre lines and dots on her face. She seemed supernatural, as if he'd entered another plane when he came inside. He wondered if she actually was a witch and she was charming him with a spell.

"Was your *abuelita*, your grandmother, a murderer?" she asked.

"No!" Ty exclaimed. "Are you kidding?"

"Then was she a prostitute?"

Ty was shocked. "Nothing like that. She's a sweet old lady who raises a garden and loves cats. I'm just concerned about her."

Lucia gave him a doubtful look. "Your story sounds like bullshit, Ty. Why are you wasting my time? Ask me what you really want to know."

"Why would you say that?"

"Santa Muerte is virtually the patron saint of the underclass, the downtrodden. She protects the people society has forgotten or turns their backs on. She is typically not the saint of sweet little Anglo cat ladies."

Ty let out a deep breath. So much for his plan. "Fair enough. It's not about my grandmother. I do need to know a little about Santa Muerte."

"Why?"

"Does it matter why?"

Lucia gave him an assessing look, which looked odd on such a highly decorated face. "It matters now, since you lied to me once already. I have to be sure of your motives. Are you a reporter or something?"

Ty met her eye. "I'm not a reporter. I'm trying to find someone who disappeared. She was kidnapped and I have reason to believe that the person who kidnapped her is involved in Santa Muerte."

Lucia considered this a moment before replying. "You have to understand that crime is not a *component* of Santa Muerte, though she is revered as the saint of killers, thieves, sex workers, and drug dealers. It is part of the acknowledgement that death is always close when you live that life."

"I'm from the east," Ty admitted. "I don't know anything about it."

Lucia reached to a nearby shelf and removed a statue of Santa Muerte about a foot tall. She placed it in front of Ty. The statue was wearing a bright red robe with a hood. He noticed that she was depicted differently in several of the little statues.

"She has various names. The Skinny Woman, The Bone Lady, Saint Death, and others. I personally prefer to use the name Holy Death. While her roots are ancient, the modern worship of Santa Muerte goes back to the 1950s. It's said to have come from Catemaco. Do you know Catemaco?"

"No."

"It's a city of witches in Veracruz. Male witches. *Brujos.*"

"A city of witches?" Ty repeated, having trouble picturing such a thing. He couldn't imagine someone casually referring to a city in America, say somewhere in Nebraska, as being a city of witches. He had no idea there were such things.

"Yes. It's a very powerful city. They have supernatural festivals there every year. They didn't invent Santa Muerte, though. It's suspected the practice goes back farther, perhaps all the way back to the ancient Aztec goddess of death. That's why the Catholic Church does not acknowledge Santa Muerte. They condemn it as devil worship. As black magic."

"Is it?"

Lucia looked him in the eye. "There is dark and light in everything, Ty. There are people who take it to the extreme. Some ask very big things from Santa Muerte and she demands large offerings in return."

"Like human sacrifice? Human remains?"

Lucia got up from her chair and went behind the counter. She retrieved a stubby black candle, placing it beside the statue on the table, and lit it with a wooden match. "We do not keep black candles on the shelves. People who need black candles know to ask for them. A black candle burned in devotion to Santa Muerte will ensure her protection. It will also help if you are seeking vengeance."

"Is this a ritual? What you're doing now?"

Lucia locked her eyes onto his. The candle flickered hypnotically. Ty couldn't look away from her. From somewhere she produced a small card and propped it against the statue. Ty dropped his eyes for a moment and saw a picture of Santa Muerte looking like the grim reaper. The card read "Holy Dead" across the bottom.

"Most Holy Death, I ask that through this image you will cover this man with the cloak of your protection, that you will always take care of him, that you will guide him through snares and dangers. Give him your blessing so that he will never lack the things he needs. Give him strength, health, prosperity, and protection."

Ty sat up straight in his chair. "Okay, that was definitely a ritual."

Lucia smiled at him. "You paid for my time. With the questions you are asking, you will need protection. It's the least I can do."

Ty reached into his shirt pocket and removed the piece of paper. He unfolded it and slid the picture of Fidelia Mendoza across the table. "Do you know this woman? They say she's called Tia. Is she a customer of yours?"

Lucia didn't touch it. She looked from the picture to Ty without a word.

Ty leaned forward and said urgently, "Look, I came here all the way from Virginia in search of a missing child. She was abducted from a truck stop where I was working. This woman was involved." He tapped the picture with his finger for emphasis. "I know her name is Fidelia Mendoza and I know she worships Santa Muerte because the police found a shrine in her home. There was a dead child on it, if that means anything to you. Has she been in here buying any of those black candles from under the counter?"

Again, the beautiful eyes stared at him. Not angry, not defiant, just observing. Did this woman even blink?

Ty reached into his pocket and withdrew a hundred dollar bill. He tossed it onto the picture. "Can you tell me anything about Fidelia Mendoza? Please?"

Lucia studied the money for a while before coming to some conclusion. She placed an elaborately decorated nail on the bill and pulled it toward herself. She folded it, tucking it into her bra, along with the money he'd already paid her. She tapped the picture with another pointed fingernail, the tapping loud in the silence of the room. "This here is a bad bitch. You don't mess with her. I know she looks old and shit but she's dangerous. She used to run a neighborhood north of here and she's still got juice."

"Why do you think she'd be involved in kidnapping a child? Is that her business now? Is she involved in human trafficking?"

This was the first thing Ty said that provoked any measurable reaction from Lucia. She sat back in her chair and crossed her arms in front of her. She waved her nails through the air in some kind of nervous gesture, a flair of color that was almost subconscious.

"I don't know anything about what people do. I don't ask because *their* business is not *my* business. All I know is that Tia is devoted to Santa Muerte and comes here sometimes for supplies."

Ty bored into her. "Look, you have *all* my money. I'm trying to find a child who was taken from her mother. Is there anything else you can tell me?"

Lucia took the prayer card with Santa Muerte on it and slid it across the table to him. "You should put that in your pocket. It carries a blessing and you're going to need every bit of protection you can get. The only other thing I can tell you is that you should go home. Go back east and forget Santa Muerte. Forget Tia. Forget this child."

Ty slid the card into his pocket and stood. "Thank you for your time. If I leave my number, will you call me if you hear anything?"

She shrugged noncommittally. "I can't stop you from leaving it."

He went to the counter and took one of her business cards, writing the number to his burner phone on the back. She took a beaded rosary from a hook and slid it across the counter to him. He noticed that instead of a cross, the rosary held the shiny skeletal visage of Santa Muerte.

"Take it. You paid for it," she said. "You'll need it."

He shoved it in his pocket with the prayer card and mumbled a thanks. He suspected she had more information than she was sharing but she wasn't parting with it. He couldn't blame her. This was her land and her people. He was an outsider who could be putting her in danger. He headed toward the door, uncertain of what his next step was going to be.

"Please come again," she said, not sounding at all like she meant it.

Ty opened the heavy steel door and the heat slammed into him, the light blinding. He paused to fumble for his sunglasses, slipped them on, and went outside. He found himself staring down the barrels of three handguns, three cold faces hovering behind weapons.

"Hands up!" one of the men ordered.

Ty did as he was told.

The men searched him but he didn't have any weapons on him. The FBI had his Glock and he hadn't seen his knives since Barger took them. He had his Tavor X95 rifle in the truck but that didn't do him a hell of a lot of good right now. One of the men cuffed his hands and shoved him between the shoulder blades. "In the fucking car."

The car was a late 70s Pontiac four-door in mint green. The engine was running and the AC was cold. Ty was shoved into the back, falling across the vinyl seats. With his cuffed hands in front of him, he pushed himself upright as one of the men took a seat beside him. The other two piled into the front.

Ty could tell these men were of the same cut as the two sicarios he'd fought in the desert. He didn't know if they were assassins sent to kill him, but they were hard men. They handled their guns comfortably, like soldiers, and that told him something. It told him they used them often.

He should probably have been afraid. He could well be on the way to his death. In fact, that was the likely outcome. Where else would they be taking him? A woman with Tia's history was not going to have a beer with him, tell him to pack his shit, and get out of town. There was only one reason these men would be here for him. That was to make him disappear.

Ty forced himself to relax. To some extent, this was what he'd been hoping for. The only way he was going to find Gretchen without law enforcement was if Tia found him. Apparently the bait he'd thrown out at the corner store had worked. The boy had told someone Ty was headed for the botanica and, rather than call him, they came for him. He appreciated that kind of efficiency and decisiveness. It was the way things got done.

"Where are we headed?" he asked, his voice casual, conversational.

The temples of his sunglasses partially obscured his peripheral vision. That may be why he didn't see the gun butt coming at him from the side. It collided with his forehead, a solid blow that left him dazed. He felt blood running down his forehead and along his cheek.

Was it his delivery? Had he sounded sarcastic?

Once that gate was opened, the blows kept coming. A second caught Ty above the ear and he slumped into the seat. Everything faded to black.

39

A bucket of fetid water dumped over his head brought Ty back to the world of the living. He lay on a concrete floor, his hands cuffed in front of him. He tried to sit up but his head protested, sending him reeling. Forget a concussion, he'd be lucky if there weren't shards of skull driven into his brain like chips into dip. He wondered if he could shake his head and hear it rattle like a maraca. His scalp burned from scabbed wounds that tugged and tore as he moved his head.

He found a well-dressed man who looked like a rancher in front of him. He was Hispanic but no one Ty had seen before. He held a cattle prod in his hand, tapping it into his palm like a guard eager to wield his truncheon. A line of men stood behind him and Ty recognized a couple of them from the ride in. One grinning face belonged to the man who had so viciously pistol-whipped him.

"I hear you've been asking after my mother?" the rancher asked.

Ty squinted. This must be Luis. The stinking blood-tinged water ran down Ty's face, into his eyes and open mouth. He tried to shake his head but the gesture caused a wave of blinding pain. "Is your mother Tia?"

"First things first, I am the one asking the questions here." To emphasize his point, Luis jabbed Ty with the sparking cattle prod.

Ty screamed as his body went painfully rigid, jerking uncontrollably. The motion exacerbated the stabbing pain in his skull. The line of men laughed and taunted him as he attempted to regain control of his body.

When Ty made eye contact with him, Luis was satisfied that he could continue. "I'm going to be asking you some questions. I suggest you answer truthfully. We have done horrible shit in this building, *amigo*. Your screams would not be the first to echo off these walls."

That image penetrated the fog of Ty's brain. These men would kill him. That was not the optimal outcome. "I have no reason to lie."

"Who are you?" Luis asked.

"My name is Ty. I was a security guard at the truck stop in Virginia where a child was abducted. I have reason to believe your mother was involved. I followed the trail here."

"I don't keep up with my mother's affairs but she's a retired old lady. She spends her days knitting shit and going to church."

"I doubt your mother goes to church. She prays to the Santa Muerte."

The cattle prod crackled as it hit Ty in the ribs.

"NO!" Ty screamed. Then he was paralyzed again, unable to control his body as millions of nerve endings registered the pain.

When he recovered, Luis was shaking a finger in his face. "You only answer questions, Ty. That was unwelcome commentary. Now, let's try again. Why would my mother go all the way to Virginia to steal a child when, if she wanted one, there's plenty of children in Arizona?"

Ty was getting tired of explaining this. "I don't know, but I have evidence."

"What kind of evidence?"

"Evidence she was in Virginia." Ty struggled to make his muscles work, his neurons scrambled by the high voltage. He moved his cuffed hands to his shirt pocket, pulling out the folded picture from the Petro Panda. He held it out toward Luis.

Luis came forward and snatched the damp picture from Ty, unfolding it. He stared at it for a moment before smacking his fingers into the image dismissively. "All I see is an old lady with a dog. What does this prove? Where did you even get this picture?"

"The Virginia State Police," Ty lied. "The FBI has it too. They have reason to believe this lady used the puppy to lure the child into her RV."

Luis shrugged dramatically. "If that's the case, my friend, then why are you here and not the FBI? Are you such a big deal that they send you to do the government's work for them? Are you some kind of super-agent or something? Super security guard?"

Some of the men laughed appreciatively as Luis played to his audience.

"I'm not alone," Ty said. "You already know men raided your mother's house this morning. If you are as plugged into that neighborhood as it appears, then I'm sure you know they're combing through the house right now. In fact, I was at the FBI field office for a meeting this morning. They were trying to determine the identity of the dead baby found on your mother's altar. You think they're going to let that go? You think they're going to forget a dead baby on an altar?"

That information took Luis by surprise. He approached Ty and knelt down, glaring at him. "What dead baby?"

"They said it was old and dried out. Possibly a newborn."

"If you're lying to me, you'll die screaming," Luis promised. "I'll peel you alive."

"I'm not lying. Ask Tia who the baby was. Was it one she stole? Was it one of her own? Could be it's your own brother that she killed and offered to Santa Muerte."

Luis stood up and whipped the cattle prod back, ready to strike Ty with it. His eyes burned into Ty's, his mouth taut. Ty didn't flinch. He was enjoying the disturbed look on Luis's face. Was it the idea that his own mother kept a dead baby on the shrine in her bedroom that so disturbed him or was it the idea that it may have been a brother to him?

"This still doesn't explain why you're the one going around and asking questions, *gringo*. You're not a cop. You're not FBI."

"I'm asking questions because you know the feds have their heads up their asses. They can't do anything without meeting about it. By the time they're done meeting about this, Gretchen Wells will be dead." Ty intentionally used her name, hoping he could make them see the victim as a person.

Luis hesitated, scratching his chin as he thought. He seemed unsure of what to do next.

"That's her name," Ty repeated, latching onto the opportunity. "Gretchen Wells. She's ten years old and likes puppies. You have any children, Luis? You have any little girls? How would you feel if your daughter was stolen like that? What would you tell your wife? Would you shrug it off because that's the business you're in?"

Luis launched himself across the room and grabbed Ty by the bloody stubble of his hair. He drew the cattle prod back, ready to pound Ty in the face with it. Ty didn't try to turn away.

"That is *not* the business I'm in, my friend."

"Then convince your mother of that. Tell her to let Gretchen go. Return the child to her mother."

Luis released Ty and backed away, pointing a blood-stained finger at him. "You're never leaving here alive. I've heard enough of your lies. Enough of your bullshit."

"I don't care if I leave here or not," Ty said, his jaw set. "With the shit I go through every day, I welcome death."

Luis nodded his head in Ty's direction, as if granting him a favor. "Then you shall have it, my friend. Don't let it be said we're not gracious." He turned away from Ty and headed from the building.

As he passed his men, he said, "Cuff him to a post. Put a man on this building. The rest of you get back to work. You all have jobs to do. The cops could show up at any time."

40

C liff Mathis had just gotten off a conference call with his attorney when his secretary buzzed him.

"Mr. Mathis, I have a lady on the phone who says her name is Jessica from the Wasteland. She wants to speak to you."

"I'll take the call."

He figured his receptionist had to be wondering what this "wasteland" business was about but she knew better than to ask. He dealt with a lot of people who didn't use real names because of the nature of their work. She probably assumed it was code for something.

He picked up the call. "Cliff Mathis."

"Hey, Cliff, I know you're busy and I apologize for bothering you, but I'm worried about Ty. I know this isn't your problem but he hasn't been active on social media for an unusually long time. I tried calling his phone but he didn't answer."

Cliff sighed. "It's a messed up situation, Jessica. The guy's heart is in the right place. It was a ballsy move, chasing these people across the country when no one believed him, but there's been a hitch."

"What kind of hitch?"

"The case broke open last night. I can't say a lot about that part of it, but basically Ty stuck his nose where it didn't belong. Now there's no doubt that he was right. He found the proof he was looking for."

"Thank God."

"There's a problem, though. They had a task force meeting about the case this morning. I was invited in as a consultant since Ty reached out to me. Ty was there too. There was the FBI and some local PD. Turns out Ty has some legal issue hanging over him in Virginia. He has an assault charge pending against him."

"You're kidding!"

"I wish I was. The investigator who flew in from Virginia to consult on the case insisted on pursuing it. She had papers to extradite Ty back to Virginia."

"That's messed up. He was just trying to help. Doesn't that matter?"

"I don't know the story," Cliff said. "All I know is they were going to ambush him in the meeting with an arrest. Everyone there thought it was bullshit. They assume the real reason behind it was that Ty must have embarrassed the cops. They were pissed at him for being right and making them look bad."

"So did they arrest him? Is that why I can't reach him?"

"He's not in jail. I don't know if he overheard something or his spidey-senses went off, but he excused himself to go to the restroom and never came back. They couldn't find him. The investigator from Virginia was pissed. She wanted to track him down but no one was willing to devote resources to it when a little girl is missing."

"I'm concerned about the girl but I'm concerned about Ty too," Jessica admitted. *"He seems like he's together, but he suffers from the same problems a lot of us do. That's a pretty raw deal to spend your own time chasing down a lead and then get arrested. He deserves better than that."*

"I know the FBI agent running the case," Cliff said. "I'll give him a call and follow up. I walked out of the meeting today after they mentioned extraditing Ty. I don't know how things ended. They might know something more."

"Can you let me know if you hear anything?" Jessica asked. *"I know you're busy, but I'd like to know he's safe."*

"I'd be glad to. I'll call him as soon as I get off the phone."

After he hung up, he found Agent Esposito's number and shot him a text:

Hey, this is Cliff Mathis. Don't want to bother you but did Ty Stone ever turn up?

His phone rang about fifteen seconds later. It was Agent Esposito.

"Hey, Cliff," Esposito said when he answered, "*my mouth works faster than my fingers. Just wanted to let you know that Stone hasn't turned up but we're not really looking very hard. That investigator from Virginia is an asshole and no one wants to cooperate with her.*"

"Any progress on the girl?"

"*We're trying to locate a piece of property supposedly owned by her son but we can't get a handle on it. He doesn't have the same last name as her and it's probably buried under layers of corporate entities. We can't get a warrant if we can't find the damn place.*"

"Well, I know you're busy but do you mind to let me know if Stone turns up? He's got people worried about him. I guess I'm one of them. Kind of a raw deal to get this far and end up in jail."

"*Roger that, Cliff. I'll keep you in the loop.*"

Cliff placed his phone on the desk and settled back into his chair. He laced his fingers together and stared at the wall, deep in thought. Reaching some conclusion, he stood and placed his palm on a biometric scanner, unlocking his wall safe. He pulled out several phones, checking adhesive labels on the back until he found the one he was looking for. He closed the safe and returned to his desk, powering up the phone.

One of the things about a company like Door Kickers International was that they weren't limited by some of the same constraints that law enforcement was. There were certain things DKI couldn't easily do, like get court-ordered access into someone's financials or phone records. However, there were other things they could do more easily than law enforcement, such as maintain stables of paid confidential informants. That got too sticky in law enforcement. There were too many strings attached to money when it flowed from the government to criminals. Cliff wasn't encumbered by those same issues. He dialed a number.

"Hello?" answered a cautious voice.

"This is Cliff Mathis. Can you talk?"

"Give me a second." Cliff heard the guy mumbling as he made some excuses and moved to some place he could talk freely. *"Go ahead."*

"There was an old woman gangster in Barrio Libre that went by the name Tia. She has a son who lives in the area. I think his name is Luis but I don't have a last name. I've got 5Gs for you if you can get me his address in one hour."

The man on the other end hesitated, thinking it over, probably trying to decide whether pursuing this information might expose him to any life-threatening scrutiny. *"Okay, I'm on it. Call you back at this number?"*

"Affirmative."

They ended the call. Cliff picked up his other cellphone and called one of his contractors. "John, this is Cliff. Can you get us three more local guys who can work in one hour? The job is unconfirmed but it's local. They'll only need their personal gear. We'll be using the chopper so have it ready."

"Roger that, Cliff. See you in an hour."

41

"Did it ever fucking occur to you that kidnapping a child from a crowded truck stop might *not* be the best idea?" Luis asked. "Since when is this the way you do business?"

Tia sat in a lounge chair in the shade of Luis's back porch. She was sipping agua fresca with a splash of tequila and smoking a cigarette. She wore a blue sweat suit, a handful of rings, and a chunky beaded necklace. Her wraparound sunglasses hid her eyes. "I don't tell you how to run your business."

Luis was ready to pull his hair out. His mother had never liked anyone telling her what to do. Surrendering her neighborhood to the cartels had been a bitter pill to swallow, and she hadn't been the same since. Now he had to wonder if she was losing her mind, going soft in her head. To make matters worse, she was intentionally obtuse with him. There were never any simple, straight answers. Every response was sarcastic, accusing, or derogatory. He honestly didn't know why he bothered with her. It wasn't like she'd ever made an effort to be a mother to him.

Luis stood up and lit a cigarette. He paced the wide patio. "I've never known you to snatch a girl off the street, Mother. You always find girls who want to come with you. Correct?"

"That's true," Tia replied. "It didn't work out this time. The girl I was supposed to pick up didn't show up. We drove all that way, all the way to Virginia, and she quit answering her messages. I'd promised El Clavo a girl and to come home empty-handed would make me look bad. I'm done with looking bad."

"Look bad to whom?" Luis asked, waving his arm with a flourish. "There will always be other girls. They're born every day. Why take this kind of risk?"

"I prayed to the saint. I asked for a girl and she gave me one. When I saw the child, there was no doubt. She was put there for me."

Luis took a drag off his cigarette. "Santa Muerte?"

Tia sipped her drink. "Don't act like you don't know which saint I'm talking about. Don't act like you've never asked her for anything. You know how she works. You know she answers prayers."

Luis brushed it off with a wave of his arm.

"Don't insult Holy Death," Tia whispered. "You know better."

"It's a superstition of old ladies and the ignorant!"

"So that's what you think of your mother? An ignorant old lady?" She flipped her cigarette butt into the yard, something she knew irritated Luis. Especially when there was an ashtray beside her.

Luis frowned at the smoldering butt. "Don't get all sentimental on me now, Tia. You were never a mother to any of us."

"I raised you to be what you are now."

Luis laughed. "You did no such thing. I did this! I earned this!" He indicated his estate with a sweep of his hand. "With my own two hands, I earned this. If I learned anything from you, it was from the bad examples you set. I learned how *not* to do things."

Fidelia stuck out her chin and turned away from her son. "You are ungrateful to your mother and disrespectful of Santa Muerte."

"I call bullshit where I see it, Mother. Now I have to fix this problem you've created. I will not have your sloppiness put me at risk any more than it already has. I'm going to deal with this once and for all."

"How do you intend to do that?"

"You're going to Mexico for a while. You've poked the hornet's nest and I can't keep you in my home. We'll find a safe place for you in a small town where no one talks."

"What about the girl? What about the money she'll bring from El Clavo?"

Luis finished his own cigarette, crumpling the butt into an ashtray, and giving his mother a pointed stare. "You'll get no money. Tonight, my people will kill the man who followed you here from Virginia, the girl too. I'll stick them in a hole in the desert far away from here. Then hopefully the trail goes cold and this will all just fade away."

Tia stood in a huff. "If you can just hang onto her for a few days, she'll bring good money."

"Are you crazy?" Luis demanded, raising his voice. "I expect the police to show up here tomorrow because of you! They're probably working on a search warrant right now. I have to devote all my resources to making sure there's nothing illegal on this property. This is extra work you created. You're costing me money."

Tia waved Luis off and walked away. She wanted to stomp off, but as an overweight old woman in Crocs the gesture lost some of its impact.

"Where are you going?"

"If your mother might trouble you to borrow a car, I need to go into the city."

"What for?"

Tia stopped and replied without turning to look at him. "The botanica. I need a few things if I'm going to Mexico."

"Surely anything you get at a botanica here, you can find at a botanica in Mexico. Probably even cheaper."

She was hearing none of it. "Can I borrow a car or not?"

"No," Luis said. "You've been drinking and you can't be trusted. I'll have someone drive you." He wasn't going to let her out of his sight.

"Fine then," Tia spat. "I'll be in the kitchen. Have them meet me there."

Luis pulled his phone from his pocket and punched a number from his contacts. "I need you to run my mother into the city."

Though the man agreed, Luis could hear the reluctance in his voice. It was a job no one wanted. The old lady could be a handful.

He replaced the phone in his pocket. His mother had become a pain in the ass over the last couple of years. She wasn't as cautious as she should be. She didn't understand technology well enough to take the proper precautions. She was going to end up getting herself thrown in jail, possibly even implicating him in the process. He should probably be burying her in the desert too.

Though he'd meant it sarcastically, that was a thought worth considering. She was his mother but what had that ever meant in the context of their relationship? She hadn't been warm and nurturing. He'd been tucked into bed by *putas* who worked for his mother. She was more likely to cook meth than bake cookies. Then there was the time he'd found a human head in the freezer when he was looking for a Hot Pocket.

Luis pulled his phone back out of his pocket. He dialed Ramon, the man he'd left watching Ty. "Hey, Ramon, have a second barrel handy." He ended the call and headed for his office. He had a lot to think about.

42

I t was Alvarez who showed up in the kitchen as Tia's driver. That was fine with her. Alvarez had come up as an enforcer in her crew, when she had a crew. He collected payments and drove off pimps who tried to steal her girls. He was a physically powerful man, even with a few years on him. Perhaps not the sharpest knife in the drawer but that was not a detractor in a business where loyalty mattered more than brains. Besides, no leader wanted soldiers smart enough to plot against them. It was better to hire men who were comfortable as followers.

Alvarez wasn't spooked by Tia in the way many of the younger men were. Everyone knew she prayed to Santa Muerte, as did many of them, but some thought her to be *bruja*, a witch. How else did a woman become so powerful in a man's business? Command such respect? Her appearance, with the crazy eye makeup and the long, sharp nails, didn't help.

While Tia had heard the whispers, she didn't care if they thought she was a witch. She was long past caring what anyone thought of her. All she wanted was the money and respect she deserved. Aside from that, they could think whatever they wanted.

"Where are we going, Tia?"

"A botanica in the city."

Alvarez nodded thoughtfully. "I know one closer."

She shook her head. "That's not *my* botanica. Mine is in Wakefield and that's where I need to go."

Alvarez shrugged deferentially. He didn't care. Work was work, and at least this was in an air-conditioned vehicle. It beat helping the other men clean out the ranch.

Soon they were on the highway heading toward the city. While Alvarez would have been completely comfortable not speaking at all, Tia intentionally engaged him. She brought up stories from the old days, when they were both young and hungry.

"You were so scary," Tia teased. "No one wanted to mess with you. No one would steal my girls when they found out you were protecting them."

Alvarez cracked a smile at that. He'd been young and crazy, anxious to make a name for himself.

"You remember that night we went to the casino to party because we'd scored big? We all felt rich and dangerous, like we were big time gangsters. I took you as my bodyguard because it made me feel important to need a bodyguard, like I was a celebrity or something. You remember that, Alvarez?"

He gave a single nod, not taking his eyes from the road.

"You remember how that night ended, *el amor*?" Tia gave Alvarez a coy look, then reached over and tweaked him on the thigh.

He indeed remembered. The grin spreading on his face and the sparkle in his eye told her he did.

"Cocaine, tequila, and passion," she whispered in a throaty voice.

Alvarez cleared his throat. "I was much younger then, Tia."

"We both were, but you were an animal." She fanned herself, as if the memory threatened to overcome her.

"I was drunk. Had it not been for the cocaine, I'd have passed out on the floor."

"Well, you didn't pass out. You left me with a memory that puts a smile on an old woman's face."

Alvarez's grin faded as he lost himself in the old memories, floating like motes of dust stirred by Tia dragging him through the past. Much had happened to both of them since then. Some of it good, some it not so good. They rode in silence for the remaining twenty minutes, each lost in the grainy highlight reel of their youth, until Alvarez rolled to a stop in front of the botanica.

"You wait here," Tia said. "I have prayers and they're personal."

"As you wish," Alvarez said. He cracked his window open and lit a cigarette.

Tia sat looking at him. "Are you going to open an old lady's door or have you forgotten all your manners?"

Alvarez sighed and opened his door. He stood, hitched his belt, and went around to Tia's side where he held the door open for her. With a little effort, she worked herself out of the car and stood. She took a moment to straighten her clothes. Alvarez looked away, patiently waiting for her to move along so he could close the door and get back into the air-conditioned interior.

When she was clear, he shut the door and watched her shuffle toward the botanica in her baggy sweat suit, white socks, and yellow Crocs. He recalled a day when the view from this side had been much better. He shrugged, walked around the car, and got back inside.

Without knocking, Tia twisted the knob, calling out as she entered. "Lucia! Sweetie, are you home?"

Tia knew she was, otherwise the door would have been locked, a note left on the door. Lucia rushed around the counter, took her by the arm, and escorted her to the small table where she did readings.

"I'm so glad to see you in good health, Miss Tia," Lucia said. Though she had watched the man from Virginia being taken away, she didn't mention it. You survived in this neighborhood by not seeing such things and, most certainly, by not talking about those things you didn't see. She wouldn't bring it up unless Tia did.

"Good to see you too, Lucia. That pink looks amazing in your hair. If I was a few years younger, I would wear colors like that."

"You still could," Lucia said. "I know a girl who's good with colors."

"Too much trouble for me these days." Tia patted her hair. "I like simple."

"Well, if you change your mind, you just let me know."

Tia settled into the wobbly little chair, setting her purse on the floor. She became serious, pausing before continuing. "I'm so glad you were in today."

Lucia slid into the seat across the table. "Miss Tia, I'm always in for you. If I'm not here, you call me, and I'll come in just for you. You know that. I'll take good care of you."

Tia reached across the table and patted Lucia on the back of her hand, a gesture of appreciation. She withdrew her hands, resting them on the table palms down, fingers flared, displaying her nails.

Lucia took the hint. "Oh my God, Miss Tia. Your nails are so beautiful."

Tia smiled. "They're a lot of trouble. It's my one indulgence." Her smile faded. "There is so much, child. I don't even know where to start."

Lucia lit a candle between them. "What weighs on your heart?"

Tia sighed. "I'm wondering if I have disappointed Holy Death in some way. If I have fallen out of her favor. She blessed me for several years now and I honor her with my tributes every day. Several times a day, in fact."

"I know you are a devout and spiritual woman."

"Thank you," Tia said. "I like to think so, but I recently had a business matter fall through. It's nothing I want to go into detail about but Holy Death has always looked after me in matters of business. Yet everything around this venture has gone wrong. Now I have to leave the country for a...family matter. I am not certain when I will be coming back."

"It sounds like you require a strong blessing."

"I do," Tia said, nodding adamantly. "Perhaps more."

Lucia rose from the table and selected several multi-colored candles. They began as one color but all had black bases. One began burning as red but ended in black. Another began burning as gold then turned to black. She found a glass bottle with a corked lid and a handwritten label. She tipped a drop of the amber oil onto a fingertip and anointed each candle. She placed them at the base of the life-sized Santa Muerte that dominated the room, then placed two pillows before the statue.

She went to Tia and helped her up. "We need to kneel. I will say a prayer and you need to repeat each line after me."

Tia nodded, her joints cracking as she got to her feet. She stood before the shrine, slowly lowering herself to the pillow with Lucia's help. When Tia was comfortable, Lucia joined her on the second pillow. She began rocking back and forth, her eyes closed, the candle-light flickering on her face. She moaned and whispered while Tia sat beside her, eyes shut in her own beseeching.

"I will pray now," Lucia said. "Repeat after me."

Tia did as requested and the pair prayed until the candles melted. When the flames flickered noisily in the puddles of melted wax, Lucia rose and helped Tia to her feet, helped her to a chair, and took the seat across from her.

"This will help you. It was powerful. When you return from wher-ever you're going, come see me. Let me know if this helped. If not, we'll try something else."

"Before I leave I need some herbs," Tia said.

"What condition are we treating?"

"Rats," Tia said.

"Rats?" Lucia asked, raising an eyebrow. "Have you considered traps?"

Tia directed her gaze toward the young witch. Gone was the feeble old lady, replaced by the commanding presence she concealed beneath. "Rats are stealing my lemonade. I need something I can put in there that will take care of them. It should be something rats won't detect until it's too late. No taste, no odor. Do you have anything like that?"

Lucia nodded. "I do. Such tinctures are very powerful and very expensive."

Tia dug into her purse and removed a roll of bills secured by a rubber band. "Have I not always treated you well?"

"You have, Miss Tia, and I meant no disrespect. I just wanted to make sure you knew in advance. It will take me a few minutes to prepare the tincture. Do you want to pick it up later or wait?"

"I'll wait. I'm not sure when I'll be able to come back." She pulled a pack of cigarettes from her purse and looked around. "Can I smoke in here?"

Lucia nodded. "*Si*, but The Skinny Lady requires a tobacco offering if you use it in her presence."

Tia removed two cigarettes and pushed up from her chair. Lucia started to rush to her aid but Tia held a hand up. "I got it."

She lit two cigarettes, placing one in an incense holder at the base of the tall Santa Muerte statue. She returned to her chair with the other, watching as Lucia meticulously crushed herbs with a mortar and pestle. Tia licked her thumb and counted out a thousand dollars in worn bills. She fanned them on the table and used the glass candleholder to weigh them down, then banded the remainder of the bills and tucked them back into her purse.

Fifteen minutes later, Tia departed with a warm hug from Lucia. The sunlight was blinding after the dark interior of the botanica and brought a stabbing pain in her head. When she finally got her wrap-around sunglasses on, Alvarez was at her side. He reached for her bag but she yanked it away.

"I got it, I got it," she said. "Just get me home before Luis starts whining like a little bitch."

"He's already called once," Alvarez said, opening the car door for her.

"See? I told you." Tia slipped into the cool interior of the car and leaned back in the seat. It was heavenly.

After Alvarez got in the car, they drove in silence. Tia was tired. She'd like to have a nap that afternoon, if she had time. She thought about her visit to the botanica. So many good things had come her way when she began worshipping Santa Muerte. When she placed the bones of her dead child on that altar, it was like plugging the passcode into a vault door. The world opened up to her and she found her little niche in providing girls to El Clavo. Although it was not like running a crew again, it was something. She was earning money and she was in the life.

The idea that she could buy such power by offering Holy Death a cigarette and an anointed candle was laughable. She'd thought the puppy, an actual living creature, might get her something. Maybe it had. She wasn't locked up and she wasn't dead.

She'd received a response to her prayers in the botanica. At one point, she'd cracked her eyes open and was certain the jeweled eyes in that skull were looking directly at her. Santa Muerte was telling her that only blood bought power. A black candle might buy you protection from an enemy's bad juju but that was it. If you wanted big things, you made big offerings. She needed to offer blood.

Tonight, before Luis whisked her across the border, Santa Muerte would have her blood.

43

———

Ty was secured around a support pole, his hands cuffed in front of him. To conserve energy, he sat down and leaned forward, resting his shoulder against the pole. The man assigned to watch him played on his phone, took a few calls, and smoked the remainder of a crumpled joint he pulled from his shirt pocket. Ty bided his time. The cuffs weren't a problem but he couldn't get out of them under the watchful eye of his guard, a man they called Ramon.

Ramon's phone rang and he must have been receiving instructions because all of his responses were limited to a single word. When the call ended, he checked Ty's cuffs and verified they were secure. Satisfied, he left through the wide rolling door and Ty heard his boots crunching on the stone road. Unsure of how much time he had, Ty reached for the cuff of his jeans and groped around. A non-metallic handcuff key was inserted into a slit in the hem. Were he to be wanded or pass through a metal detector, the key wouldn't draw any attention. A single stitch kept the key from slipping loose. Ty tugged on the key and the stitch broke easily.

He deftly unlocked the cuffs and stood, rubbing his wrists. He rushed toward the sliding door, taking cover and glancing out. He heard metallic banging in the distance, then found his guard headed in his direction with a steel drum balanced on his shoulder like a keg of beer.

The man staggered toward the door, grunting from the effort of balancing the awkward barrel. Ramon wore a handgun on his right hip, the holster exposed. If Ty could get control of the gun before the man set the barrel down, that would be ideal. Above all, he didn't want any shots fired. That would only draw unwanted company.

As soon as Ramon was through the door, just as Ty prepared to step in behind him and slip the gun from his holster, it all went sideways. Ramon immediately noticed the missing prisoner, the cuffs in a pile at the base of the post. He went to set the barrel down so he could get a hand on his gun. Anticipating this, Ty charged at him, trapping the barrel between his body and Ramon's. Forced to backpedal, Ramon had both hands on the barrel, trying to push back against his attacker. It was pointless. Ty hit him like it was football practice and Ramon was a blocking sled, shoving with short, choppy steps.

Ramon lost his balance and fell backward, his hands staying on the barrel as he tried to prevent it from rolling over his face. Unfortunately for him, that left everything below the waist unprotected. Ty dropped on the man's groin, crushing it beneath his knee. There was a hard exhalation and Ramon's body tensed, the barrel rolling noisily away from them.

Ty had a hand on Ramon's gun now and yanked it free of the kydex holster. Ramon was slowed by the groin strike but not out of the fight. This was clearly not his first brawl. He clutched desperately for control of his gun. Ty shifted his body, throwing a knee across Ramon's neck and cutting off his air. That worked. Ramon's hands flew up to shove at Ty's knee, attempting to move it enough to open his airway.

Ty shifted the gun in his hand and brought the butt down on Ramon's forehead, stunning him. A second blow followed, then a third, and Ramon's head tipped to the side, lights out. Ty climbed off Ramon, then dragged him to the pole where he himself had been secured. He wrenched the unconscious man around, cuffing him with his back to the pole. Ty unbuckled Ramon's belt, yanked it free of the loops, and lashed it around the man's neck, strapping him to the pole. He didn't tighten it completely, wanting Ramon to be able to breathe. He needed him alive a little longer.

Ty frisked the guy, finding and keeping two spare mags, his cell-phone, a fixed blade knife, and a ring of keys. Ty used Ramon's own fingerprint to unlock the phone, then disabled the password. He wasn't certain he remembered any phone numbers off the top of his head, other than 9-1-1, and it was too early for that. He needed information first. He needed to find out where the girl was. Were these some of Tia's associates? Did they work for her son? Had she sent the cartel after him?

He placed his knuckles against Ramon's sternum and rocked them back and forth, applying intense pressure. The man squirmed, attempting to twist away from the pain, and his eyes cracked open. Rivulets of blood ran down his forehand and from the shattered bridge of his nose. He gave Ty a scowl, a look that said this wasn't over yet.

"Where's the girl?" Ty demanded. "Is she here?"

"I don't know anything about a girl."

Without warning or preamble, Ty unsheathed the fixed blade knife he'd taken from Ramon and buried it in the man's thigh. He was certain it struck bone. He left it embedded there, allowing Ramon to see what had been done to him, allowing him to taste a little of what Ty was capable of.

Ty leaned closer. "You can see that I'm not in the mood to fuck around. I'll ask again. Tia took a child in Virginia and I need to find her. Where is the girl?"

"They'll kill you," Ramon hissed.

Ty yanked the knife free from the man's thigh and immediately drove it into the top of the other thigh. He slapped a hand over

Ramon's mouth, turned his head away, and waited for the scream to subside. Ty removed his bloody hand and grinned. "You've got a lot of places to cut and I'm not squeamish. I suggest you start talking."

"I can't—"

"I don't have time for this!"

Ty yanked a cowboy boot off Ramon's foot, then peeled off a rancid, sweaty sock. He shoved the sock into the protesting man's mouth. Ramon gagged and pushed at it with his tongue but couldn't remove it.

"You're going to need that," Ty whispered. He moved back down to his foot and locked it in his powerful grip, momentarily second-guessing his choice. Did this dude ever wash his feet? They smelled like a dumpster. With his other hand, Ty shot a powerful palm strike aimed at Ramon's big toe.

Ramon's body arched and contracted as the big toe snapped. It stuck out at ninety degrees to its original position, now pointing at Ramon's face.

Ty smiled. "Hurts, doesn't it? Remember there are nineteen more fingers and toes."

Though Ramon couldn't speak, his tearful eyes revealed the level of pain he was experiencing.

"This is where we test your level of commitment, Ramon. I'm going to twist that broken toe until it separates from your foot like a tomato coming off the vine. Can you imagine what that feels like? The bone grinding? The muscle tearing?"

Ramon started to jabber, trying to speak around his gag.

Ty reached up and yanked the sock from his mouth. "Talk to me, Ramon."

"The house," he groaned. "They're keeping a young girl in the basement of the house. I don't know if that's who you're talking about or not but that's all I know. She just showed up here last night." He began sobbing, fixated on his mangled toe.

"If you would quit staring at it, it might not hurt so badly," Ty said. He shoved the sock back into Ramon's mouth, ignoring the protests.

"I'm leaving you alive, Ramon. If I find you've lied to me, I'll be back, and we'll talk again."

He removed the knife from Ramon's leg and cleaned the blade on the man's pants. He stashed the knife in his belt, ran to the door, and slipped out into the brutal heat of the day.

44

When they parked on the circular stone drive at the house, Tia remained in the car, waiting for Alvarez to walk around and open her door. As he circled the hood, he gave her a sideways glance to let her know what he thought of the demands she put on him. She smiled broadly, her lips caked in fresh pink lipstick, but he didn't smile back.

"Thank you," she said when he tugged the door open and held it for her.

"You're welcome. Will you be requiring anything else? Do you need me to carry your tiny little bag to the house?"

"No, smartass, I got it."

"Then if you'll excuse me, I have matters to attend to." Alvarez closed the door behind her and returned to the driver's seat. Luis didn't like the front of the house cluttered up with cars, preferring they park them all around back.

Tia headed toward the door in her ambling, unhurried gait, Crocs flapping against the sidewalk. She opened one side of the massive hand-carved entry doors and stepped inside. The house was cool and dark, the walls thick enough to muffle the sound of the car pulling away from the house. She never cared for this gigantic house with its fancy furniture and expensive decor. She didn't know who her son thought he was that he needed such a house.

"Hello?" she called, uncertain if anyone was even home.

"In my office," Luis replied. "I need to speak with you."

"Give me one minute. I need to set my bags down." Tia walked to the kitchen, placing her purse and shopping bag on the table.

The house was quiet. Luis's children were in school. They were technically her grandchildren but she wasn't that close to them. She suspected Luis kept them away on purpose, which was fine with her since most kids were brats. Her daughter-in-law was gone shopping in the city, something she did every day. Tia didn't care for her either. Aside from Luis's men, it looked to be just the two of them on the property. That was perfect.

She made two tall glasses of lemonade. To hers, she added a long pour of tequila. To Luis's, she added the special tincture she'd obtained at the botanica. She took a careful sip of hers, since the addition of the liquor had filled it to the top of the glass. She picked up both drinks and headed toward her son's office.

He was on the phone when she went into the expansive room with its exposed beams and large desk. She placed one of the glasses of lemonade on his desk. He frowned at her, surprised by the gesture. It wasn't like her to do things like that. He suspected she was trying to butter him up, perhaps trying to change his mind. She sipped from her glass and looked out the window while she waited for him to complete his call.

"Jesus Christ, Tia. This smells like straight tequila," Luis said, placing his phone face down on the desk.

"That's mine you smell. I need a little tonic each day before my afternoon nap. Yours has no tequila."

He took a sip of his lemonade, eyes on Tia, confirming his drink wasn't half-tequila, like hers. Satisfied that it wasn't, he took a longer drink. "There will be no afternoon nap today, Tia, unless you take it in the back seat of a car. You're leaving as soon as we're done here." He took another sip of his lemonade and placed it on his desk, sitting back in his chair to measure her reaction.

"What about the girl?" she asked.

"I'll clean up your mess."

Tia took a seat across from his desk, settling into a nice leather chair. "That's not what I mean, Luis. She's my property and if you're taking her, I'm owed money. That's the way this works."

Luis pounded a fist on his desk. "You're owed nothing!"

"When one pimp steals from another, payment is customary." She was aware putting it in those terms would infuriate him.

Luis rolled his eyes heavenward. "This is not me stealing your girl. This is me covering your ass to protect myself."

"That's not how I look at it."

"I don't care how you look at it. You're lucky I'm not sticking you in a hole in the desert, because I fucking considered it. You're a crazy old woman who thinks she's still a player but you're not. You're old news, Mother. You're history. You cause me nothing but trouble and inconvenience. I'm done with it. You're leaving for Mexico and you should consider that payment – the fact I'm letting you live."

Simmering, Tia took a sip of her drink and wouldn't meet his eyes. "I can't believe you'd talk to me that way."

Luis erupted into a loud, genuine laugh. "Don't even go there. Don't even play the 'mother' card with me, Tia. You've never been concerned with anyone but yourself. It's too late to pretend there's any feelings between us."

Tia didn't deny it. "If you won't let me sell her to El Clavo, how about we ask for a ransom? They do this in Mexico all the time, right? It's big business, kidnapping."

Luis was shaking his head in frustration. He took a sip of his drink, rested his elbows on his desk, and let his head sag into his palms. "There's a reason that's successful in Mexico. The cartels control the whole fucking country. It may work here one day but we're a long way from that point."

"What if I take her to Mexico with me? I can hide her out until you have the ransom. I'll split it with you."

"No!" Luis shouted, shooting to his feet. "This is *done*. This was your last screw-up, Mother!"

With those words, Luis froze, his face turning bright red.

Though she'd been averting her eyes, his sudden silence caught her attention. Tia turned to look at him and saw his eyes bulging from his head, his mouth contorted into a violent rictus. His skin was flushed a brilliant red. Tia took a sip of her drink and watched placidly.

"Help...me," he gasped, staggering. He tried to sit down but couldn't control his muscles. His rigid body pushed the wheeled chair away and he dropped onto his back on the floor. She could see his feet jerking as he began to have a seizure.

Tia considered getting up but didn't need to see this. She had a suspicion of how it ended, if the tincture was all it was promised to be. She heard steps behind her and craned her neck around in a panic. She hadn't expected anyone.

Alvarez was standing in the doorway, eyes wide. He could hear the gurgling and choking sounds coming from behind the desk. "What's going on here?" He rushed around the desk and crouched at Luis's side. "What's wrong?"

Luis was unable to answer, clutching desperately at Alvarez's arm. White foam filled his mouth and ran down his face. Blood vessels were bursting in his eyes.

"I think he's having a heart attack or something?" Tia said, getting to her feet, and taking another sip of her drink. She made no attempt to hide her lack of concern.

Alvarez popped up from behind the desk. "And you're just sitting on your ass watching? Why haven't you called 9-1-1?" He reached for the phone.

As he picked the desk phone up from its base, Tia placed her hand on his. Alvarez paused, looking from Tia's hand to her eyes. She pressed his hand back down and he conceded, hanging up the phone. He understood now what was taking place. Tia was letting Luis die.

"We're not calling anyone. There's nothing to be done," Tia whispered.

When Tia reached forward and picked up Luis's lemonade glass, awareness dawned on Alvarez. "You did this to him?"

Tia stepped to the French doors and flung the contents of the glass onto the patio. It would evaporate in minutes. Uncertain of what to do with the glass itself, she tossed it into the landscaping. When she turned around, Alvarez was in her face.

"What the *fuck* did you to do him, Tia?"

"I did to him what was done to me. One day you're the dog, the next you're the rock other dogs piss on. I got tired of being pissed on," she said flatly. "Luis is no longer in charge here."

Alvarez turned away, rubbing his temples with his fingers, pacing frantically. "You just can't do things like this. This is not a street gang he works for. This is the cartel! They'll kill you. They'll kill all of us!"

"I have no fear, Alvarez. I'm protected by The Skinny Lady. I cannot say the same for you."

"You crazy old bitch," Alvarez mumbled.

"I can make this simple for you, old friend. You return my property to me and you give me a car. Once I'm gone, you call his bosses and tell them whatever you wish. Blame me, if you want. I don't care."

Alvarez returned to Luis's side and confirmed he was dead. The time for getting help had passed. "What about his wife? What about your grandchildren?"

Tia shrugged. "Tell her there's been a problem at the house and it's not safe for them to return. Put them in a hotel with a guard. If she understands Luis's business, this life, she'll respect the seriousness of that."

Alvarez looked at Luis's body, refusing to believe what he saw. "You are a cold woman, Tia. I've known you for a long time but I can't believe you killed your own son."

"I killed a man who stole from me. Now are you going to do as I asked, Alvarez, or do I need to be concerned about you too?"

Alvarez turned and found Tia had removed a shiny automatic from her purse. It was leveled in his direction. He looked into her eyes. "I am no threat to you, Tia. We go back a long time and I respect that history."

"I feel the same way. Killing you might even bother me a little."

Alvarez laughed but there was no humor in his eyes. "What do you want me to do?"

"Leave me with Luis. I need to say my goodbyes to my niño. Then bring me a car. I expect the girl to be in there. Can you do that?"

Alvarez nodded. "What about the prisoner in the barn?"

"Kill him as soon as I'm gone. Bury him somewhere off the property. Then I would advise you to call your cartel associates and let them know Luis had a heart attack. Let them decide if they want you to call an ambulance or not. They'll give you instructions. I suggest you not let the men see him. You don't want them asking questions. You don't want them starting rumors this wasn't a natural death."

Alvarez gave his dead boss a final, grim nod and left the room. He closed the door behind him.

Tia stepped around the desk and stopped in her tracks, momentarily frozen by the gruesome visage of her dead son. His red face and frothy mouth, his open, sightless eyes. She fished a small statue of Santa Muerte from her pocket, then awkwardly knelt on the floor, using the desk to lower herself. She held the tiny statue in such a way that the empty sockets gazed upon the dead body of her son.

"Can you see this, Holy Death? Do you see what I am willing to do for you? I give you the flesh of my flesh. The blood of my blood. All I ask is your blessing. Protect me and grant me what I ask."

She used the desk to raise herself back up. The motion left her lightheaded and she stood there for a moment, gathering herself. When she was done, she drained her glass of lemonade, belched, and left the room.

C liff Mathis was barreling toward the airport in his 1979 Bronco when the phone in the passenger seat rang. Had the phone in his pocket rang, it could have been anyone. *This* ringing phone could only be one person. He hoped like hell there was some good news. He snatched it up and took the call.

"Mathis."

"Gray Mesa Ranch. Take I-19 to West McGee Ranch Road. It's about ten miles out. There's a sign."

"You sure?"

"Positive. Talked to someone who'd been there."

"What's the security like?"

"He's cartel. What do you think?"

"Got it," Cliff replied.

"When do I get my money?"

"If your info is accurate, I'll have it for you tomorrow. You still have that card I gave you?"

"Yeah."

"I'll put the five thousand on it tomorrow if this pans out. Thanks." Cliff powered the phone down, stashing it in the center console.

In ten more minutes, he hastily parked by DKI's private hangar. A shiny black Bell 412 had already been rolled out. The chopper was leased for Cliff's company by a charity that supported their anti-trafficking efforts. A team of men sitting in the hangar stopped talking at his arrival.

"I've got an address. You guys ready to scramble?"

"We're ready. What's our loadout?" John, the man who'd assembled the team on such short notice, replied.

"Non-lethal," Cliff said. "Baton and stun guns, entry tools and optics. We'll pull up satellite footage when we're in the air but I don't have much to go on."

"What's the mission?" Badger asked. He was a burly guy known for his tenacious grappling. He was a brawler and would go toe-to-toe with anyone.

"Not much to go on," Cliff said. "More of a hunch than anything. Brother of ours from Special Forces tracked a missing child here on his own dime. The FBI now confirms her DNA is present in the RV suspected of transporting her. The woman who allegedly snatched her is MIA. Cops raided her home this morning. The ranch we're dropping in on belongs to her son and we're going to see if the suspect is hiding out there, possibly with the missing child."

"So there hasn't been a confirmed sighting?" John asked.

"Negative," Cliff said. 'This is all a hunch. I'm doing this to support a brother who put a lot on the line to get things this far. He's dropped off the radar so we're carrying the ball."

The men nodded. They got it.

"Law enforcement joining the party?" Badger asked.

"I'm going to send them the address when we're in the air. It'll take them some time to verify it and get warrants in place, but we're not waiting. I'm not sure we have that kind of time."

"We're going rogue!" said another of the men, pumping his fist.

"Which is why we have to do this right," Cliff said.

46

W hen he was brought to the ranch, Ty was blindfolded and barely conscious. He was unfamiliar with what lay outside the barn where he'd been kept. He hurried to the outside corner of the metal structure and paused to look around. The sun was blinding, making his battered skull ache. In the distance, perhaps five hundred yards from his position, was a low, sprawling dwelling that had to be the main house. There was some decorative fencing, a watering trough, and some scattered red boulders along the road separating them, but not enough cover to make Ty feel safe. It was an exposed approach with very little cover if things got ugly.

Numerous other structures were within sight and he suspected some of them had to contain people. When he'd been interrogated by Luis, the man had backup. Ty couldn't assume the men he'd seen had been the extent of Luis's forces. There could be several times as many men as he'd seen.

He also had to assume these men would not hesitate to use the weapons they carried. These weren't ten dollar an hour security guards like Ty had once been. These were killers used to pulling the trigger and burying the evidence in the vast Arizona desert. This was dirty cartel business, the world of black magic, skinned bodies, and decapitation. Ty had seen some ugly things over his years of deployment but this was a match for any of it. The Taliban had nothing on the cartels when it came to brutality.

Deciding the only thing that might break up his silhouette was the fence, Ty ran alongside it. The heat was ruthless, the sun pounding on his neck. Running along the ranch road, his adrenaline high and his mind laser-focused, he kept flashing back on Iraq. With such a callous, cruel enemy and such inhospitable terrain, that was exactly what it felt like. In fact, it was almost easier to believe he was back there than to think he was in the US again. He was not in the land of superstores and fast food. He was on a mission, and missions were part of his old life, not his current life. That was where he was in his head and it became harder with each passing second to overlay reality onto the situation in which he found himself.

Somewhere between that barn and the house, he quit fighting it. He let the struggle go. What did it matter where he was? What did it matter if this was the United States, Afghanistan, or Iraq? The mission was the same either way. Find Gretchen Wells and get her home. If he had to kill people, he'd done it before. If he faced dying himself, he'd done that before too. With that realization, that acceptance, he felt freer than he had been at any time since leaving the military.

Ty spotted a few men as he moved along. The place was a functioning ranch and men were working with horses or loading stock trailers. They didn't spot Ty and he pushed on, head down. As he neared the house, he crouched amidst a cluster of tall cacti and a pinyon pine, taking stock of his surroundings.

He realized that once he passed that point, the landscape opened up and there was even less cover. When he ran for the house, he'd be committed. There were no approach angles shielded from the view of the house. Once he bolted, he was exposed and there was no turning back. If this turned into a firefight, it would be a face-to-face gun battle with both luck and skill having a say in the outcome.

As he prepared to launch himself into the open, a black

Suburban came from the back of the house and parked around front. A man Ty recognized from his interrogation got out, disappearing through the front door of the house. Deciding it was now or never, Ty bolted from cover and sprinted toward the house.

When he reached the driveway, he flattened himself against the Suburban, pausing to listen for activity. When there was no indication he'd been seen, he eased around the vehicle. He continued up the short sidewalk and stopped at the front door, intending to listen for signs of life, but doubted he'd hear any through the massive door and thick walls. He put a hand to the lock and pushed down on the ornate iron thumb lever. There was a solid click and the door unlatched. Ty shoved and let it swing open of its own accord, his body concealed behind the fixed panel of the double door.

When no one reacted to the opening door, he peered around the edge and into the house. The deep foyer area was empty. Ty slipped inside, then eased the large door closed behind him to cover his tracks. The floors were polished concrete and he placed his feet carefully so he made no sound beneath his shoes, no squeaks to give him away.

He took one step, then another.

Loud talking came from behind a door to his left. He paused to listen. It was only one voice, not two. The speaker was beseeching. Pleading. Ty wondered if Luis was getting ready to kill someone and they were begging for their life. Then Ty realized it wasn't talking.

It was praying.

His pistol at high-ready, Ty walked toward the sound and pressed his ear to the cool surface of the wooden door. The voice was definitely coming from inside the room. He took a deep breath, turned the knob, and stepped inside. He opened it casually, hoping that whoever was inside would think he was someone with a legitimate reason for entering the room. He kept his gun close to his body in case there was anyone ready to make a grab for it, but there wasn't. The only occupant of the room was the woman standing behind a desk.

Although she had her back to him Ty could tell it was *her*. It was Tia – Fidelia Mendoza – the woman he'd chased across the country. He recognized the hair and the shape of her. She was even wearing the same type of cheap sweat suit, just in a different color.

Her hands were clutched together in front of her chest and she emitted a wailing prayer in Spanish. Uncertain of exactly what she was doing beyond praying, Ty circled to the right, never taking his gun off her. As he moved, the body on the floor came into view. He was shocked to see that it was Luis.

Tia's prayers ceased. She had detected his presence, possibly heard his footsteps, but her eyes remained shut. "I asked to be alone with my son, Alvarez."

"It's not Alvarez, Tia," Ty replied.

The unfamiliar voice startled her. Tia's eyes popped open and she staggered over Luis's body, nearly tripping. She threw a hand to her chest. "Who are you?"

"I'm the man who followed you here from Virginia," Ty said. "I'm the man who's come for the girl you kidnapped."

Tia recovered some of her composure. "You've come a long way and wasted a lot of your time. You've also caused me a great deal of trouble."

Despite her age, her eyes were alert and full of menace. They were the eyes of an animal preparing to attack. "You've caused me some trouble too. Not to mention what you've put the girl's mother through."

Tia shrugged. "In this business, somebody always has to be on the bottom. Someone is always getting hurt. The trick is to make sure it's not you on the bottom."

"You'll know all about that soon, Tia. It's over for you. You'll probably die in prison and I doubt anyone will shed a tear when you do." He cast a glance at Luis. "It looks like the only one who might have is dead."

Her mouth tightened at that comment. "I have money. What would it take to make you go away?"

Ty shook his head. "I'm not for sale."

"The girl has already cost me more than she's worth. All I have left is my freedom and that's worth a lot to me. How about I give you fifty thousand dollars and you walk out of here? You go on with your life and forget you ever saw me."

"Not happening," Ty said. "You're taking me to the basement, to the girl. On the way, I'm going to decide if I turn you over to the police or if I go ahead and kill you myself."

"You think you can live with that blood on your hands? It's one thing to talk hard but another to live it."

"There's already a lot of blood on my hands. One more body won't make me sleep any worse."

Tia squinted at him, studying him intensely. "There's some darkness in you, isn't there? Would you like to come work for me? A man willing to kill is always in demand."

Ty wondered if she saw the struggle inside him. Did she sense the trauma? The pain? Then he realized it was nothing like that. Her eyes were on his chest. Ty looked down and saw the beads he'd been given at the botanica were dangling from this pocket. The Santa Muerte prayer beads.

"Have you asked the Holy Death for assistance?" she asked. "If so, we're more alike than you might imagine. She's the only saint who cares for our kind. The only one who hears our prayers. She forgives the darkness, protects our endeavors."

Her voice had an almost hypnotic quality that disoriented Ty for a moment. Was she right about the darkness? The psychologist at the VA clinic said one of the symptoms of PTSD was a detachment from emotions. He'd certainly experienced nothing when he'd jabbed the knife into Ramon in the barn.

Ty snapped out of it, closed the distance, and Tia recoiled at his approach. "We're done talking," he said, pointing the gun at her face. "Take me to the girl now."

Tia smiled. "It's too late. She's leaving with my friend Alvarez. He's taking her into town." She nodded toward the window.

Ty looked outside and saw a large man loading the girl into the passenger seat of the Suburban. "Fuck!"

With Ty distracted, Tia took the opportunity to grab for the pistol in her waistband. It was a chrome .32 automatic, her Saturday Night Special from the old days. Ty caught the movement, the reflection of light off the shiny gun. It was nearly pointed at his center mass before he reacted.

"NO!" he bellowed, sweeping her gun with his left hand as he pushed himself to the side.

The gun fired and the sound exploded in the confines of the room. The hot slug ripped along the underside of his bicep, nearly punching a hole in his chest. She grabbed at the gun with both hands as Ty attempted to twist it from her grip. When she didn't let go, he smacked her in the temple with his handgun, knocking her to the floor.

Tia rolled onto her side, clutching at her face. Blood streamed between her fingers. Ty looked out the window and saw Alvarez had heard the shot. He'd hustled the girl into the vehicle and was deciding his next move. Ty shoved Tia's automatic into his back pocket and raced for the front door. He flung it open and sprinted onto the porch.

The appearance of the armed and enraged man running in his direction helped Alvarez choose his course. He hurried around the front of the Suburban and scrambled into the driver's seat.

Ty threw his gun up and leveled it on the vehicle. "Dammit!" he shouted in frustration.

There was no way he could fire. With those tinted windows, he couldn't see his target. The last thing he wanted was to injure the child he'd come this far to save. He dropped his point of aim to the front tire and sent a round into it. There was a pop and hiss.

He closed on the vehicle and grabbed at the passenger door handle. Alvarez started the engine and floored the gas pedal. The door handle yanked free of Ty's hand and he reacted out of pure instinct, grabbing at the roof rack, the only thing he could reach. He pulled his legs onto the running board and tried to swing himself onto the roof but Alvarez, with the flat tire's assistance, was swerving all over the place.

Ty attempted to shove the handgun into his waistband so he could hold on with both hands but the vehicle veered wildly and he nearly lost his grip. His legs and free arm were waving in the air, one white-knuckled hand all that kept him from falling. When he got four points of contact firmly back on the vehicle, he found he'd lost Ramon's gun. That wasn't optimal but he had Tia's pocket pistol.

Having trouble steering with the blown tire, Alvarez whipped the vehicle back and forth, trying to shake Ty free. When that failed, he aimed the vehicle at the landscaping, intent on using a ten foot cactus to scrape Ty from the side. Ty could only imagine what that might feel like.

He dropped a hand and opened the fuel filler door. Using it as a step, he launched himself onto the roof. He drew his feet up just in time, barely missing the vicious cactus spines raking the side of the vehicle like claws.

Ty rolled onto his stomach, spreading his feet to brace himself into the roof rack. Alvarez kept trying to shake him free. With his left hand locked onto the roof rack, Ty dropped his right to his back pocket and came up with Tia's automatic. He crawled forward and aimed the gun down through the roof, directly over the driver's seat.

He figured he had one chance at this. Once he started firing, Alvarez would likely attempt some type of evasive maneuver. Ty opened fire with the tiny pistol, pulling the trigger as fast as he could. Ty managed to get off three puny rounds before the driver locked the brakes up.

It wasn't the type of action a dead man took. Ty had either missed the guy or the ineffective .32 caliber rounds had failed to incapacitate him. Ty had no time to react to the change in direction. He sailed off the roof, bounced heavily off the hood, and face-planted on the dusty gravel road.

He lay there stunned, dust whirling around him, wondering if he should just roll into the ditch and let the man go on his way. Any second he was going to stomp the gas again and that would be the end of Ty, snagged beneath the vehicle. The mission would end in failure. He raised his face from the road and felt the burn of hundreds of scrapes and gouges. The gravel had chewed him like sandpaper. Blood from his flattened nose poured into the dust beneath his face.

The door swung open.

47

Alvarez shoved open the door and stumbled out, struggling to get his gun from his holster. He carefully touched his left hand against his stinging head and it came back drenched in blood. His ear was mangled, nearly ripped loose by the bullet now lodged in his shoulder. He took a single step and pain exploded through his leg. He grabbed the door to right himself. One of the bullets that tore through the roof had buried itself in his thigh. Blood soaked the leg of his jeans but it was not gushing. While none of his wounds would be fatal, each brought its own bouquet of pain and suffering.

He was going to repay the favor when he caught this *cabron*. This ended here and it ended now. He wasn't fleeing the property. If he did, what the hell would he do with this girl? Where would he take her? Children were not his business.

No, he was finishing this man and then he was returning to the house to finish that crazy Tia. This was all her fault. She'd killed her own son and Alvarez wasn't letting her him kill too. To hell with the old woman and her witchy bullshit.

He limped to the front of the vehicle, gun at the ready, and swung around the bumper. The man wasn't there. Alvarez sucked in a breath when salty sweat ran over his wounded ear. It stung like crazy.

He examined the ground. The man had been there. Alvarez had seen him sail off the roof, and there were droplets of blood all over the ground. Had he circled the vehicle? Was he coming up behind him now?

Alvarez spun wildly, ready to start blasting. There was no one there. Could the man have run off into the desert? Alvarez sagged against the grill of the Suburban and mopped at his face with the tail of his blood-stained shirt. He threw back his head and yelled, "You can't get away, you bastard! I'm going to find you!"

Alvarez gave a sudden intake of breath when he felt a strange impact on the back of his legs, then two sharp stings. He looked down, thinking he might have been bitten by a snake or stung by a scorpion. Instead, he found a bloody knife in motion, having just severed his Achilles tendons. Alvarez screamed and dropped to the ground, the pain finally penetrating his already pain-drunk mind.

Then the man was on him, scrambling from beneath the vehicle. He climbed onto Alvarez's chest and held the bloody knife to his throat. He wrenched Alvarez's gun from his hand and shoved it into his own belt. Alvarez caught a glimpse of the bloody face, the gritted teeth, and the determined eyes, but could find no words. Another spasm of pain seized his body and he cried out.

48

Ty hastily searched the man but was unable to keep him still. The pain from the severed tendons was too intense and he writhed on the ground like a man possessed. Ty found a spare mag for the Kimber .45 he took from him and a .22 magnum revolver hidden in an ankle holster. Although getting the ankle gun required a serious effort due to the contortions, there was no way he was going to leave it with the guy.

Gasping for breath and unsteady from the adrenaline dump, Ty got to his feet and stashed the weapons on his body. Blood ran into his eyes. He was certain his left thumb was broken and possibly his collarbone. There was so much pain it was hard to separate out the individual sources. With a hand on the fender to steady himself, he limped to the passenger door and threw it open.

Time slowed down.

The seat was empty but there was a body slumped on the floor. A blood-stained face with flat, expressionless eyes stared back at him.

Ty reeled. Not again.

He threw back his head and screamed.

A roar filled his head and dust blinded him. He fell onto his back and screamed at God, forgetting even to breathe. Bloody spittle flew from his mouth and he pounded the earth with his outstretched arms, clawing at the ground. He thought of the gun in his belt and reached for it. He'd once wondered how much he could take before he broke and now he knew. He was there.

This was the end.

Then there were hands on him. He assumed the main body of Luis's men had caught up with him. They were going to kill him and he didn't even care. As long as they did it soon, they were welcome to. The roar he'd assumed was in his head diminished as a chopper lifted off and headed in the direction of Luis's house.

In the absence of rotor wash, the desert breeze swept the dust away and Ty saw men in camouflage fatigues tending to him. They had medical kits and were assessing his wounds. Ty imagined he was back in Helmand Province again, the medics tending to his blood-soaked body after they pulled him from the van where the Pakistani girl had died. Any minute these men were going to pull Gretchen's body from the vehicle and he'd see those accusing eyes again.

"Just kill me!" Ty begged. "Just kill me!"

The men tending to him spoke but he couldn't understand their words. Another man, wearing a tactical vest and eye protection, came out of nowhere. He said something to one of the medics Ty couldn't hear. The man walked toward the Suburban and stood in the passenger door. When he slid his goggles up Ty saw it was Cliff Mathis. He reached inside the vehicle.

Ty screamed again and tried to get up but the men held him down. Then Cliff was standing over him with the girl in his arms. She had a hand up to her mouth now, tugging on her lip. Cliff was using a wipe to clean blood from her face. Ty could see now that it was only blood splatter from the driver he'd shot. It wasn't her blood. She wasn't dead.

"Is it her?" Ty asked through tears. "Is it Gretchen?"

Cliff nodded. "They cut her hair and I think they've drugged her. She's got some needle marks. She should be fine."

Ty barely heard the words. All that mattered was Gretchen was alive. He'd found her.

Beyond that, he only remembered bits and pieces. There were sirens and a few scattered gunshots coming from the main house. At some point, he was loaded into an ambulance. They tried to load Gretchen into a second vehicle but she begged to ride with Ty. Cliff Mathis convinced them to allow it.

The last thing Ty remembered was the large, dark eyes of a child he didn't know, staring at him between the bodies of the EMTs working on him. He wondered if she was aware how far he'd chased her.

49

Four hours later, Ty was in a hospital room. He'd been in and out of consciousness, the edges of his world fuzzy due to the pain medication in his IV. He saw lots of bandages on his body and a splint on his left hand. His skin pulled in an odd way when he tried to move. He remembered that feeling. There had to be stitches somewhere.

"How are you?" a nurse asked, typing something into a laptop.

He hadn't even noticed her, too engrossed in taking inventory of his condition. Ty shifted in the bed, wincing at the surge of pain that fought to overpower the medication. "What the hell happened to me?"

"You don't remember?" she asked, stopping her typing and flashing him a concerned look.

"No, I remember *how* I ended up here. I mean, what's the damage? What's wrong with me?"

"Three broken fingers on your left hand, a spiral fracture of your left arm near the wrist, and nineteen stitches underneath your left arm from a bullet wound. You have a mild concussion, a broken collarbone, and some nasty road rash from bodysurfing on gravel. A little blood, some fluids, some rest, and you'll be good as new in no time."

Doubtful, Ty raised an eyebrow. Even beneath the pain meds he could feel the dull throb of his injuries. It was like someone punching him really hard through a pillow. "If you say so."

"How is your pain level?" the nurse asked. "Are you experiencing double vision?"

She continued through a checklist of symptoms, all of which Ty responded to.

"How long am I going to be in here?" he asked when she was done.

"You'll have to ask the doctor," she replied. "He'll be coming around shortly. In the meantime, you have some insistent visitors outside. Do you feel like company or should I tell them you're asleep?"

"Who is it?"

"Two FBI agents. There's a woman with them who looks like a cop."

Ty sighed. He couldn't avoid this any longer. He assumed the cop was Whitt, ready to lock him up. "You can send them in. Do you know anything about the girl I came in with?"

The nurse smiled and patted his arm. "Why don't we let the agents fill you in on everything? They don't have to follow the same privacy policies that I do."

Ty nodded, flinching again at the undercurrent of pain stirred by moving his head. He gritted his teeth. "Good enough."

"You take it easy, Mr. Stone. No moving around. If you need anything, push the call button."

The nurse rolled her cart with its laptop and medications out of the room, spoke to someone in the hallway, and then the door opened. Agents Esposito and Cornell entered. Whitt tagged along behind them, looking a little uncomfortable.

Ty started to nod a greeting but caught himself. He'd learned his lesson. He needed to keep his head still. "The girl?" he asked. "Is it Gretchen?"

"It's her," Esposito said. "Her mother had her fingerprinted once as part of a child safety event at her school. Gretchen told us who she was but those prints confirmed it."

Ty was uncertain what he felt. It was a mixture of redemption, satisfaction, and accomplishment, although there was no happiness in the cocktail of feelings. He'd assumed there would be. Instead, a void remained in the space his obsession with the mission had occupied. "Where is she now?"

"She's here in the hospital," Esposito said. "Fidelia Mendoza was injecting her with drugs to keep her compliant. She's a little dehydrated but in good shape overall. They want to monitor her for a few days to make sure there aren't any complications."

"Is her mother here?"

"Not yet," Whitt said. "She should be soon. Someone gave up their seat on a flight to let her squeeze in. She doesn't know the whole story, but I did let her know that you were the one who found Gretchen. She told me to thank you, but I'm sure she'll want to express that herself when she gets here."

"I guess you're here so you can arrest me, Lieutenant Whitt? You going to cuff me to the bed so I can't sneak off again?" Ty made no effort to hide his sarcasm.

"I'm sorry about that whole mess, Mr. Stone. I've spoken to the Commonwealth Attorney in Washington County and they've dismissed the warrant. They spoke with the man you allegedly assaulted and, considering the circumstances, he agreed to drop the complaint."

"Well, I guess that's good news," Ty said.

"I took the liberty of calling your sister," Whitt added. "I hope you don't mind. She booked a flight and should be here tonight. I also have a message from your niece."

Ty frowned. It irked him that Whitt was acting like she was being helpful. He'd liked her when they first met, but she'd quickly gone from wanting to help him to wanting to arrest him. That tended to sour their relationship. "What's the message?"

"She said to toughen up, butthead."

Ty almost laughed but even the thought made him hurt. However, he did crack a smile. He missed that kid and she obviously missed him too.

"I need to ask you something," Esposito said. "Did you see Fidelia Mendoza at the ranch when you were there?"

Concern flashed across Ty's face. "Yes. She was in the house, in Luis's office, when I left. She tried to shoot me with that pocket gun so I clocked her in the head. She was laying there when I saw the Suburban leaving with Gretchen. I assumed Mathis's men found her."

Esposito scratched at his forehead with a crooked finger. "We went over that house with a fine-toothed comb and couldn't find her. We even brought in tracking dogs. We found the man you left cuffed in the barn, which we also have a few questions about. We arrested several of Luis's crew for outstanding warrants and weapons charges. There was no Mendoza."

Ty exhaled hard. He gritted his teeth, enraged. "I should have fucking killed her. I should have put a bullet in her head in Luis's office. I could have ended this."

"Your head was in the right place," Cornell assured him. "You were focused on the missing girl. If you'd let Gretchen out of your sight, who knows if she'd have ever been seen again?"

"Besides," Esposito chimed in, "people have a right to a trial. You can't simply execute people because that's what you want to do. And as long as we're on the topic of rogue behavior, the same goes for torture. You should have called us the minute you were able to."

Esposito was referring to Ramon, of course, and the knife wounds in his legs, but Ty had no regrets. He'd done what he had to do. He wasn't law enforcement, and therefore wasn't bound by their rules. "I don't know what you're talking about."

From the raised eyebrows around the room no one was buying that story.

"At any point in your contact with these people, did you ever over-hear *why* they took Gretchen?" Whitt asked. "We're still unclear on motive."

"No idea," said Ty. "Luis seemed to be in the dark about the whole thing. I got the impression it was Tia's work and not his. I don't know what happened between them, but when I found her in Luis's office, she was praying over his body with a little statue in her hands. I didn't understand everything she said, but she was gesturing at Luis like she was offering him up to the saint or something."

"That would be consistent with what we found at the altar in her home," Cornell said. "She was not above blood sacrifice. We've confirmed the infant skeleton was related to her."

"Maybe the saint helped Tia escape," Ty mused.

"I think you've had too much pain medication," Cornell said. "That Santa Muerte stuff is bullshit."

"She got away somehow," Ty pointed out.

"These are cartel people," Esposito said. "Who knows what escape plans they had in place? They could have caves or tunnels, or she could have even headed out into the desert on a horse."

"Are you still looking for her?" Ty asked.

"Definitely," Cornell replied. "She's got warrants. This is a national story now. We've got her photograph in the facial recognition databases. She'll turn up."

"What about the guy I fought on the road? The guy who had Gretchen?"

"His name is Antonio Alvarez," answered Esposito. "He used to be an enforcer for Tia back in the day, but started working for Luis when Tia got shut down by the cartel. We're hoping we can press some information out of him, but these guys are tight-lipped. If he talks, he knows they'll kill him in prison."

"Let me talk to him," Ty said.

Everyone in the room got a laugh out of that and Ty looked at them curiously. He didn't get the joke.

"By the way, we found your truck at a rest area on the interstate. We'll need you to review an inventory to make sure nothing was stolen. I'm guessing everything is there since they left some pretty nice gear behind," Cornell said.

"What was your plan anyway?" Esposito asked. "We found a

suppressed bullpup rifle in there. What were you going to do with that?"

"My plan was to find Gretchen and bring her home," Ty said. "Whatever it took."

Esposito shrugged. "Mission accomplished, my friend."

50

W hen Tia heard the approaching chopper, she knew it was all over. The cops were coming. She struggled up from the office floor, reeling from the blow to her head. She steadied herself against the desk for a moment, then hurried to her bedroom, Crocs scuffing on the concrete floor. She grabbed her suitcase and purse, then headed for the basement. She flicked on the light switch and carefully negotiated the steps.

The large house required a substantial heating and cooling system. Tia looked for the filter panel that Luis had once shown her, proud of his planning and foresight. She located the panel and swung the steel door upward, where it locked into position. Beneath it was a large HVAC filter. She removed the filter and set it to the side.

She placed her suitcase and purse in the opening, then shoved them as far back as she could reach. She groped around on top of the unit for the flashlight Luis kept there. She turned it on, shoved it inside with her belongings, awkwardly crawled inside the passage, then pulled the filter in with her. This was no easy task. Her body was a lot stiffer than it used to be and crawling was not part of her regular routine. Reaching out, she closed the steel door behind her, then slid the filter back in place. If anyone checked, nothing would appear amiss.

She put the flashlight in her mouth while she got herself situated. The ductwork was cramped and it was hard to move. She shoved her suitcase and purse further down the tunnel. After a few feet, the duct made a sweep to the right. Just beyond the bend, a sheet metal door was on the left side of the ductwork. Tia opened the door, shoved her belongings inside, then negotiated her own bulk through the opening. When she was inside, she closed the steel door behind her.

Just beyond it, the tunnel changed from ductwork to a larger corrugated steel drainpipe. There was not enough room for her to fully stand up, but she could walk if she remained hunched over. She waited for a moment, catching her breath. This was more exertion than she was used to. When she recovered, she took her purse in the hand with the flashlight and used the other to tow her suitcase. She ambled off like a troll packing up for greener pastures.

She couldn't remember that Luis had ever told her exactly where the tunnel came out. Wherever it was, it had to be better than sticking around the house waiting for the cops to arrest her. She advanced slowly, keeping a careful eye out for rattlesnakes, scorpions, and spiders. She had to stop multiple times due to her back cramping. When she finally got to a safe place, she planned on chasing a couple of pain pills with a stout tequila. She was too old for this shit, but not old enough that she'd give up without a fight. If the cops wanted her, they were going to have to earn it.

When she reached the end of the tunnel, she found a backpack hanging on a hook by the exit door. She wasn't ready to make a break for it yet, so she stopped and sat down, afraid a chopper or tracking dogs might find her if she headed out in the daylight. She figured she was safe in the tunnel until it got dark enough to flee. They were unlikely to find the entrance in the basement without some thorough searching, and she assumed Luis had camouflaged the exit as well as the entrance.

She dug into the backpack and found it contained another flashlight, some food, water, a handgun, and ammunition. There was a sleeping bag, a jacket, and five thousand dollars in cash. She smiled. Luis had figured this was what he'd need to escape if the cops raided his ranch. She decided to eat some of his food and drink his water. He wasn't going to need it.

There was no way she could carry the backpack, so she added his cash to the pile in her suitcase. She also took the gun since hers had been taken by the brute who hit her. With nothing to do for the next couple of hours, she fished around in her purse and found a pill bottle. She took a Lortab and washed it down with a swig of tequila, rolled out the sleeping bag, and laid down for a nap, using the back-pack as a pillow.

WHEN SHE AWOKE, she checked her watch. It should be dark by now. Her plan was to cut across the ranch and intersect the highway. From there, she would make a call on her cell phone and have someone come pick her up. She had money to buy a safe bed for the night. Tomorrow, she would probably take Luis's advice and disappear across the border. She could find a place to lay low until people forgot about this story.

Tia unlatched the welded steel door covering the end of the escape tunnel. When the door wouldn't freely swing open, she kicked it with both legs until it broke loose. Dirt spilled around the opening and a cloud of red dust engulfed her. She lay there for a moment, coughing and catching her breath from the exertion.

She shined her light out of the opening and found she was in a ravine, hidden on all sides. The location would be concealed enough that she could use the flashlight while she got herself together and figured out which direction she needed to go in. Once she headed out, she was traveling in the dark, just in case cops were still at the house. With a little moonlight to help her, she should be fine. Being a city girl, however, she wasn't excited about the creatures that crawled around the desert at night.

She staggered out of the tunnel and stretched her back. Despite the pain pill, her back was stiff and her legs sore. She took a sip of tequila from the bottle in her purse. She had water now but who drank water when you had tequila? She carefully climbed to the lip of the ravine and located the ranch house in the distance. Now that she had her bearings, she knew which way to walk.

Gathering her gear, she turned the flashlight off, and clipped it onto the collar of her sweatshirt. She made certain Luis's gun was loaded and had a round in the chamber, then put it in her purse. While she was in there, she removed the little effigy of Santa Muerte.

"You helped me escape, Holy Death. Please help me find my way to safety tonight. Please bless me for my offering."

She replaced the statue in her purse and let out a deep sigh. She grabbed the handle of her rolling suitcase, took up her large purse in the other hand, and ambled off into the night.

51

"*Badger for Cliff, Badger for Cliff.*"

"Go for Cliff."

"*I've got a two-legged heat signature traveling east from the ranch house. It's about three hundred yards out. Figure appears to be short and overweight, pulling a suitcase. Not moving too fast.*"

"Roger that, Badger. Everyone stand by."

Cliff had a small team scattered in a large perimeter around the ranch house. The cops had pulled out already, planning to resume the search in the morning. Cliff wasn't done.

Each man was using a thermal optic to scan the terrain for any targets. So far, they'd seen a lot of rabbits, a few coyotes, some burros, and a couple of birds, but there was only one target they were interested in. This was the first human signature they'd come across and it was moving in the right direction. Hopefully, this was the person they were looking for. Cliff pulled his cell phone from his pocket and made a call.

In less than a minute, he was back on the radio addressing his team. "FBI says to make the intercept. They've got men on the way. If we can detain the target, they'll pick us up with ATVs to haul her in."

"*You sure it's her?*" John asked.

"Negative," Cliff said. "I don't have a visual from my position. It's somebody, though."

"*It's her,*" Badger said. "*Either her or Humpty Dumpty, judging by the shape. Too short for a sasquatch.*"

"She using any lights?" Cliff asked.

"*Negative,*" Badger replied. "*Humpty's in stealth mode.*"

"I want you and Riley to get in position ahead of her. I'll start moving toward you guys. I want the rest of you to remain in position and monitor for other targets."

52

Tough as she was, Tia was already beginning to question her ability to trek the distance to the road. She didn't remember walking being this difficult. She was committed, though. It was either keep going or lay down in the desert to die. Even if she called for a ride at that very moment, it wasn't like they could come searching for her in the middle of the ranch. She was going to have to tough it out.

She pulled her Santa Muerte effigy from her purse and shared some tequila with her. She replaced the statue and the liquor in her purse, then set off again. As she walked, she prayed aloud. She asked for a new life; asked for the ability to rise again and be a respected member of her community; asked for the strength to haul her tired old ass across these last few miles of dark desert.

Several times she thought she heard noises. She was aware that the desert was alive at night. During the day, most animals took shelter from the heat. At night, they came out and moved around like she was doing.

She was deep in prayer when a man popped up from behind a rock. He blinded her with a powerful strobing flashlight while barking orders at her. She didn't even think of the gun in her purse. It was pure reflex to drop her bags and raise her hands up in front of her face. Anything to block the painful flashing light.

The man was screaming commands in English. She figured he had to be a cop but she couldn't see him. He was ordering her to put her hands over her head but that would only allow him to further blind her with the light. Did he think she was an idiot? She wasn't moving her hands.

Tia felt a sting at her back, and for a moment she thought a scorpion must have gotten beneath her shirt. Then she heard the crackle of high voltage electricity and her muscles quit working. She went rigid and toppled over into the dirt. Her bladder let go, dampening her sweatpants.

Strong hands rolled her onto her face. She tasted the dirt embedded in her smeared pink lipstick. Her hands were gathered behind her and flex-cuffed. When the cuffs were secure, the hands rolled her onto her back. The bright light hit her in the face but it was no longer strobing. The blinding beam made it impossible to open her eyes. Although she scrunched her eyes closed and tried to twist her head away she could find no relief.

"Are you Tia?" a voice demanded. "Are you Fidelia Mendoza?"

"Fuck you," she hissed. "Get that light out of my face!"

"It's her," a different voice said. "It matches the photo. We got her."

The beam of light moved from her face, lowering to her torso. She cracked her eyes open and saw a man speaking into a microphone attached a helmet. She wondered if she'd been captured by the Army. Did they think she was so dangerous that they'd sent the military after her? She found that to be funny. At least someone had a little respect for her.

"This is Badger. Subject in custody. I've got a visual confirmation from the photograph. This is our target."

53

Getting uninterrupted stretches of sleep in the hospital was proving impossible. There were constant visits from nurses wanting to take his vitals and ask about his pain. His biggest pain was the inability to sleep, to which they were contributing. By morning, Ty was ready to bolt. The only good thing about the night was that the pain medications interfered with his dreams. There were no nightmares and no sensation of waking into a hyper-vigilant panic state.

The next morning, he'd already given up on sleep when he got a text message from Cliff Mathis.

We got her. She's in custody.

No explanation was required. Ty knew what that meant. They had Tia.

He was typing a response, wanting details, when the door flew open and Aiden marched in with Deena on her tail. Aiden's arms were full of tiny fast food bags, which she deposited at the foot of his bed. She started to leap onto Ty, to give him a flying hug, but Deena grabbed her just in time.

"He's hurt, baby. You have to be gentle."

Aiden rolled her eyes. "Oh, I forgot he's a *baby*." She flashed Ty a wicked grin.

"What's in the bags?" Ty asked.

"She insisted on bringing you some food," Deena said.

"They're Happy Meals," Aiden said. "To make you happy."

"How many are there?" Ty asked.

"Six," Aiden said.

"What about that one in your hand?" Ty asked. "It doesn't look like a happy meal."

She frowned. "I don't eat Happy Meals. *I'm* not a baby." She winked at Ty and dug into the adult-sized portion of chicken nuggets she'd gotten for herself.

Deena rolled Ty's tray table into position and began laying out the tiny containers of chicken nuggets and French fries for him. Aiden could barely stifle a grin. She pulled out her phone and took a picture, cackling as she stared at the image she'd captured.

"How are you feeling?" Deena asked.

"Like I got hit by a truck."

"Poor *baby*," Aiden whispered.

Ty considered throwing a nugget at her but wasn't prepared for the consequences. He was in no condition for any kind of battle at the moment, even if it was simply a food fight. "The orthopedic surgeon came by for a consult earlier. He said I might have to have some pins in my wrist but they won't know until the swelling goes down. I'll have to follow-up on that when I get home."

"So when are they releasing you?" Deena asked.

"I don't know but I hope it's today. I think they were just concerned about my head injury."

"Your head is pretty hard," Aiden quipped. "You'll be fine."

There was a knock at the door and it opened enough for a face Ty recognized to appear in the crack. It was Heather Wells, Gretchen's mother.

"Can we come in?" she asked.

"Please," Ty said.

Heather pushed the door open and stepped aside to let Gretchen enter the room. She was wearing pajamas with a hospital gown over them. She hesitated inside the door and her mother put an arm around her. They approached the bed together. Deena moved to Aiden's side, giving Gretchen and her mother room.

Ty smiled at Gretchen. "Would you like some chicken nuggets?"

Gretchen looked at the half-dozen boxes, then at her mother.

"Are you sure it's okay?" Heather asked.

Ty nodded. "Definitely. They're a gift from my niece Aiden. She wants me to be very, very happy, but there's more than I can eat."

Aiden nodded as if it were the most obvious thing in the world.

Ty scooted two containers of nuggets and two packets of fries in Gretchen's direction. She opened a container and sampled one.

"They're better than the hospital's," she said.

Ty smiled at her. "I'm sure they are."

Heather gently placed a hand on an uninjured portion of Ty's arm. "I can't thank you enough. You were the only one who figured it out. If you hadn't hung in there..."

Ty didn't know what to say, uncomfortable with the praise. "I didn't have any choice. I couldn't let it go."

"I'll let you rest, but I'm going to get your information before we leave. We don't live that far away from each other. I could make you dinner when everyone is home and healed up." She looked at Deena and Aiden. "You all too."

"That sounds great," Ty said. "I'd like that."

"In the meantime, if there's anything we can ever do for you, just ask. We are eternally in your debt."

"Oh, he needs all kinds of help," Aiden said. "Trust me."

"Aiden!" Deena hissed. "Be quiet."

Heather smiled. "It's okay. I'm used to little girls."

"Tweens!" Aiden insisted. "Not little girls."

"Thank you for helping me," Gretchen said. "And for the nuggets."

"You're welcome, sweetie," Ty said.

Heather gave him a very gentle hug and left with her daughter. When they were gone, Aiden gave him a look.

"Eh, so you saved a girl. Don't start thinking you're a bigshot or anything."

Ty grinned. "No chance of that. I have a feeling you'll keep me humble."

"I don't even know what that means."

"It means, we're going to leave now and let Uncle Ty rest," Deena said. "I'm sure he's exhausted."

"We just got here," Aiden groaned.

"It's you," Ty said with an evil grin. "*Your presence* is exhausting."

"If you weren't such a *baby*, we'd fight," Aiden said. "There'd only be two hits. Me hitting you and you hitting the floor."

Ty started laughing but winced when the movement caused a sharp pain in his collarbone. Aiden stood and Ty instantly stiffened, afraid his rowdy niece might pounce on him. Instead, she patted the back of his hand with a dramatically delicate gesture.

"Hope you feel better, little baby," she cooed.

"I love you, Aiden. Thank you guys for coming."

"Love you, Uncle Ty."

Deena gave him a kiss on the cheek. "Call me the minute you know anything about your discharge."

54

T he doctor discharged Ty that afternoon. Before leaving the hospital, he went by Gretchen's room and said good-bye to her and her mother. While seeing those two reunited gave him a sense of accomplishment, he was wary. He was waiting on the letdown, the depression that would come crashing down on him now that this all-consuming mission had been completed. What was next for him?

The FBI put him up in a hotel so he could meet with them the next day. They wanted him to provide a detailed statement on what took place from the time he ducked out of the task force meeting, up until the point Cliff Mathis's team showed up at the ranch. Now that he was certain he wasn't going to be arrested, he was fine with returning to the field office.

Deena and Aiden were already at the airport, waiting on their flight home. Deena had invited Ty to stay with them for a couple of days when he got home but he assured her he'd be fine. He was anxious to get back to his own bed and his own space, as long as it didn't swallow him. If depression took hold, he wasn't sure he was in any condition to fight back.

Lying in bed at his hotel, eating pizza, Ty caught Jessica up on the turn of events through text messages. He assured her he hadn't told anyone how he got Barger's address. She told him the Wasteland had been relatively quiet as of late, which he was pleased to hear. They made plans for him to stop in Oklahoma so he could buy her that dinner he promised.

He shot Cliff Mathis a couple of messages inquiring about Tia's capture, but hadn't heard back from him. He had to assume the man was involved in something that was keeping him away from the phone.

The next day, the meeting with the FBI was tiring. Ty was fighting pain and taking meds for it, although he was aware he needed to get off those pills as soon as possible. He'd seen too many friends become addicted and he had enough problems already. The last thing he needed was an addiction to go along with it.

After making a day-long recorded statement, the FBI delivered Ty back to his room. They told him they were done with him for now, but he was free to stay in the room until he was able to travel. If they needed anything further from him, they'd reach out. Depending on how things went with the legal case, he might have to return to testify or make further statements.

Once back in his hotel room for another evening, Ty was trying to decide on his dinner plans. He was starving. He'd been reunited with his truck and it was parked outside his hotel so he was mobile again. He was wavering between driving somewhere for dinner or simply having pizza delivered to his room. He was searching his phone for dinner options when it rang, startling him. It was Cliff Mathis.

"Hello, Cliff."

"Hey, Ty. How you holding up?"

"Feel like I got dropped out of a chopper. Pretty rough. The FBI told me how you guys found Tia. Very fucking impressive."

"We figured she was holed up like a rat. It was just a matter of waiting her out. When it got dark, she scurried out of her hole."

"That's a relief, Cliff. Going home with her on the loose felt wrong."

"I was wondering if you might be up for dinner. My treat."

Despite being tired, Ty had begun to worry that the hotel walls were going to close in on him at some point. He was due for an emotional crash. "I'd love to," he said.

"Where are you?"

Ty gave him the address of the hotel and thirty minutes later they were heading down the street in Cliff's Bronco.

"What do you have a taste for?" Cliff asked. "Mexican? Sushi? Steaks? Barbecue? You name it, we got it."

"Mexican would be great."

"I know just the place."

When they got there, Cliff ordered a beer while they studied the menu. Ty ordered an iced tea, hoping the caffeine might perk him up a little. The pain meds had him feeling a little thickheaded.

"You did good work out there," Cliff said. "I wanted to tell you that."

"Thanks, but you guys probably saved my ass," Ty replied. "I was a fucking mess when you rolled up. If Tia had sent out reinforcements from the ranch, I'd probably be in a hole in the desert somewhere. Who knows where Gretchen might have ended up."

Cliff took a sip of his beer. The waiter returned with chips, queso, and salsa. He took their orders and departed.

"If you don't mind me asking, Ty, how are you adjusting to civilian life? I know it's hard sliding from the tip of the spear to somewhere in the outfield. Some people make the transition easier than others."

"It sucks. Most days, I wish my life had gone differently. I kind of feel like I don't belong anywhere now. I can't go back to the military and the civilian world doesn't feel right either."

"How are you doing emotionally?"

Ty was a little uncomfortable with that question. He didn't know this guy well enough to go spilling his guts to him. He was a guarded person by nature and emotional crap was not something he was used to opening up about. "Well, you know I'm a member of the Wasteland. That should tell you something. We've all got our burdens to bear."

Cliff scanned the room, a gesture that seemed more habit than concern. He was a man who liked to stay aware of his surroundings. He leaned forward, his gaze intense. "Ty, I'm not going to beat around the bush. I'd like to offer you a place on my team. I'd like you to join the company."

"Door Kickers?"

Cliff nodded.

Ty hesitated before answering. "I appreciate the offer, seriously I do, but I have...history, and I'm not sure you want that on your team."

"I checked into you, Ty. I know what happened. I know about the dead civilians, and I know you took the heat for that. Everything I've learned about you makes me think you're exactly the right person for our team."

Ty stared at his tea, tracing lines in the condensation on the glass with a damp finger. "I saw her in that Suburban at the ranch, Cliff. When I opened that door, I thought it was happening all over again. It was just like in my nightmares. Another dead child. I'd failed."

"That's okay, buddy. She wasn't dead. You saved this one."

Ty kept shaking his head, staring at his drink. "It's not okay. I had a meltdown. I totally lost my shit."

"I need you to listen to me. That feeling you're describing is not who Tyler Stone is. That feeling is a symptom of a condition that can be dealt with. You need to distinguish between the two, and I might be able to help with that."

"How?"

"I have a doctor I want you to see in Virginia. He's worked with my people before. He's good but you have to be honest with him. Don't be afraid to tell him the truth when he asks hard questions. The only way he can help you is if you're honest. Will you call him?"

Ty looked Cliff in the eye. "Are you sure you want me on your team?"

"One hundred percent," Cliff said. "However, medical compliance is required. You want to be on my team, you see the doc, and you do what he tells you."

"How would being on the team work? Would I have to move here? I mean, I help my sister out and I'd hate to leave her in a lurch."

"You don't have to move," Cliff said. "We put you on salary. You get full benefits. You just have to be ready to deploy at a moment's notice to anywhere in the world. It's like being back on a team, only with a different mission."

"What exactly *is* that mission? What would I be doing?"

"We go wherever in the world people are being trafficked. We rescue victims and help local governments arrest the offenders. We kick down doors, we drop out of choppers, and we set up sting operations. We provide non-lethal operational support. You'll take down bad guys and give victims a chance at a new life."

"You sure the other guys will be cool with me coming onboard? They saw me falling apart when I found Gretchen. What if they don't think they can depend on me?"

"You don't have to worry about that. My company doesn't just save victims," Cliff said. "It saves veterans. At some point, every man on my team felt like you do. They were waiting for a mission that never came. Now here's your mission. Are you up for it?"

Ty imagined himself returning to Virginia. To his bleak apartment. To his search for another depressing job. To only feeling alive in the gym or on the range. That wasn't the life he wanted. He extended his hand.

"I'll accept your offer."

Cliff shook his hand, a genuine smile on his face. "Welcome aboard, Ty."

Printed in Great Britain
by Amazon